DIVIDED

LIZZIE GREENAWAY

ALSO BY LIZZIE GREENAWAY

Consent

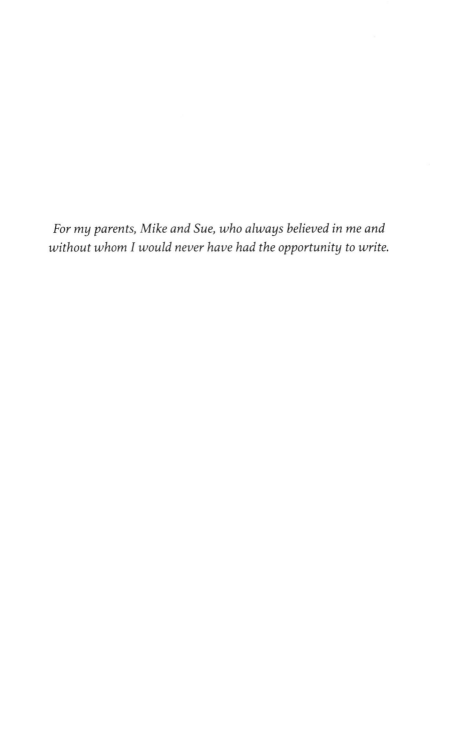

For my parents, Mike and Sue, who always believed in me and without whom I would never have had the opportunity to write.

PROLOGUE

Jon

Jon was late. The weather was threatening rain, so he had turned back to get his umbrella. It only added two minutes to his journey, but it meant he missed his usual tube and the next one would be eight minutes later.

He'd left Evelyn in bed; she never worked Mondays. Her dark hair had been strewn down her back and her face hidden in the pillow. He kissed her head and whispered, "I love you," before he slipped out that morning. He had not wanted to wake her.

Nothing was unusual about this particular Monday. He had showered and shaved as always, dressed in the shirt and trousers he'd ironed the night before, and grabbed an apple for his breakfast as he left. He glanced over at the remnants of last night's meal, and he silently cursed himself that he'd not woken earlier to clean up, so Evelyn could just relax. He sent her a message and told her to leave it; he'd clean up after work.

He was dreading the rest of the day: there was a company attempting to broker a deal with him, and their passive-aggressive stance was wearing him down. As he approached Highbury and Islington tube station, the heavens opened and he was drenched before he had a chance to open his umbrella. He ran into the station, his morning blighted by his wet jacket.

Jon scanned his Oyster card and made his usual descent down the escalators towards the tube. He scrolled through his unread WhatsApp messages whilst he waited on the platform, realising he'd arranged to meet his brother for coffee before work. He'd totally forgotten, but a caffeine hit would be welcome.

He looked at his watch. The tube should be approaching. He was going to be ten minutes late now. As soon as the doors opened Jon jumped on. There were no seats. It was rush hour, so he was crammed in between others on their way to a new working week – weary with the thought of another five days before the weekend.

As the tube set off, he shifted his position across slightly so he was no longer sandwiched up against the door. The lady to his left was wearing a fitted red dress and his eyes rested on her feet; he rarely looked ahead or around on the tube. Maybe if he had studied his surroundings he would have seen him, he would have noticed the bag, not that it would have mattered at that point because it was already too late.

A flash of light, a loud noise, a powerful surge and then it all went black.

Evelyn

The flat was cold this morning. I could feel the beginning of autumn in the air. Even though it was August the heat had already evaporated from the city. As I padded down the hallway,

I realised it was probably time I flicked the underfloor heating on.

In the kitchen I noticed Jon hadn't done the dishes. I thought about texting him, but then I'd have to turn my phone on. I turn my phone off on my days off – I attempt a digital detox. Otherwise I am forever reading work emails: brides don't understand that Sunday night is not an acceptable time to query someone about work. As a wedding planner, I am meant to be available at all hours. There is nothing more important to a bride than *her* wedding.

It was my first day off in two weeks and I was immensely looking forward to relaxing. I'd had two weekends straight of weddings, and the stress and pressure on the days had taken it out of me. I was ready for a duvet day of mindless films and comfort food. I made myself smashed avocado on toast and took my coffee into the lounge. Idly I put the TV on.

I waited for Sky to load. I intended to do as little as possible today. I was irritated the news interrupted *This Morning* when the TV powered to life. I did not care for politics today, or the news of the never-ending saga that was Brexit.

It took a while to realise what I was seeing and hearing. The screen was full of images of our closest tube station. The sound of sirens deafening, an abundance of emergency services. People stumbling in disbelief, covered in blood. Chaos. The word *bomb* repeated over and over again. The tube. A bomb. Jon. Our tube. Jon's tube route. A bomb. My hands began to shake. *Jon, I must call Jon.* My phone would not power up quick enough. *Please, Jon, please, Jon.*

I held my breath in anticipation of the ringtone. *Please, please, please.* It went straight to answerphone. I checked my messages – nothing from Jon but a message about dishes. I checked my WhatApps – nothing from Jon. His signal would have gone. Of course, everyone in London would be trying to contact their loved ones; of course the network would be down. I sat with my phone glued to my head, waiting over and over for the line to connect. I stared at the TV in disbelief as the scene played out before me. *A terrorist attack: A bomb. Our tube. Please, Jon, please don't be on that tube.*

Max

Jon was late. He was rarely late. Max had been in the café half an hour already, and he was growing increasingly frustrated. He had already drunk two coffees and he was reluctant to get another. He hadn't seen his brother for three weeks and he missed his company. Their last meeting had been fraught. Max and Jon had always clashed when it came to politics, their differing views coupled with too much alcohol, had resulted in an unpleasant argument at their previous get-together. In retrospect Max had probably gone too far when criticising Jon's values. He knew he needed to apologise today.

The waitress approached his table and took his empty cup. Max scrolled through his Instagram. Images of lives he cared little for filled his screen. He should come off social media: it was a wasteful drain on his time. He placed his phone down.

Another coffee later and Max was still waiting. Jon's phone was going straight to answerphone. He was probably on the tube. Well at least he was on his way. Max was hoping he could convince him to stay for breakfast. He had barely eaten on his night shift, and he needed some sustenance. His phone rung. Finally. He picked it up and was surprised it was Evelyn, not Jon. He hadn't known she'd be joining them, and he was mildly disappointed. He had wanted some alone time with his brother, without having to watch them affectionately fondle each other.

"Is he with you? Is Jon with you?" Evelyn was breathless, panic in her voice.

"No, he's late. Is everything okay?"

"Have you seen the news, Max? Have you not seen the news? There's been a bomb again on the tube. Jon's tube route. I can't reach him. I can't reach him."

Max was running then, the phone still pressed to his head. "Where, Evelyn? Where?" The police training in him took over. He hung up. He was running faster now. As he approached his station he saw two colleagues entering a patrol car, their movements urgent. He ran towards them, signalled he was joining them. As he jumped in the back he voiced his concerns.

"It's my brother, lads. I think he may be on the tube."

Amy

Today is different. My phone beeps incessantly. I know something is wrong: it only ever does this when people are concerned for my welfare. I can normally go days without contact from my friends or family. I open the news first, ignoring my inboxes. I am not shocked. It is part of my every day. Terrorist attacks, and protecting those wrongly accused of it, is my world.

I was fifteen years old when the twin towers were blown up. I had not heard of the twin towers before. I did not really understand the global magnitude of the event. It was the years of education that proceeded that informed my understanding, and, when I think of it, my career.

I remember George W. Bush's rhetoric shortly after the twin towers had fallen. I even did an A-level piece comparing it to Lloyd Wilson's speech at the beginning of World War I, but I did not understand the impact of that day. I had no comprehension how it would inform our society. I had not thought of all the innocent people it would implicate. I did not think of all the Muslims who would endure racism. I did not think of *us* and *them*. What I hadn't realised that day was that the war on terror that followed began with a war on Muslims.

I search my news app for information on the attacks. The news only has the skeleton of the story so far. There was an explosion on the Highbury and Islington line, the injured are in their hundreds, the number of deaths is unconfirmed. There is no suspect yet. I trust the security services will have rectified that within hours. We will have a name by tomorrow at the latest.

I grab my coat and bag and leave the office. I can't stay here.

Celine

I have been sitting in the café for twenty minutes and he is still not here. My palms are sweating and my legs shaking. I had checked with him twice. It is unlike Jon to suggest lunch, especially somewhere so public near his home. He prefers to stay at my flat, to eat at the restaurants and cafés around Soho.

I look at my phone. Time seems to move so slowly. I am waiting to hear, waiting to hear whether it went as planned. It was a big sacrifice, but something had to be done. Where is Jon? He should be here by now. I had made sure to find out what time his tube was; I had checked what time it would arrive. He should have been here, leaning across the table kissing me on the lips.

We should be looking at the specials, discussing our Friday night plans. It had been a while since Evelyn had been away for the weekend and he had become increasingly flaky about committing to seeing me every weekend. I had planned to discuss it with him today. I was sick of his lack of commitment.

I keep checking my news feed. I tap my foot uncontrollably, waiting, just waiting for Jon to burst through the door. He was meant to be here by now.

My heart sinks. I push the chair back and the bile rises in my mouth. I run to the toilet where I vomit until there is nothing left inside of me. The acid burns my throat and nose. When I have rinsed my face and regained some colour, I return to the table. I had hoped he would be sitting at the table when I returned. He isn't. I dial his number and it goes straight to answerphone. *Oh, please no. Please no, not Jon.*

PART I

"If you are neutral in situations of injustice, you have chosen the side of the oppressor."
— **Desmond Tutu**

1

14 AUGUST 2019

.

Evelyn

I want to dive into the ocean and feel the salty sea flood over my being, I want to close my eyes, open my lungs and let it all in before I float dreamingly to the deepest depths of my soul. And when I wake up I want him to be holding me, telling me it is okay, he has me now. I just want to feel his hold, his strong taut arms guiding me back to the safety of him.

When I was five years old I moved school. I left the familiar swings and slides of my past playground, and I was put in a classroom with an itchy carpet and a step I would always trip on. There were no swings or slides in the playground, just a mass of green lawn. The teacher would pick on me to answer questions in class, apparently to decipher my ability: I hated her. I had to make new friends. I didn't like new people. I had to find my way again. The school seemed so large, and I had to be new: I had to create a new me. I hated it. I hated having to wade through the unknown. I hated the thought of not knowing what lay before me each day, not understanding the routine. I hated that suddenly everything I knew became everything I didn't.

I am five years old again. I do not know what I am doing, where I am going. I lost my navigator.

Max

He had been envious of Jon. His brother had found true love just as Max was falling out of love. The timing had made the demise of his relationship all the crueller. It had taken years before they finally divorced, but he vividly remembers on Jon and Evelyn's wedding day that the cracks were already apparent.

Max's ex-wife was shrewd in her approach to the final proceedings, and he had lost most of what he had worked for. He had found their break-up difficult; he'd spent most of his twenties dating and had hoped to spend his thirties in a cocoon of marital bliss. Max liked a plan. He liked to be in control and now he suddenly found himself single and in a tailspin.

He had met Nancy aged twenty-eight. She had been vivacious, funny and alluring. A woman who drank rum on the rocks and excelled at everything. He had found her intoxicating. She was the life and soul of the party when he initially met her – everyone wanted to sit with her, be with her. He craved her attention, and he was captivated by her dry humour.

What Max hadn't realised until he got to know her more was the outgoing façade actually masked a deep depression and sombre mood. The mask of fun she wore for the outside world was merely that – a mask. He had tried to lift her, he would spoil her with flowers, trips away, and he never forgot to compliment her. He had found it frustrating when they went out and she was able to turn on her charm, he wished she was the same character behind closed doors. He could not understand how she could switch her moods so drastically as soon as she was with other people.

He suspected she suffered from bipolar disorder but found it strange she seemed able to control it. It had ground him down over the years. By the time he was thirty-three they'd been married for two years and their relationship had become draining. The thought of the years ahead coping with her mental illness had crippled him with sadness. He felt trapped and guilty all at the same time. He could not help her; yet he could help himself.

He had not meant to begin an affair, but the police force is a notoriously easy profession in which to enjoy one in: the long hours, close working conditions and stressful situations meant it wasn't hard to forge bonds that could quickly escalate. The other woman had been much younger than him. When he looked back, he saw his feelings for her for what they really were – desperate and juvenile. He realised rather rapidly that he'd just needed some light relief. The other woman was carefree; she had none of the baggage his wife carried.

He hadn't intended Nancy to find out. He never wanted to hurt her, especially as she was so fragile, but he had been careless. He should never have begun messaging her. He wasn't practised at deceit so had forgotten to delete the images of her lithe young body sprawled on their bed.

He can barely remember the words that followed the discovery, his wife's pain etched on her face as she screamed at him whilst hurling objects across the room.

He had moved out that night, gone to stay with Jon and Evelyn. Their disgust at him and his behaviour was intense, and he had rented his own apartment pretty rapidly, desperate to rid himself of their contempt. The other woman had become less attractive after that. She had only been a distraction, an escape, but then he no longer had anything to escape from.

It all seemed so trivial now. He felt a huge amount of guilt that he'd ever envied Jon.

He had not known what to do with himself in the days that followed the attack: he can barely remember them now. He'd identified Jon, he knew that much, but when he tried to conjure how that scenario played out he couldn't recall whether it was reality or imagined.

He remembers the panic, the intense fear whilst he tried to contact his brother. He remembers holding Evelyn, reassuring her they'd find him. He recalls speaking to his parents who were focused on contacting all the hospitals in the vicinity, but the bits in between, the hours that made up the days are unknown to him. He became numb very quickly. He wonders some days if he'll ever regain feeling.

Amy

"Amy, Amy, Amy. What are you doing? Human Rights? That's not a proper subject. The world's gone mad." My grandfather had always thought my career choice foolish. I had completed a research paper on corporate complicity and human rights violations before deciding to leave academia. Initially I thought I'd prefer the academic side of the profession, but I missed working with the public. I missed helping those in need. I am a human rights advisor now, my cases vary, but part of it is helping people who are under investigation for connections with ISIS.

I'd gone to university on the coast of Wales, and after living by the sea for nine years it was a shock to be back in London. But then, life had been a big shock in general at that moment in time. I'd been with Jasper throughout university and the following years: nine years in total. Jasper was wayward and elusive. I'd always known he was bad for me. He'd barely paid me any attention, but just enough to keep me coming back for more. I had hated him and loved him in equal measure. I suppose I still do. When I left him and Wales, it had come as a shock to me. An unexpected decision I hadn't realised I was about to make.

I'd been listening to the radio on my way home when the song came on. I'd spent a whole day reading UN Special Rapporteurs reports on corporate greed and my head was full of information. Jasper's behaviour over the weekend wasn't at the forefront of my mind, but I was tiring of his disappearing acts and disrespectful behaviour. "Crazy for Loving You" suddenly blasted from the speakers and I cracked. I saw with vivid clarity how toxic our relationship had become. I left him that night, quit my job the next day, and I moved to London a week later.

I have been so busy since I barely allow myself to dwell on my past with him – I'm not sure if this is a good thing, to avoid the feelings that sometimes threaten to break the surface. I have been drowning keeping up with my workload. I have thrown myself into others' problems, so I do not have to deal with my own. It has been varied, among the citizens I have interviewed are those accused of being ISIS members. There are some cases that stay with me longer than others, those that I am haunted by: Aminah was one of those cases.

Aminah had moved to Turkey with her husband for his work. Whilst there she had two young children. In 2014, when she moved, Islamic State were encouraging people to cross the Turkish-Syrian border to join its caliphate in Syria. Whilst Aminah was in Turkey her passport was stolen. Not being able to show your passport was a red flag for the authorities in Turkey. It was the catalyst for her deportation back to Britain on suspicion of terrorism. Members of ISIS frequently burn their passports as a statement of loyalty to the group.

Aminah and her children were taken to the Izmir removal centre. She was placed on the ground floor, the "jihadi brides" wing, where all the women were suspected of terrorism. Then she was deported and arrested in Heathrow. She was held, alongside her children, and questioned before being accused of travelling to Syria to join ISIS.

She had already spent months in a Turkish detention centre. There was no evidence she was part of any terrorist activity, but there was also no evidence she wasn't. Aminah's story was far too similar to others who have been radicalised; she aroused suspicion.

But, Aminah was innocent. Since 2012, the Home Office states 900 men, women and children from the UK have relocated to areas in Syria and Iraq occupied by ISIS. Forty per cent have returned home, but how are the security services to know who has been radicalised or not?

They can be monitored, but it is very difficult to determine who travels for humanitarian reasons and who travels to become involved in violence. To date, forty people have been prosecuted upon their return. Aminah was one of those. It is my job to protect people like Aminah, to fight for her human rights. It is my job to defend her right to follow her husband with work, and then to return to her country of birth without being deemed a terrorist.

2

Evelyn

I put his pyjamas on – I lie in them all day. His smell is fading, I don't know how to conjure him if I cannot smell him. *Where did you go, Jon?* My body aches for him. Physically aches. I miss him with every fibre of my soul. Who am I now? How can I be without him? My grief weighs down upon me. I am not motivated to get out of bed, I am not motivated for anything. I can't remember the last time I washed my hair.

In the days that followed Jon's death, there was an unwelcome flurry of visitors in our flat. I didn't want them there, but friends and family felt obliged to come with well wishes. I stared at them vacantly, my memory of what they said is muted. I don't know how long they all stayed for; time seems like such a strange concept right now.

It is quieter now. I prefer it that way. I do not want to go out. I don't want to be around anyone. I am more than satisfied to stay here with my grief. Max rings most days. I tend to appease his concern, but then I go back to our duvet, mine and Jon's bed. Making dinner seems pointless, there is no one to cook for.

I think it is Wednesday, not that it matters. It could be any day: they are all irrelevant now. My mother has threatened a visit before the funeral again. I need to pacify her urge to see me before it is too late.

I cannot stop thinking about our last night together. It had been the Wednesday before the Monday he had died. I knew I wouldn't see him all weekend, so I had planned a nice meal in one of our favourite French restaurants. Jon had been distracted.

I had spent most of the evening on my phone. I'm incensed that is how we spent our last moments together. I did not know. I did not realise that all my future questions would go unanswered by Jon. I had no idea I would never be able to share new experiences with him again. I'd not even imagined that night would be the last time we ever really conversed with one another. I would do anything to have that dinner all over again.

He had a little lump on his clavicle from his youth, a rugby game gone wrong, a broken collar bone never treated. He had the softest, sandy blond hair: I would stroke it for hours. He always wore his shoes in the house. He was messy. He was forever thinking about tidying up. He loved playing cards at Christmas and he would always cheat, I'm sure. His favourite drink was Heineken in the summertime and Guinness in the winter. He loved toad-in-the-hole on Mondays after work. I'd make it every week for the two of us. He would throw his head back hard when he properly laughed, his eyes crinkled with happiness. I loved his laugh. When he'd had too much to drink he would fixate on subject matters – it used to drive me insane. He was a terrible cook, truly terrible. He loved drawing, but he seldom told anyone. He read a book every week: he told me that it was like a holiday, it transported him somewhere else for a little while.

I am trying to remember everything. It seems so important: all the minute details that made him whole, all the little things that created my husband. I am terrified I will forget; I may forget all the moments, the memories, the smell of him – oh the smell of him. It is already fading. I sleep with his jumper. I wake with his jumper. I sit with his jumper. I smell it repeatedly just trying to rouse the memory of him. I wish I could smell his neck one more time. Just one more time.

My thoughts are in flux: a plethora of information is trying to reach me and none of it makes sense. My mind is distracted, rambling, and then totally blank. I am confused, yet the clarity of his loss is immeasurable. I cannot fathom what it is I am meant to do from here on in. Go to work? How can I ever work? It is not possible to function without his presence. I cannot imagine ever functioning again.

Max

Max had always known he wanted to be a police officer. Ever since he was three years old, and he would play cops and robbers with his brother, Jon. Maybe it was the authority or the power, or the sense of purpose that appealed to him. He had always liked order. He was a believer that things must be done a certain way, in a proper manner. Jon was more of a risk taker. He would fly by the seat of his pants. Max would never dream of not following the rules, the correct code. But Jon would get on a train without a valid ticket: Max never would. Jon would skip a bar tab: Max wouldn't dream of it. Jon was spontaneous: Max wasn't. Whenever they played the game Max was always the cop and Jon the robber.

Jon's spontaneity had frustrated and excited Max in equal measure. He recognised the wanton urge he harboured to be more carefree. It was only when he was with Jon he indulged it. His older brother gave him permission to let go on occasion.

Since his death Max has lost himself in more ways than one. The days after his divorce when he had drunk beer after beer have resurfaced. He drinks every day to oblivion, to the place where he no longer thinks and he can extinguish the pain that threatens to emerge every waking minute. He misses him so much.

Amy

I had not intended to look into Islam extremism when I pursued my masters. It had been a subject I was mildly avoidant of. I had been far more enamoured with indigenous tribes and the threat to their existence due to land grabbing. But I had found myself enthralled in cases involving anti-terror laws. I became more and more invested in the young people who were penalised, and whose human rights were violated due to a minority of extremists. Such is often the case in life: I found myself on a path I hadn't intended to tread.

Islam extremism has mistakenly been equated to the Muslim community as a whole, hence islamophobia. A phobia is irrational. It is a hateful prejudice. Islamophobia is a blanket judgement about an entire group. I think that is why I was drawn to the field. It is the everyday injustice, the casual prejudice that I cannot stand.

I see it in my friends who assume their comments are justified when they talk about flying: "When I get on the plane I always glance around to make sure no one looks like a terrorist. I'm not going to get killed because I'm meant to be politically correct. You can't see what they've got under their veils. Who knows what they are trying to hide."

I cannot help but draw comparisons with the rise of anti-Semitism. There are similarities between the rise of anti-

Semitism in the twentieth century and anti-Islam in the twenty-first century. In the twentieth century there was the formation of nation states, and now there is an increase in European integration. It makes me question whether integration gives rise to racism and intolerance. At the beginning of the twentieth century there were negative portrayals of Jews. Can the same be said in the twenty-first century in regard to Muslims? A collective view against a group influenced by the media, governments and world leaders that results in unrest.

In Germany, the newspapers warned against a Jewish invasion. There are parallels with Europe now. A president vowed to expel all Muslims from the United States of America. Hitler vowed to expel all Jews from Germany. In classical fascism, it is thought spoken words were more important than written text. Trump and Hitler are examples of how effective this can be.

My colleague sat with me on his lunch break yesterday and commented on how forlorn I appear: "I don't know why you're surprised, Amy, the rise of the right and extreme xenophobia is increasing. The Muslim immigrant seems to have replaced the Jew in terms of racist targeting. Syria is just a modern-day Auschwitz – it's just a country instead of a camp."

I cannot help but think of this every time there is another terror attack in the UK. Immediately the media scapegoat Islam, I've been privy to many cases where the evidence of involvement is questionable to say the least. Those investigating the tube bombing have released a name today – Mohammed Osman, a twenty-three-year-old British national. It is a story that has been told numerous times before. A British citizen radicalised through the community or the internet. A young man so disillusioned with the Western world he took people's lives. I wonder what evidence they currently have, if any, on Osman.

I also know from experience that attacks on innocent

Muslims will increase in the city now. Every time there is an incident there is a backlash on the Muslim community as a whole.

I decide to walk home that night: it is only fifty minutes to my flat and it is a beautiful August evening. The parks are full of young people and families enjoying picnics. I think of all the innocent Muslims in the city, how their fear will have amplified – every time there is an incident I'm aware there is the possibility of a backlash on the Muslim community as a whole.

3

Evelyn

You never think it will be you. You fear it, but you never really think it will be you. It was a constant in my mind – pushed to the back where it didn't disrupt my day-to-day too much – of course after every attack the fear would enlarge slightly and the anxiety that occupied me would swell, but then you would carry on. Push it back again. Keep going. You never think it will be you.

My mother always worried. She would ring me weekly to discuss her concerns about the danger I was exposing myself to. She thought it foolish, moving to London. She could not understand my decision to leave the country, to move away from the greenery and towards the concrete jungle, as she called it. She wanted to cocoon me with valleys and vast fields of green. She wanted me nowhere near the threat of terror. My mother believed that if I moved to London it would be inevitable, I'd end up a victim of a terrorist attack. But she does not understand that terror is everywhere – it is the nature of this war, we cannot identify its presence.

I grew up in a two-up, two-down terraced cottage shielded from the news and the world beyond me. It was a terrible shock to hit adulthood and realise the enormity of sadness that encompassed this planet, so much so I am surprised I did not simply turn off the news, ignore the papers and stay where I was safely ignorant of it.

It is fitting the sky is crying today. But I want to hear the land sob and the sea scream. I want the whole world to mourn my loss loudly: my pure desperation from the disappearance of him. His photo stares back at me from the order of service. He is smiling, his dimples deep and his eyes wrinkled. I am so confused. How can it be his face looking out at me with an end date? How will Jon not be here today to hold my hand, to guide me through the moments of pure desperation? How will he miss the drinks to him, the distasteful guests who just came for a day out? The pain is too deep, I cannot cope with the idea, yet alone the reality.

It is only when the service is over, I realise I cannot remember it. I cannot cope with his death, there are too many questions. Too much grief. Sadness envelopes me, all-consuming, all-encompassing: it is suffocating. What is the point? Where did our love go? I despair. I feel so desperate – I cannot go on without him. This morning I woke to the horrific realisation that he will not see all the world has to offer, that he will have only scratched the surface. Since Jon left there are questions swarming in my head about mortality I do not wish to answer or think of. We are all so insignificant in the scheme of things: Jon and I, our story, now irrelevant.

I was so glad the weather was fitting. It seemed right that it was as bleak as I felt. An impenetrable grey dampness filled the horizon as we left the crematorium. The clouds looked menacing and oppressive: a landscape of despair. I had been dreading today, but more than dreading today I feared tomorrow, and the panic that filled me with was too cumbersome to bear. Tomorrows seemed impossible.

Max

Today as he wakes up his first thoughts are of what lies ahead. He knows he needs to get through today, but he cannot comprehend how he will. His chest feels like it is being crushed. He is hoping there won't be any press there, but then the media seems to have attended all the funerals of the other victims so far. He does not wish for their grief to be public. He does not want anyone to see him cry for Jon. His loss is something he needs to compute in solitude.

During the service, he is choking on his rising emotions. It takes every ounce of him to suppress them. He sits next to Evelyn whose skin colour is increasingly pale. She does not talk, just gazes ahead, as if she does not occupy the same room.

The day left him with little peace. He could not understand the loss of Jon, or accept it.

Jon's friends speak, someone reads a poem, there are songs. Max wishes he'd been able to express the words to honour Jon. He had wanted to speak today, but he can't, and he regrets it immediately.

It was a blur of rage and sadness and grief, an uncommunicable disbelief that the day was happening. He wonders when reality would resume, because this feels so far removed from it.

The wake is a blur of handshakes and polite platitudes. He does not care to be there. Evelyn was shrouded by her friends in the corner; a cloak of comfort. He has barely communicated with her today. He wonders whether she has been assisted with a doctor's prescription for the funeral: she seemed so vacant.

Shortly before the last of the mourners leave, Max makes an escape for his room. For the wake, they had hired a rather formal hotel. He is glad of the bedroom and the isolation it afforded.

He orders room service and drinks whisky into the small hours, willing his mind to blank out the fact he is now an only child. He wants his brother back.

Amy

The story gains momentum. The media reports intensify daily. The death toll reaches twenty-three. I reach the news-stand and pick up the *Metro*.

"Send them back to where they came from, I say." A man next to the newspaper stand is, I realise, directing this rhetoric at me. "We don't need that kind in our community, our country."

"I'm sorry, I don't know what you mean."

"Muslims – the bloody terrorists. I've had enough of it, coming into our country..."

I turn my back. There are some arguments I know I won't win. My tube arrives, and I stand in the carriage looking at the front of the city's newspaper. The faces of the victims stare out at me. It is tragic, and I hate the world we live in, a world where events such as these occur. But I also worry about the other side of this story. The innocent people who will be targeted due to a minority group of extremists.

We're all aware in my line of work that there is substantial evidence of collective blame – the idea that all Muslims are responsible for the acts of very few extremists. And this gives rise to the collective fear that they will be collectively punished. Collective fear works both ways though: innocent Muslims worry they'll be targeted or attacked by other members of the public, and those members of the public equally fear a further attack by a Muslim extremist. The vital point here is the word "extremist". It often gets used in the narrative when the media describes the perpetrators: they are identified by their faith.

When I think of 9/11 and where I was, I used to think of how it affected the West. I would think of those living in America. I would think of the UK and other countries I perceived were threatened. That was until I met Gael online during my research for my masters. He told me about his experience of 9/11 and its aftermath. He'd just graduated from high school in Lebanon, university was at his feet. He was having a haircut in the city centre when Al Jazeera, the international Arabic news channel, came on TV. The breaking news was of a plane crash into the first of the twin towers. As he watched the TV the second plane hit. Like the rest of the world he was shocked. He did not understand what had happened. Within a week, he did. Suddenly he found Arabs and Muslims everywhere were blamed for the largest attack in the USA's history since Pearl Harbour.

He remembers the intense vilification. Some of his friends had been accepted into US universities. Suddenly their visas were cancelled: their lives forever changed. His relatives in the US spoke of the need to keep a low profile. It was not just the Western world's lives that fell that day. 9/11 rippled across the world. I felt for Gael: America had lost lives and suffered a huge atrocity, but 9/11 and the world's reaction ripped from Gael and his friends the future they'd planned, that they'd worked so hard for.

The world is a geographical lottery from which many of us have won a fortune. Those like Gael did not. The reaction, the wars since, I believe have ensured that the then hundreds of terrorists have gone on to spawn thousands.

4

Evelyn

In the weeks that followed I would try to recall Jon's funeral and there would be a void in my memory. It was if I had never been there. I cannot remember. My grief was a mess. I was permanently exhausted. My bed was my favourite place. I spent days watching mindless programmes, not even registering their content. On the odd occasion, I would leave the house for a brief walk, but I found myself floored by the amount of energy it consumed. I just wanted to sleep through this moment in time.

I dreamt of him, of course. I would wake after these dreams and the longing for one more day with him would be too profoundly upsetting. I longed for one last walk, a coffee and an ice cream by the sea; a holiday; a meal out; an evening on the sofa: one last moment of togetherness. I longed to tell him my news. I longed for him so much it caused me physical pain. When I thought of time stretched out before me without him, I would lurch: my body collapsed in on itself my grief was so immense.

I could not understand where he had gone. I had not

understood the permanency of my situation originally. I realise now it was shock protecting me. I would play out our memories in my mind like a film reel. My favourite memories I would repeat endlessly. I wasn't sure whether I'd eroded them through overuse.

Why do you love me? I would ask him on a regular basis. I needed this man to reassure me. I needed him to tell me what it was he saw. Through his eyes I learnt to love myself a little bit more. He observed things about me that I did not notice. He told me stories of the person I did not realise I had become. He made me see myself clearly for the first time, and for the first time he made me realise that I liked what I saw. I'll never be able to ask him again.

I have always known every love story ends; there is no such thing as eternal love, for we are not immortal. All our stories will cease to exist one day. They will be heard through surviving relatives for a time. They will flicker through their imaginations; a vague awareness of people who they "should" find familiar. Our love stories are all evaporating into thin air. The loves of all of us disintegrate as time ticks on. I can't comprehend that this is my forever, though. I'm not ready for our goodbye. I'm not sure who is going to stop me falling. I'm not sure who is meant to catch me now.

Max

"Evelyn, you look awful."

He hadn't been able to reach Evelyn immediately after the funeral, and when he finally managed to, she appeared not to have showered for days. She had lost too much weight. Her skin was sallow and her eyes sunken. She had always had a willowy look about her, reminiscent of a catalogue model, but she looked too drawn.

"Well, thanks, Max. Nice to see you too." There was no intonation in her voice.

"Sorry, I didn't mean to be blunt, but you don't look like you're taking care of yourself."

"I don't really see the point. It is not as if I'm going anywhere or seeing anyone."

Max sighed. He knew how hard it was to motivate yourself when you were despondent – he understood how these small tasks could seem impossible.

"I'll run you a bath: trust me you'll feel better for it." Max got to work. He found a clean towel and some bubble bath and prepared it for her. When he re-entered the living room, she was slumped back on the sofa.

"You have to now, Evelyn. It's ready. There is a fresh towel in there too."

He cleaned her living room and kitchen, not that there was much to tidy away. He had no idea what she had been living off.

By the time she emerged she looked so much better.

"Coffee? A walk?"

"I'm not sure, Max. I haven't left the house for a while. I don't really want to."

Max insisted. They strolled to Hyde Park where he bought her a coffee from an outdoor vendor, she stared at the cup vaguely, as if she no longer understood the concept.

Max had been granted compassionate leave. He should have taken time off after the breakdown of his marriage, but he had the misguided idea that it took a stronger man to carry on. It actually took a far braver man to admit he needed some help. Now, he found his grief had compounded, the loss of his wife and brother had amalgamated into a messy ball of sorrow that he could not work his way under or over.

Max had always been a problem solver. He wanted to find the answers and resolve any issues as quickly as possible. He couldn't fix this. Evelyn had shrunk before his eyes, in every manner possible and he felt entirely helpless. He needed to do something to guide her through this pain. It would have been what Jon wanted. He had to find a way that would focus them both.

The doctor had signed him off for three months initially, and the emptiness of those days stretched out before him. Maybe they needed a holiday? Maybe a distraction, some sun, a week away would do them both some good. He began to think of where it would be hot in October, when he suddenly remembered a conversation Jon used to have over dinner with him and Evelyn.

If I die before you, take me back, darling. Take me back and leave a little bit of me behind where we made our memories. Evelyn would naturally turn the conversation on its head, and Max would watch on enviously as Jon kissed her forehead and made her promise to him she would. He would joke about it. But, Jon had voiced in his lifetime he wanted a little bit of himself to be scattered everywhere he had been with Evelyn. It was typical of Jon's ego really, but it had given Max the idea.

Amy

The newspapers are now awash with the funerals of the victims of the tube attack. Their faces still stare back at me as I head to work and pass the news-stand. A reminder of the real human cost of this atrocious attack. It is such a senseless waste, an evil act that should never have happened, but I cannot help but think of the other backlash this will cause, the fall out for Muslims in the city this week, as they are yet again blamed for the actions of the minority who use their religion as a mask for their motivations.

The question of what it means to be Muslim has faced intense scrutiny since national and international events. There is a great deal of complexity surrounding Muslims and their identity. How the world responds to Muslims has changed. That is why my job is so important. Marginalised groups need protection, especially with the increased hostility and suspicion they face.

After the tragic *Charlie Hebdo* attack in Paris 2015, where two brothers, armed with assault rifles entered the magazine's office and violently killed twelve people, there was a significant increase in attacks towards Muslims with women suffering the most from this explosion of hatred based on their faith. The "Muslim identity" is being socially constructed by the media; they are portrayed as extremists – bearded haters of the West. My colleague is of the opinion this was a problem created by the West centred around the need for power and control.

I thought back to the broadsheet that ran a story demonstrating our country's innate racism. It documented the story of a white Christian child who was taken from her family and "forced" to live with a niqab-wearing foster family, in a home where she was allegedly encouraged to learn Arabic. When the council in question complained, it was found the article was inaccurate. There was no evidence of distress, no evidence of speaking Arabic. It was also falsely reported she'd been banned from eating pork. The girl's maternal grandparents were, in fact, Muslim, but this fact was omitted.

What I can't understand is why this story was negative. In a country founded on tolerance and democracy, what is wrong with diversity? If the headline had been reversed and read: *Muslim child placed with white Christian family*, I'm sure the lessons of teaching alternative languages would have been praised. The foster parents would have received encouragement and been commended for being foster carers.

A newspaper proprietor once said the secret to his success was: "I give the people somebody to hate every day." This was thought to have been uttered by Alfred Harmsworth, the founder of the *Daily Mail* in 1896. The truth is, in the 1980s and 1990s the press did not write much about Muslims, but after 9/11 and the London bombings on 7/7 that all changed. The press gave the people Muslims to hate every single day.

I am obsessed with this new rhetoric and how it is spreading. I actively research the effect it is having. It is important. It affects my job. Only yesterday I read that the five most common nouns linked with British Muslims in the media are: *terrorist, extremist, Islamist, Cleric* and *suicide bomber*. The most common adjectives were: *fanatic, extremist, fundamentalist, radical* and *militant*. Sensationalism sells. The media stoke the suspicion about Muslims daily for their own agenda.

5

SEPTEMBER 2019

Evelyn

The phone rings, startling me. I answer mechanically. I am not having a good day. Some days are much worse than others: today is one of those days. Before Jon's death, I seldom allowed myself to stay in my pyjamas all day, but now it is a regular occurrence. I do not seem to be bothered about functioning on a basic level – that is, washing and dressing.

"Are you in?" It is Max. He rings most days. I'm not sure whether it is for my benefit or his.

"Yes."

"I'll be there now." He hangs up before he hears my response.

I am not in the mood for visitors, but I suppose Max is different. He has seen me in the majority of my worst states of late, so I am not particularly concerned with my unsightly appearance. Max is breathless when he reaches the door ten minutes later. He pushes through to the kitchen with a sense of urgency. His tall frame fills the room. He was taller than Jon, although they were both over six feet.

"I know what we need to do," he says.

I have no idea what he is talking about. "We need to do about what?"

"Jon. What we need to do about Jon."

I have been avoiding this conversation since the funeral: I want to keep Jon close. I know it is not fair on the family, but I assumed they were going to wait until I broached the subject, until I told them my wishes. I do not respond.

"We have to do what he wanted, Evelyn, we have to take him back." I stare at him all the more confused. "Remember what he used to say to you? He used to say: *Take me back, darling. Take me back to all the places we've been and leave a little bit of me there.* We have to take him back, Evelyn, to all the cities, all the places you travelled together, and scatter a little bit of him there."

I am dumbfounded. Of course, I remember Jon saying this, but he was joking. It was only ever a joke. He wouldn't have meant it. How on earth would I manage to take his ashes in my suitcase across Europe. It was always a ridiculous idea. I walk to my bedroom and close the door. I don't want to talk with Max anymore. I look around the room. Photos are strewed all over the floor. Jon and I on our wedding day, our holidays, days in the park, moments long gone now. Days surrounded by friends, nights cuddled on the sofa. A life. Our life. How will there be no more photos, no more memories, no more tomorrows?

Max

It hadn't taken long to put his plan into action. What with his spare time, he'd researched and booked flights and accommodation easily. He'd asked Evelyn's parents who seemed ambivalent, but they were also at a loss as to how to support her and seemed pleased by any suggestions concerning her well-being. They both needed to get away from the constant reminder of the terrorist who had killed Jon; they needed to escape the news and the endless reports about what led to the attack.

The trip was slightly obscure, in the sense their flight paths crossed over countries; but he'd opted for the cheapest connections. When he'd finally finished the plan, he'd been eager to tell Evelyn. He was excited by her reaction. He hadn't thought to share the idea with her, as he knew she may resist. The first flight was next week, which gave her enough time to get everything in order.

She wasn't working at the moment, and he knew Jon had left a substantial sum for her in his will. She'd handed over all her weddings to another planner. There was nothing stopping her. She had to start living again.

He'd booked a hotel on Las Ramblas for their first trip – back to where Jon and Evelyn had begun. Max remembers the moment Jon had told him he was going on a date to Barcelona. He had dismissed it. It was commonplace for Jon to charm different women one week to the next. Upon their return, he and Nancy had met with Jon, and Evelyn was all he could talk of. This Evelyn became a fixture of every conversation for weeks before they met her.

It seemed Jon had not only lost his heart to Barcelona but to Evelyn too. Max had never been. He couldn't wait to explore the city. He had already read the guides. He didn't know whether it was best to leave Evelyn to her own devices when they arrived – he didn't know what to expect at all.

Amy

I arrive at the office. It is frenetic, and paperwork is piled high. The phones ring constantly and there is an air of disorganisation.

"Morning, Amy." One of the directors rushes past me. Our receptionist greets me with a thumbs up. She is busy scribing down notes from a telephone conference. She pushes a handwritten note towards me.

Amy, meeting at 11am. Sister of non-active subject of interest in terrorist attack.

I hadn't been expecting her, but then I often found out about prospective cases after they'd been assigned. After a morning of catching up on the backlog of emails from the weekend, there is time for a coffee before she arrives. Just before 11am, there is a faint knock at the door and I welcome Zahera. She looks bewildered, clearly frightened by the situation. I try to make her comfortable and then I ask her to tell me her story. I can see the fear in her big, almond-shaped hazel eyes, framed by full eyebrows. She is petite, with olive skin and thick silky dark hair.

Zahera was sleeping when the police arrived. She hadn't understood at first. They had woken her little sister too. She could hear Naila crying through the partition wall. She ran to her, desperate to protect her from the intimidating scenes. They had not rung the bell or knocked the door. They had barged into her home with force.

She had reached her sister, her eyes wide with terror. As she wrapped her arms around her little body she could feel her shaking uncontrollably beneath her embrace. All she wanted was to keep her safe. She watched on as the police ransacked their family home. They overturned drawers, emptied wardrobes, seized her computer, her laptop and her phone.

They took her mail, any scrap of possible correspondence in her home was taken. She did not understand what was happening.

"I cannot believe it. I will not believe it. My sweet little brother would never be capable of such a thing. It is just not possible, Miss Lions."

I reassure her I'll look into the case. I'll find out what evidence may contradict the fact that Mohammed Osman is the killer here. I do not give her a time scale, I am contending with a heavy workload as it is, so I would not like to say the exact timings on when this may be.

6

Evelyn

When I first met Jon, I did not know what love was when he entered my life. I had no idea. What I felt for my ex-boyfriend was only a fragment of what I felt for Jon. I did not know of all-consuming, can't sleep, can't eat love. I did not know of longing so strong it keeps you awake in the middle of the night. I did not know of desire so fierce you daydream about seeing someone again. I did not know that love and respect are mutual. I did not know that there was more to life than the men who went before him. I did not know that happiness with another like this existed. I did not know. And, then I met Jon.

I had not been looking. I was sworn off men: my last ex and I had an acrimonious split; he'd taken most of my things and treated me with disdain for months. I'd decided to have a year celibate. Recovery. I'd been out with my friends when I saw him. It was no rush of electricity, there was no moment of certainty, but he had registered.

I have never had a problem speaking to strangers, but then I never assume it is anything other than friendship. I do not remember how we started talking, but we did. He was handsome. The more I spoke to him, the more I realised how handsome he was. Tall and rugged with sandy blond hair and a chiselled jaw. He clearly worked out. He was out of my league.

I could see him trying to read me. I'd denied his advances that night. I wanted nothing more than to go home with him, but I never had the confidence of other girls. I always refrained in that respect, too shy to reveal that much of myself. I did not really understand what he saw in me, why he had chosen me in a bar full of beautiful women. I'm nothing special, a typical English rose complexion, but I'm no supermodel. I didn't know why he'd approached the girl next door, when he could have had the girls on the screen.

He'd pestered me for my telephone number. It hadn't taken much for me to surrender my contact details at the very end of the night.

I did not think he'd ring, but he did. The next day he'd called first thing and told me I was meeting him for brunch. His confidence made me laugh. I realised it was a little arrogant, but I was taken with him. I'd found myself on a bus to Shoreditch an hour later. I suppose that was our first date.

Max

Jon hadn't always been so committed. Evelyn was the only relationship he had been faithful in. He'd wanted to change for her; that and maybe youth had passed. Max hadn't believed it would last. Jon had a habit of falling as fast and hard into love as he did out of it. But his conversation was always scattered with her name.

Max didn't dislike Evelyn, but he just wasn't convinced she was a permanent fixture. These women never were, and Max had learnt to keep Jon's girlfriends at arm's length if he did not want to be involved in the fall out of Jon breaking their hearts.

But Evelyn was different, and when she kept on turning up on their nights out and he saw the way Jon looked at her, even he was finally convinced Jon had changed.

Max thinks of the first time he met Evelyn and how strange it was now they were about to embark on a trip together. How peculiar mutual grief was: the loss of the same person meant something so different to each of them.

Amy

Zahera tells me the first time it had happened to her, she was laden with groceries, carrying home the weekly shop for her Mum. She had never been spat at before. He shouted with venom at her, "Go home, terrorist bitch. You people make me sick."

She had been terrified. He was taller than her, so he towered above her. He was in his forties, smartly dressed. He appeared wealthy, educated and his friends had laughed alongside him.

She was seventeen years old. "I wanted to tell him that I am, in fact, British, that my parents are British. I am home. But I froze. I had no words. Then I turned and ran away from him."

"You must have been terrified, Zahera."

"Yes, I was. That was only the first time though. There have been many others."

She tells me about the incidents in the ten years since that initial attack. She has had her hijab pulled off forcefully. She removes it now out of fear for her safety. She has had "Kill them all" sung at her on the tube. She feels unsafe every day. She has got used to the micro-aggressions. She came off Twitter because of the trolls who hurled abuse at her. Since 7/7 it has become part of her daily life. It has become part of many Muslims' lives. Her religion, her belief has been under scrutiny. Her dress, her lifestyle is questioned constantly.

"I am not a terrorist, Miss Lions. I hate terrorists, yet I am treated like one at every turn."

7

Evelyn

Our first date was more than I imagined. Brunch turned into a day-long affair hopping from bar to bar. By the time the evening came I was delirious from laughter and alcohol. Jon's charm was alluring. At around eight o'clock he reached for his phone and said he had a surprise.

Ten minutes later a car pulled up outside and we were whisked to the Shard for champagne. He was always extravagant. As I stood overlooking the city it almost felt this existence wasn't real.

"Champagne, this view and you," Jon whispered. "What more could I ever want?"

Our courtship felt like the movies, almost unreal in perfection. He'd stayed at mine that night, and it was the beginning of what I thought was my forever. Jon introduced me to so many activities in the early days: climbing, hot yoga, art galleries I'd never visited. He explained the history of the city to me whenever we went for a walk. He expanded my world like no one had before. It had been intoxicating.

Max

"Do you really think this is a good idea, Max? Evelyn is so fragile." His mother is still in shock and seems dazed whenever he sees her. It is as if she is speaking about another family this has happened to, detached from the fact it is her son.

"It will do Evelyn good to get away, Mum. We agreed a break from their flat would help."

"I know. I just worry it'll all be too much – reliving their past."

"It's fine, Mum. It is what Jon would have wanted."

"Is it? Or is it your misguided guilt, Max. Your way of trying to make up for the last time you saw him when you argued and you both said things in the heat of the moment?"

"I don't know what you mean, Mum, it was just politics, it was a silly argument."

"I think you do, Max. I know you hate that you didn't get to say sorry, that it was the last time you saw him. You have to forgive yourself, like you said it was a silly argument. Anyway, I'm meeting your father, so I'll leave you with that. It's not too late to back out."

His mother had left, and in her wake, he could not help but wonder if this ridiculous plan was his way of proving to Jon he cared, that he deserved to be spread across the globe, that his life had mattered.

The last time he'd seen Jon, the three of them had meant to go out for dinner. Evelyn had cancelled at the last minute – an emergency with a bride. He'd been looking forward to Thai food all week, but Jon had changed the restaurant at the last minute to his favourite Italian. Max hadn't been there before, and he wasn't overly impressed. It was authentic, but the food lacked the essence of the flavours; the food was missing love.

Jon was agitated. He had stared at the kitchen doors for the majority of the night, as if awaiting the arrival of the food was stressful. Max had thought Jon had wanted to tell him something, but he never pushed his brother on matters of the heart. He imagined it may have something to do with their lack of a family, but he had hesitated to ask.

He wishes he could ask him all those unanswered questions now. He wonders what he had wanted to share, what was happening with him.

It was three weeks before Jon's death and unbeknown to Max it would be the last time he ever saw his brother. The evening had passed over beers and tortellini.

He and Jon had got into a brief spat: they held very different political views and it was a subject Max tried to avoid. He didn't understand where Jon's beliefs came from. His intolerance of those different from him was not an attitude their parents had instilled in them. Max had veered off the subject as quickly as the conversation had started. He could not quite believe they were related when they discussed their views on immigration.

"Two tequilas, please," Jon had shouted at the waiter, his voice raised.

"I don't think either of us need them." Max was keen to leave.

"Live a little, Max. If you're going to sit here lecturing me with your left-wing views, I sure as hell am going to drink through it."

The waiter had returned with their shots. Max remained silent as Jon ordered more, he just wanted to go home.

"Your problem, Max, is you're too soft. You need to grow a backbone. At least I care for our culture and preserving it." Jon was testing Max's patience.

"I thought our culture was one based upon empathy, understanding and acceptance, but correct me if I'm wrong, Jon. It seems to me your idea of 'our culture' is based on thinly veiled racism, ignorance and intolerance."

Jon had guffawed and necked both the shots that had arrived at the table. He attempted to order more drinks. He had been reluctant to leave the restaurant. Max did not really understand why considering the atmosphere, but his brother in some sense was always a mystery to him – and now he always would be. Max had stood and placed cash on the table to cover his bill.

"I'm off, Jon. You can drink by yourself."

It had been the last time Max saw his brother.

Amy

I'd spent the week looking into what sort of case counterterrorist police may have against Mohammed Osman, also trying to find out if they were trying to build a case against Zahera. If Mohammed was named as the bomber, it was likely they'd look into complicity with regards to the plan, even if she wasn't directly involved. They had to make sure they knew the extent of the network.

Now it is the weekend and I have come to a bar around the corner from the office. I am seeking escapism.

The irony did not escape me that I now searched for men to fix me, when I'd inflicted on myself for so long the one that broke me. There was something about Jasper that I knew I would never recapture with anyone else – not that I wanted to – but there was an uneasy equilibrium to the relationship that I strangely craved.

Jasper had always wielded the power, had always been willing to put me down, humiliate me. I had wound him up. I was desperate for his attention, his affection, and sometimes I received it, but secretly I knew he wasn't enough. Always had.

I thought back to all the nights he'd disappeared, or the friend's girlfriend he spent too much time with, the nights when he arrived at 4am unable to explain where he'd been. The money he'd lent. The help he'd asked for. He was so reliant on me for years, so reliant on me just being there. It had taken everything for me to sever the tie, but I had suddenly become acutely aware that it was now or never. I saw with such clarity how he was destroying me. I saw my life laid out before me, the pain, the embarrassment, the loss that I'd have to suffer, and I realised I cared more about myself than him.

Maybe it was self-preservation. Ultimately, we all have an innate urge to survive. Maybe deep down I knew he was destroying me. Now with the knowledge gained with time, I kick myself for not leaving him sooner. I kick myself for letting the cheating go, kick myself because I hadn't been stronger. I hadn't realised the habit of working myself into the ground had been because of him grinding me down slowly, a means of burying my head in the sand. Chipping away at my confidence and self-esteem, slowly breaking me so he could behave in such an abysmal manner and I would still stay.

I'd seen his new girlfriend online. She appeared very quickly, but Jasper wasn't capable of being on his own.

I wondered if she, too, put up with his behaviour. I had a glimpse of their relationship once. I saw the girl had the same weakness as me: him. I could see that both of us were outwardly self-assured, confident, humorous. He had a way with women like us, attracted to us, but as he was unable to build us up, he preferred to batter us down.

About nine months into his new relationship, he had accosted me outside a friend's wedding. "You know she is nothing compared to you," he drunkenly slurred.

"I'm sorry? What?"

"My girlfriend. She is nothing compared to you. I miss you, Amy. I miss you looking at me like that."

"Like what?" As far as I was concerned I only looked at him with contempt.

"I still love you. I don't love her. I want you."

I had laughed in his face, unable to believe he was so cruel. I wondered how many times he'd said similar to girls behind my back. I could so clearly see him for what he was and it made me shatteringly sad.

Four months later the new version was pregnant. I did not wish bad upon her, I was strangely worried for her, I wanted to warn her. Warn her to not let the behaviour slip, to go hard line, to watch him with women, watch the mania that arrives in summer and recedes in winter. I wanted to warn her that he may break her heart, too.

I'd come face to face with him three years later, married with a child. He was devastatingly drunk. He'd inappropriately and repeatedly tried to hug me, asked me how I was over and over again – although I was positive he didn't want to know. Jasper struggled to acknowledge that my life continued after him.

I had seen the new wife, wary now, I'd seen the panic on her face and I'd wanted him to stop, to stop using me the way he used to use others to get at me. I did not want to be part of his game. But, his wife had seen. I saw she had seen, and secretly I was glad he'd revealed some of his true colours, because at least forewarned she could be forearmed.

8

Evelyn

Anger surges through me, I pull over the car, the urge to hurt something, or inflict pain, is so great. I am furious, the injustice, the unfairness of it all overwhelms me. I do not know what to do with my anger – I want to throw it away, but it clings to me. It will not leave. I had wanted to come here before we fly tomorrow. If Max insists we scatter Jon's ashes where he made his memories, then this should be the first spot. I park my car and see Max already waiting by the gate.

I thought back to late summer 2013. The park had been brimming with families, all enjoying the last scenes of summer. Jon and I were eating scotch eggs, honey-roast ham and gherkins. I had made a variety of sweet treats that we were going to devour as the afternoon passed us by. We lay on a blanket, the newspapers strewn out before us, drinking fruit cider from plastic tumblers. Our limbs flopped upon one another. It was the most perfect of Sundays.

As the sun set and the noise of children disintegrated Jon rolled back and smiled. "What shall we do now, Evelyn?"

"I'm happy here," I said.

"Me too, but maybe we should do this now?" With that Jon produced a diamond ring from his pocket and rising to his knees he kissed me and said, "Maybe now, we should get married?"

I was delirious with happiness; unadulterated joy overcame me. Our whole future lay before us. I was twenty-nine-years-old, engaged to be married to the man I loved, and full of youthful hope.

I sit here now, my face turned to the sky, and close my eyes. I try to remember everything about that afternoon: the noises, the smells. I need to wrap myself in the blanket of that moment. Such a simple pleasure of a picnic had turned into one of my favourite memories of us. The proposal had been so comfortable, so understated, yet so profoundly perfect for me. The urge to go back to the afternoon engulfs me.

Max holds me as I rock with grief for the moments I have lost to the past.

Max

Evelyn's grief is so raw that he feels he shouldn't be party to it. Max does not know what to say. He isn't qualified to deal with her upset. They do not speak. He reaches forward to hold her. She sits in his arms sobbing. He tries to recall why this place is so significant to her. It is only later after he gets back to his flat he remembers it was where Jon proposed.

He didn't know the details of the proposal – they were always very private about their shared moments. He vividly remembers Jon's voice that day though, the joviality in his tone.

Max had wanted to feel like Jon that day. He and Nancy had been arguing for nearly a week and he had wished he could put his relationship in reverse before it entirely derailed. It made him realise how jaded he'd become. He and Nancy had met them the next day to celebrate in the pub. They'd managed to keep the façade of happiness going for the evening, helped by the fact Nancy had drunk well over five glasses of wine.

Nancy had talked about their wedding day for the latter part of the evening. She was animated as she relayed stories from the day, pushing advice on Evelyn about what she had to do, where she should get married, what suppliers she should use. This arrogance on Nancy's part did not go unnoticed. It was rather embarrassing as Evelyn was a wedding planner. They'd stayed until last orders, before Max had supported Nancy to a waiting taxi.

As soon as they entered the car, the charm offensive disintegrated. She hurled abuse at him about what a shit husband he was; why couldn't he be more like Jon; why had she even married him anyway; why had her life turned out the way it had; why was he so pathetic.

Max had remained silent, as he often did during these rages. It was easier that way: she tended to pacify sooner.

Amy

Memories of Jasper come in flashes. I had hoped after four years I would have eradicated the memories. I hated experiencing his ill treatment and emotional abuse, so I did not wish to relive it in my dreams. I had not realised at the time how much he had broken me down, how many times he had manipulated me, controlled me.

I remember the frustration, the despair trying to explain to him how his behaviour affected me: how it made me feel.

He had not listened. Or, he had chosen not to listen. Sometimes, I thought he actively behaved in a manner that would hurt me, and he claimed he could not see it, that I was being ridiculous, paranoid, jealous. He was gaslighting me.

I remembered the inappropriate female friend, Clara, how he had twisted their friendship to get to me on purpose. She had played along too. Neither of them cared for the hurt they inflicted upon me. It was a power game that I was glad I was no longer a part of. I can see clearly now how unbalanced the relationship was, how awful he had been to me so many times, how many times I had forgiven him when I shouldn't have.

I had been surprised after we'd split up that when I relayed his behaviour to people they displayed their shock on their faces. It had become so much a part of my script I did not realise how bad things had been: the time he slept with another girl in our bed; the friend's girlfriend he had an affair with; the messages I had regularly found; the fling he still messaged on the other side of the world to tell her he wanted to fuck her; the terminal pain he had put me through every summer; the drinking; the money problems I'd endured because of his lifestyle; the dependence on me during his depressive moments; the punishments if I went away, enjoyed myself or attended a festival without him.

I realised with such clarity now how utterly wrong it had all been, how destructive our bond had become. I did not doubt he loved me, but the problem was his kind of love was simply not good enough. It had taken me many, many years to realise that, and then suddenly, as if a switch had flicked, I saw him for what he was. And, it was over. As quickly as that it was over. My resolution was so strong, there was no option other than to leave him immediately.

His escapades had worn me down. Over and over again, I had put up with his actions, forgiven him, listened to his promises he wouldn't do it again, and then I had snapped. I had simply snapped. I was never a wall flower. That is why it was such a surprise when I finally realised what he had done to me. But then he had time on his side, and over those months and years it had happened so slowly. By the time I realised it wasn't right, my idea of love had become so distorted and eroded I couldn't remember it being any other way.

This is not to say I don't miss Jasper. I still think of him, I imagine his life now: him and the new version of myself.

There have been other men since, but nothing serious, I have enjoyed myself more than I ever knew possible outside of my job, which isn't hard considering my limited social life. It is a welcome escape, this light relief I seek in bars and clubs across the city. A sexual awakening ignited in me so strong that I cannot help myself after a few drinks. These men had healed me – each in their own way. I had felt appreciated on a basic level – attractive, wanted and respected again. And, I had felt in control: I had regained control over my destiny.

9

OCTOBER 2019

Evelyn

I t has finally arrived. As I trudge towards check-in, I feel heavy with this task. Max is being overly buoyant beside me, I know he is trying his hardest to be positive. I must remember he lost his brother too; maybe he needs this journey more than me.

My mother and father have accompanied us to the airport, their faces strained: my mother's lips pinched with anxiety and my father's brow furrowed. Neither of them knew what to say to me. Neither of them had form dealing with a grieving daughter. When I first saw them after Jon's death had been confirmed their eyes were filled with fear as they approached me. They did not know what to say to help me through. The fact there is no solution for my pain scares my parents, especially my father. They did not and do not know how to fix me.

I approach check-in, my phone in hand ready to scan my boarding pass. I can feel my parents' desperation to slip away: to fast-forward so the future is already upon us.

I turn and briefly hug both of them, aware that I may break if

I allow too much affection. I muster a smile, which does not reach my eyes. I want to say so much, but there are no words that could convey how I feel at that moment.

I'm almost an arm's length away when my mother's hand shoots out and grabs me. She thrusts a wad of letters at me. "I just wanted to give you these. Please, darling, maybe just try and read them whilst you're away. We all have our love stories and pain to bear."

I do not have the energy or inclination to ask her any questions. I open my handbag and shove them in without any care. I scan my boarding pass, and then I am gone. Their silhouettes are shadows behind me as I walk towards the plane.

Max

He wasn't entirely sure he would get Evelyn to the airport, let alone on the plane, so it is a relief when he hears the familiar "cabin crew ready for departure". Evelyn was a nervous flyer, so he extended his hand to her. He hoped she'd relax once they were up. She looks so strained. They won't arrive in Barcelona until early evening, but there would be enough time to share some tapas before settling in for an early night.

They are staying in Hotel 1898, a grand colonial style building. Max picked somewhere particularly nice for the first trip. He wanted Evelyn to feel comfortable. He knew that she and Jon had stayed in an apartment on their last trip, and he didn't want to emulate that experience. He'd arranged transport from the airport so when they arrived it would be seamless.

Evelyn is quiet throughout the flight, staring vacantly out at the clouds before darkness fell.

Max sinks beer as if it was going out of fashion. His nerves about the impending trip and what it meant had begun to set in.

He wonders what his brother would think of this journey. He imagines he'd be shocked Max could undertake something so spontaneous. It was far more in Jon's nature to travel.

Amy

I threw myself into the job the minute I arrived in London. I had not made any friends, but, strangely, it did not bother me. I was consumed by the cases I took on. I worked six days a week and spent the evenings bingeing on box sets, bar the occasional one-night stand.

I dealt with cases of asylum, with people who need to remain due to humanitarian grounds. People who feared persecution. People who had risked everything and given up the lives they had spent years building. People who deserted their future, their homes, their extended families, because the only other option was more horrendous.

There are so many misconceptions about immigrants. For a start a large number of people trying to enter the country are asylum seekers. They are trying to find a safe place for them and their families. To claim asylum, they must have been persecuted because of their race, religion, nationality, political opinion or anything that puts them at risk in their country, due to the cultural, religious, political or social situation in their countries. These people are not "immigrants", as the media calls them. These people are desperate, terrified and need our help.

10

Evelyn

I had suggested Barcelona to Jon on a whim. We had not known each other long, but I was caught up in the spontaneity and excitement of it all. I wanted to embrace it. I wanted to extend these perfect moments laced with lust and the promise of love. It was December 2012 when we flew: I'd booked the trip just three weeks prior to take-off. We were meeting at the airport in Barcelona: Jon was flying in from a work trip in Copenhagen. I loved the thought of three days together.

It was perfect. We ate seafood tapas and drank copious amounts of cava. We idly walked through the Gothic Quarter enchanted by the history and dramatic surroundings. We fell in love listening to an old man on a guitar, the street lights sparkling above him and the night sky an abundance of stars. We held hands. We stopped for kisses – his hands traced my waist and my arms whenever the opportunity arose. We dozed in bed for the majority of our mornings. We explored the city with the same level of thirst we held for one another, gradually getting drunker with desire.

He was like no one I had ever met. He was animated and passionate; his conversation interspersed with laughter and knowledge. His background so vividly different to mine – a man from the city, he represented all the gaps in my world from my youth. He filled the isolation I had felt growing up in the country. He was an aphrodisiac for my life in that moment. I had not intended to fall in love with him. I had just wanted his company, but that is not how love works: it sometimes appears whether you want it to or not.

On the last night, too consumed by conversation over our cocktails, we had failed to realise the time and missed the possibility of dinner in a restaurant. Instead we ate baguettes on a bench with glasses of red wine from the local sandwich shop. We were fearless of our future, totally immersed in the moment. It was the best of meals. I could have eaten baguettes on a bench in Barcelona with him forever.

Of course, it has happened here too, the irony that Max thinks Jon's last wishes would send me to a city that experienced a terrorist attack too. As I stroll down Las Ramblas, I think of the white van screeching from side to side – its momentum gathering as it ploughed into the crowds. Fourteen people were killed and 130 injured. Citizens of twenty-four countries. One Thursday in August 2017, a white Fiat van veered onto Las Ramblas promenade, travelling for 500 metres as it barrelled into innocent pedestrians. I imagine the poor victims left in the street, limbs broken and blood abundant among the injured. I can almost hear the screams of the families fleeing with their young children. Profound sadness overcomes me. I am unable to think of the three-year-old and seven-year-old children who were confirmed dead.

I do not want to live out my grief here. I do not want to think of the other atrocities that occurred here. I don't know why Max has insisted we make this trip: everywhere I look there are memories. If I close my eyes I can still hear Jon's laughter as we strolled down this street. I can feel the faint imprint of his arm around my shoulder. I can imagine his voice in my ear suggesting what we may do next, but bringing me here, bringing me somewhere that when I open my eyes it is so obvious he is no longer here is so unfair. I really want him to be here. What I'd give for him to be here.

Max

He understands now why Jon raved about the city. There is something for everyone in Barcelona, a mixture of the beach and the city, a young vibrant atmosphere, the trendy bars and restaurants would have been exactly what his brother enjoyed. He has a plan to visit the Sagrada Familia, to experience Gaudi's gardens. He cannot wait to meander through the La Boqueria food market in the morning and sample the produce – he wants to experience everything Jon had.

He has brought Evelyn to a tapas bar close to the hotel. She is brooding. He tries to talk to her of his plans for the next few days, but she is uninterested. She leaves most of her food. The table falls silent whenever Max stops his incessant one-sided chatter. He was hoping to go to a few bars with her, for her to show him the best places for a drink. But she is tired. She rises from the table and feigns excuses. Max wanders the Gothic Quarter, the lights illuminating the fantastic architecture thinking of his brother and how he'd love to explore this city with him.

He's missed out on so many adventures, engrossed with saving and not spending money. He had not appreciated how important travel was. He knows now with such certainty how precious time is. He vows to never put off a trip he wishes to take again. If Jon's death has taught him anything it was to live in the moment.

11

Evelyn

I leave the restaurant Max has booked pretty quickly. I cannot bear to be there. What Max does not realise was that the last time I was in Barcelona, I sat in exactly the same restaurant. He wouldn't have known we'd come here too, but the memories are so confronting and painful.

Jon and I had ordered so many tapas the waiter had to bring an additional table to the side of us, it was embarrassing, especially given I wasn't eating much, filled with trepidation as to what we were embarking on. I could tell already I could fall in love with him: I lit up when I was around him. We'd drunk cava and feasted on meat croquettes, padron peppers, patatas bravas, Iberian ham, *gambas al ajillo*, stuffed squid and *albondigas*.

There is nothing like the early days of a relationship when you are falling in love and soaking up new facts about each other. The possibility of our future had been intoxicating. The city had heightened the romance. I had felt euphoric the whole weekend we had spent here.

And now I cannot cope with the memories, with the

reminder that it is all over. I couldn't bear to finish the food. I stood and told Max I was tired. He was visibly disappointed, but I was not here to please Max. I did not want to stare in wonderment at sights Jon could no longer enjoy, or sit in bars he could no longer occupy.

The hotel is luxurious, I'll give Max that – I cannot fault the accommodation. I enter the room and slump on the bed. I begin to empty my bag. I am not a smoker, but I am sure I'll have a stray cigarette in there somewhere: since Jon's death I have taken up the habit on occasion. My hand fumbles across a wad of paper. I remember my mother handed the package to me in the airport, but I had only vaguely paid attention.

It is a collection of correspondence: letters, I lay them all out on the bed. On the top was a letter from my mother:

Your great-grandparents endured pain too. May you find solace in their love story, sweetheart. Try and heal.
Love Mum xx

The paper of the letters was a pale mustard: although aged, they were still in very good condition. I imagine they have been locked away for years in a suitcase, in an attic. I didn't know my great-grandparents – I had heard of my great-grandmother, Olive, but she had passed away shortly before my birth. All I knew of her husband, Jack, was from a vague conversation my mother once had with me regarding relatives lost in the war.

I sit at the edge of the bed in the hotel, the letters before me. I should probably ring Max, apologise, head back to him. I do not have the energy. I call room service and order fresh coffee and then change into my pyjamas. I settle in. I start at the beginning.

11 October 1915

Dear Jack,

Kitty told me today that she'd seen the newly erected London Home Depot in Regent's Park. Five whole acres – five whole acres to house the love letters to our troops. Thousands of women stood sorting the sweet nothings we all wish we could whisper into our lovers' ears. Kitty said they post 20,000 bags across the Channel to France each day, but I think Kitty is favourable in nature when it comes to exaggeration. I do wish God's speed with my letters, though. I picture my letters to you making their journey through the wooden hanger, as she described it. I wish I could travel alongside my letters, so I too could be privy to your touch.

I hope my letters go some way to remedy your troubles, I know letters are only a mere consolation for our distance but do know for now that I love our love story, Jack, and I love the thought of the story it is to become.

Yours always,
Olive

~

October 1915

Dear Olive,

It is quite the adventure so far. The boys all seem buoyant with the possibility of our travels.

It is funny how our fate plays tricks with our plans. This time last year, I certainly did not think I would be heading to France.

I am lying here thinking of our final kisses, between the tears, so tender. I feared that your tears were suffocating. This will be over soon, my love. We won't be apart for long. It is difficult to write as we are travelling now, so I must lie flat on the bed to pen this.

But, know that I'll be home soon, my love. I'll be home soon.
Jack

~

Christmas 1915

Dear Jack,
It has only been two months since you left, and I so hoped you'd be
back by now, at least back for Christmas. It feels awfully wrong to be
sitting down for dinner without you.
I hope you have received the hamper from Fortnum and Mason I sent.
I could not decide between the provision boxes. In the end, I chose one
of the "Sovereign" boxes. I do hope you have had the opportunity to
enjoy the delights. Chocolate, potted meats, sardines and cheddar
cheese are on their way, my love, if you have not received the package
already. I even managed to get some of your favourite Dorset
butter too.
I cannot fathom the idea of your Christmas there. I hope it is not too
miserable.
Know that you are in our thoughts and your name is spoken often.
I miss you terribly,
Yours always,
Olive

~

I must have drifted off as I wake in a panic. My dreams crowded with fear, I am sweating profusely. I'm momentarily mortified I may have damaged the letters in my sleep, but they are all still laid out before me in the same position. I fold them neatly and place the ones I have read in a separate compartment of my luggage. I drift off shortly after, my thoughts full of Jack and Olive and what became of their love story.

Barcelona passes. Max and I endure the tourist sites. He is enthralled with the city. I understand, I had been too, the first time I'd visited. But now I just can't see past the fog of my brain. It is as if the world had lost its colour.

We scatter a bit of Jon's ashes on the last night. Max has asked me several times where he would have wanted to be left. There were the grand, famous sites, but it didn't seem fitting. It didn't seem personal enough to our story.

On the last night as we make our way out of the hotel, I gaze down Las Ramblas and know the place immediately. I had put a small bit of Jon's ashes in a metal tin in my pocket. We walk towards the sea. I stop at the last moment and sit on a bench. The same bench where we shared those baguettes and red wine all those years ago. Our laughter reverberated in my mind and I think of how hopeful the future seemed as I release the lid of the tin. A little bit of Jon travels in the air – down the street where we'd first fell in love.

I sleep well that last night, a little bit relieved I'd managed to scatter Jon here. Tomorrow is our second flight: to Bordeaux.

Amy

"Can you tell me when you noticed a shift in how you were treated as a woman?" I'm interviewing Zahera about her experience as a Muslim woman in Britain, alongside looking into her brother's case.

She looks timid, unsure what to expect, but I remind her that it's all anonymous, and she replies more confidently, "It was 7/7 in 2005."

"And what has happened since 7/7, Zahera? What would you say your experience has been in your own words?"

"Since 7/7, abuse and micro-aggressions have become part of the daily existence as a Muslim living in the UK. I remember watching the news after the tube bombings, in utter disbelief that someone would commit such a purposeful attack. My family and I sat in shock. My mum always says their world came to a standstill after 9/11, and my parents knew the future of global society had shifted forever. I think that is how I felt after 7/7."

"When did you realise everything had changed, Zahera?"

"My mum remembers watching the aftermath of 9/11 on television. She relays it to me sometimes: '*Either you're with us. Or you're with the terrorists,*' announced George W. Bush, his rhetoric mimicking previous world leaders who had entered into war. Only this time she realised that she wasn't included in the '*with us*'. She was suddenly seen as a threat, considered a danger. Overnight my parents were grouped with killers. My family and I were suddenly under scrutiny – our dress, our lifestyle, our religion."

"I can't even imagine."

"I've always been told how I was repressed as a woman. I've been told that I must be made to cover up by males: I haven't. It has been my choice. My white friends have drawn comparisons with my faith and women living in Saudi who were only allowed to drive in June 2018. I've stopped being British in people's eyes. After 7/7 I was just a Muslim, a possible terrorist, a jihad. I was considered an outsider in the place I called home."

"How do you cope?"

"I've tried to explain that Islam is not the precursor for women being treated badly, patriarchy is, Islam recognises women's rights. Yet I am often shot down: 'That's what they want you to think.' After 7/7 I was either considered severely repressed, or on the verge of a mass killing spree. Yet, all the while I kept thinking the argument that Muslim women are treated badly by Islam, is clearly rebuffed when we look at the torrent of abuse I receive in this country from some non-

Muslims. I realised very quickly that to live in Britain during these times would be fraught."

I had read about the spectrum of abuse, which had become more and more common, from the everyday micro-aggressions to horrific physical attacks: a pregnant woman kicked to the floor because of her beliefs. The rhetoric from UKIP and EDL swelled around us all in our day-to-day life, giving rise to racism and increased levels of hatred towards Muslims.

"I continued as best as I could to live life as well as I could, Amy. Sometimes I cried, sometimes I let it go over my head, but when you hear 'Osama bin Laden, Paki-terrorist, go home' yelled at you daily, it wears thin."

"The sad thing is it is total ignorance on behalf of the perpetrators, Zahera."

"I know, but when I was asked in the street why I supported Osama bin Laden, purely because of the colour of my skin, it still hurt. I nipped to Tesco's to buy milk last week. As I exited, 'Afghan terrorist!' was shouted at me from a car. I had only nipped out because I wanted a cup of tea..."

Zahera's statements make me feel ashamed of some people living in Britain, I am grateful Zahera has given me the opportunity to better understand her experiences as a Muslim woman in this country. And, it makes me think how can someone from the same family have been responsible for this attack? What grounds do they have to be suspicious of her brother.

12

Evelyn

On the morning Max and I arrive, the chateau is shrouded in mist; the building is magnificent in the coat of fog. It is very different to our wedding day. Then we danced the night away under the dusky Bordeaux sky of autumn 2014, the sound of crickets echoing around us.

Jon had worn a simple navy suit and me a fishtail silk bridal dress. It was more of a slip than a dress really. We had married on the lawn with the elegant chateau looming in the background. We had written our own vows. The ceremony was interspersed with laughter, and I was overwhelmed by clarity that I was marrying the most perfect man: he was perfect to me.

We had drunk coupes of champagne and eaten delicate canapés throughout the afternoon. We had been consumed by happiness. The autumnal sunshine shone down upon us as the leaves slowly crisped before our eyes. In the morning, we had swum in the pool, floating for hours, our eyes closed to the blissful sun before emerging to get ready. I had wanted a simple affair: the decoration was limited but the food delicious. I had been to so many weddings with my job and I'd gathered a clear idea of what I didn't want.

Jon had allowed me free rein and I'd been in my element creating the perfect balance of "relaxed" and "French glamour". There were sixty guests; I'd been to weddings where there were well over a hundred people and it lost its intimacy. Our wedding had been everything I had ever dreamed of: we ate and drunk late into the night under the pretence this could be our life forever.

As we pull up the long winding drive, I can see the old Citroen Traction car we had used for the week to explore the surroundings. Chateau Rigaud is just as beautiful as I remember. The perfect mix of modern and medieval.

Max has booked us in for a wine tasting weekend. The chateau runs them twice a year. Jon and I had hoped to come back here next year to enjoy one – he never will.

We have a weekend packed with wine tasting in St Emilion and Sauternes, a trip to the market and walks in the vines. They have opened a new river restaurant since our wedding, *Au Four de la Rive*, and I am relieved to eat there in the evenings. I do not want an identical experience. I'm glad things are slightly different.

Max is quiet on the first day: he spends a lot of his time exploring the grounds, deep in thought.

I give him space. I crave it too and retreat to a corner of the sprawling gardens where I immerse myself in my great-grandparents' letters.

Early 1916

Dear Olive,
I do not know the date, but Christmas feels like weeks prior, so I know

we are into the New Year. Thank you so much for my gift, I hope it was not too dear. I know what a luxury Fortnum and Mason is. I did curse you for being so generous, but the joy I felt devouring the delights soon made me praise you. The package certainly lifted my spirits.

I am afraid I do not have much to report, my dear. It is terribly cold here. We seem to be stuck in a constant quagmire. We are laying boards on the ground soon, so I do hope for improvement. I am yet to find out my leave, but I pray it is imminent.

It will not be long before I hold you in my arms.

Jack

~

Dear Jack,

It sounds so wet there. I hope the interminable rain has given way to sunshine now. I cannot bear to think of you amongst the mud and slosh, and to think you must sleep in those conditions every night. I feel tired even considering it. I hope the boards you were laying down have helped improve your ease of walking through the trenches.

I have enclosed more potted meat, toffee, rice and candles. Please ask me for cigarettes if you should need more in your next parcel, my darling.

Pearl told me today that Edward has been granted leave. It seems an impossibility that we will ever be together again some day. I despair at the thought of how much time may pass before I can hold your hand again.

In the moments, when I think I cannot sustain this separation any longer, I worry that when we meet again we may not recognise what our eyes fall upon. I do hope that the change that has transpired in us both will not have allowed a distance to develop that we were unaware of.

Yours always,

Olive

Max

He had been dreading Jon and Evelyn's wedding. It was a stark reminder of the disintegration of his relationship. He and Nancy had decided to drive to France; she did not like flying and it would be far easier transporting all the wedding paraphernalia Evelyn wanted. In retrospect, he realised his immediate mistake. The resentment had been building in their relationship for months and fifteen hours driving in a van with no escape was the last thing they needed.

The arguments had been intense. Nancy had gone off the handle about everything, before sobbing uncontrollably. They'd stopped overnight in a French service station, where they'd had a meal cloaked in silence. Max wasn't sure how they'd managed to reside together in such a small space. It had been unbearable.

When they finally arrived at the wedding venue, they were so busy helping with the preparations that they'd barely spent any time together before the day of the wedding. Max was the best man, so inevitably he'd been occupied with photographs and speeches. He'd watched from a distance as Nancy held court. She'd been jovial and vivacious, laughing with their crowd of friends. From a distance, she looked the picture of happiness. He'd wished he could permanently make her as happy as she appeared in that moment.

When he'd finally reached her later that day, he could tell she had drunk too much. Her words were beginning to slur and there was a sharpness to her communication. He hoped no one had noticed. He was on edge and wanted to pacify her. He tried his hardest to neutralise their communication, but he knew what was coming.

He could tell Jon had noticed; he'd tried to approach him about it the next day. Max had dismissed his concerns; his brother's wedding week was not a time to broach the subject. He wonders now why he did not leave Nancy after that, why he stayed longer when the writing was so obviously on the wall.

She only ever lashed out when she was drunk. The first time it had happened he'd tried to restrain her, but had gripped too hard in his attempt to stop the blows and he had left bruises on her arms. He'd been mortified. It was easier to curl himself into a ball and let her pummel her anger out. She was not strong enough to leave marks physically, but she made him feel like the weakest man in the world in those moments. His job as a policeman was to protect people and he couldn't even protect himself. On the wedding night, he'd apparently spoken to the beautiful daughter of his parents' friends for too long. Nancy was convinced Max was trying to humiliate her; he had learnt it was best to remain quiet when she made these accusations.

He'd known he'd find the chateau a difficult reminder. His memories here are awash with sadness. He walks around the gardens now, trying to exorcise the memories. He wants to forget; the venue is too special to allow Nancy to tarnish this weekend.

Their wedding venue must be a very difficult reminder of the life Evelyn had lost, but he knew how much she and Jon loved it here. He remembers when Jon first rung him to tell him where they were getting married. He had advised against it, the red tape of weddings abroad and the hassle of travel seemed unnecessary, but Jon was insistent. He would not consider any other venue. And when Max had arrived that first time he could see why.

Amy

It's taken just over two and half hours to arrive at the hotel. The drive from London to Cardiff on the M4 has always been pretty monotonous. As I pull up at the hotel, where the party is being held. I am apprehensive. I have been emotionally exhausted at the thought of seeing Jasper who'd be here tonight.

As I walk towards the entrance there is part of me that is curious to see him yet terrified at my response and excited that he'll be impressed when he sees me. The party is in an old hotel, a reunion of sorts. I am not entirely sure why I am here. I see a group of people I now vaguely called friends and make my way over to them.

"Wow, Amy. Looking good."

"Oh, this?" I point at my dress. "It's nothing, just threw it on after work."

In actual fact I'd spent the last two months finding the perfect outfit, I wanted to look good in front of Jasper – I still did not know why it mattered so much. I scan the room. I can't see him. One of the girls in the group grabs me by the arm, I don't remember her name.

"Come on, you look like you need a drink." She pulls me in the direction of the bar. "Have you seen him yet," she whispers as if there is a conspiracy between us. I know she is talking about Jasper.

"No, not yet." I order a vodka and lemonade, I can feel my legs shaking in anticipation. The room seems too bright, I do not know why I'm here.

"I saw him earlier, he asked if you were coming. To think all those years you were together and now you have no contact whatsoever."

"Yes, I know. I suppose that is what happens. I didn't want any contact with him after everything: the way he behaved."

"Really? I'm good friends with both my exes." She raises her eyebrows as if I have failed in her eyes.

I really don't want to spend any more time with her. I turn to walk back to the group, but as I do I realise Jasper is behind me. I wonder how much he'd heard.

"Oh, hi... I didn't know you were there."

"I suspected as much." He still has the same swagger, but he seems nervous. He looks smaller. I've always remembered him as taller than me, but now I realise he is shorter. It is funny the imprint I have of him in my mind in comparison to the reality.

"How are you? It has been a long time."

"Yes, yes, it has. I'm good. You?"

It is awkward and stilted and I quickly discover I don't actually care. After all the hours I've worked myself up about coming tonight, I suddenly realise with such clarity that he is entirely irrelevant in my life now. I see his wife walk towards us, there are no jealous surges, no rushes of regret. It is such a relief. I realise he no longer holds any power over me.

The night progressed. It was rather a let-down in a reassuring way. I stood with groups of people who really no longer meant anything to me. These friends of my past were redundant in my new life. I quickly recognised my disinterest and internally decided I would not see many of them again, apart from my close-knit circle of girlfriends from university, these people were irrelevant in my new life. Since hitting thirty I had discovered the joy of discarding relationships with abandon, ones that no longer brought any value to my life. Wales represented the old me. I made my excuses and retired to the room I'd booked in the hotel. For the first time in a long time I slept well; Jasper no longer interrupting my dreams.

As I drove back to London the following morning, I knew I would not return there for some time. My old life was a chapter I did not wish to reread. I do not want to remember the years before. Years of building a future together, struggling through jobs with the hope I'd end up somewhere better with Jasper – for what? All for what?

I realised as I left that night that now the bitterness and pain had finally submerged in the pool of the past, what was left was sadness and loss. I had not expected it especially as it was my choice and the right decision at that. I thought the process was over, but maybe it never is, maybe when such a substantial relationship ends all we can do is learn how to navigate the aftermath, the life we are now left with. The life we must now create.

13

Evelyn

The following night I am relieved to return to the chateau after a day of wine tasting. It has been busy, which I have welcomed, but I want to spend some time alone in the sumptuous rooms. I am eager to return to the letters. Their story fascinates me, and I have only read a handful of them.

I tried to explain to Max my discovery, but he was not interested. I do not understand how he can dismiss such an important part of my family's history. I choose the top two letters from the pile and lay them out before me. There is not a great deal of correspondence, and I do not want to rush through them.

Somewhere in France 1916

Olive,
My heart is ravaged with sorrow. I fear the romance of war is just a myth, for nothing seems romantic about the intense longing I have for you. It is a deep pain that I think is slowly rendering my heart rotten;

the nourishment it needs has been replaced by all the horrors imaginable.

The shells drop all around us, the air is full of whistling. It is barren, desolate. The guns belch enormous flames and a plethora of smoke fills our surroundings. At certain moments it is as if the earth is screaming. I am always thinking of you, an endless longing to hold you in my arms, dreaming of your touch. If only I could hasten the end of the war, and squash the hours left in all these days to come, until I am home again.

Passions are indulged far too easily out here: the men succumb to their urges. Trust me when I say that this is an affliction, Olive, that does not apply to me. I cannot imagine desire for anyone other than you.

Jack

Dear Jack,

I know you feel weary, darling. I feel as if this war has uprooted my heart, and I am afraid it will never beat properly where it is meant to be caged again.

The land you now occupy will, I promise, become a memory, far and forgotten in your future, the horrors will be hidden, and the sunshine will break the clouds and the flowers will bloom. We will lie in fields of hay and bask in the twilight as we drink each other in once again. Love will overcome what atrocities the world is victim to right now my love.

Know that I am always with you.

Yours always,

Olive

xxx

Tears stream down my face. What sorrow my family had to endure, before my very existence. The horrors of yesterday's wars seem so incomprehensible, yet now I am the victim of a different war. The difference is my great-grandmother lived in fear of losing Jack every day; for me it was not even a consideration. That night in the chateau, I fall asleep thinking of their love story and of how lucky I was to have mine.

There has been a deep, unsettled anxiety in the pit of my stomach since I discovered Max's wishes, but with every day away it is easing. Bordeaux was easier than Barcelona. I scattered a small part of Jon under the tree in the grounds. It is often lit up with lanterns and decorated with roses hanging from its branches. It seems right he is decorated every now and again. He loved a party too; there will be a little part of him at all the celebrations in the future.

We left early this morning to travel to Granada. The ease of air travel is not lost on me. I think of my great-grandparents and the difficultly they had reaching one another 100 years ago. Jon used to tell me that travel provides an insight like no other. He was not a soul searcher by any means, but he understood the beauty of reflection and the importance of it. He would always tell me he was healed on our return from trips to Italy – as if the essence of the country was enough to mend the cracks exposed in us from our everyday lives.

Max had been brighter since Friday, when we first arrived at the chateau, and he seems much more spritely as we board the plane. I think he revisited some painful memories at our wedding venue, although we never talked about it. Max was far too private. Nancy's behaviour was not lost on me and Jon – the drinking, the temper, the extreme mood swings. I think Max preferred to pretend that we were all oblivious to the situation, but we were not.

I was disappointed in how their relationship ended. I do not condone affairs. I understood. I was actually mystified it hadn't happened sooner. I did not miss Nancy, she was too intense in every sense of the word. At first, I had found her fun, she was the girl who made everybody laugh; she was so bubbly and vivacious. However, I began to see a different side to her: the morose moods the following day, the curt words aimed at Max, her penchant for antagonising her husband. The bruises on his back he hadn't realised we could see one summer.

As the plane lands in Granada, I suddenly feel a shift, an uplifting. A very slight separation from grief. For the briefest of moments, I am free, but then I remembered why I was here, and the loss hits me all over again.

Max

He is relieved to leave the chateau. It had been a nice weekend. Drinking wine in those surroundings was always going to be enjoyable, but the reminders were still hard. He felt more buoyant as soon as he left the grounds, though. He was looking forward to their next trip to Granada: he was a fan of Moorish architecture and had always wanted to see the Alhambra.

The plane journey is just under two hours. He places his headphones in and lets himself be transported to another realm. It is the first time the trip has felt like a holiday. He has not forgotten why they are doing this, but he feels lucky to still be exploring this world, to experience such travel.

In the vain hope they will still experience the warmth of the Mediterranean sun in the latter part of October, Max has booked an apartment with a pool. With views of the Alhambra, he hopes this trip will give them the opportunity to relax as well as explore.

Evelyn seems to be relaxing more. The strain on her face is

softening. She has become consumed by her great-grandparents' love letters and he is concerned their sorrow may impact her. He hopes Granada will be good for both of them. His objectives for the trips have always had Evelyn's feelings at the forefront – he hopes the longer the journey goes on, the more she'll heal.

Amy

I return to London. I am meeting Jasmine, one of my firm female friends: she is in the city for the weekend. I have not realised how much I missed my close friends. It can be awfully isolating in London. I am already seated when she arrives in a quaint café near where I live. She walks towards me, effortlessly glamorous, sporting bright red lips as always. I stand and we embrace each other. I had forgotten how nice the simple pleasure of hugging a friend is.

"So, tell me everything. How was the party? Jasper there?" This was the thing about Jasmine she always wanted to know everything about you first, she was happy to discuss heartbreak for hours, even years in this case. My relationship with Jasper, and the breakdown of it, was minimised over the years, both by me and many of the people that surrounded me. I was expected to forget, to move on, to extinguish the nine years we'd grown alongside one another, but Jasmine wasn't one of those people. She always had the time to listen. If the word "divorce" had been applied to the demise of our relationship, I believe I would have been founded more sympathy from many people: more time to assimilate the end of us.

Instead, the subject was considered messy. People did not like to dwell or talk about it; it made them uncomfortable. The façade of bravery was far more pleasing for outsiders. It was necessary to move on, but mainly for the sake of others. Listening repeatedly to the same subject is not a pleasing pastime, so I have learnt to lock Jasper away, alongside all the memories of him. The conversation had a time limit and many friends had made that abundantly clear.

Inevitably, he came to me where and when I least wanted him. He was my night-time visitor, awakening me from sleep, interloping on my dreams. Sometimes we were still together; sometimes I was searching for him in the belief we were meant to be, and other times I was still living in the past. Every time I woke up it would take me a moment to remember my life was different now. I often think about the reaction of my younger self had I told her what lay ahead. It still seems impossible my life changed so dramatically so rapidly.

The memories come in flashes as time passes, my mind allowing these little reminders of him I had tried so hard to quash. I do not remember any intimacy though. It is as if I have eliminated all memories of sex. I cannot contemplate how our bodies once moved as one, it seems impossible. In that sense he is a stranger to me.

"It was fine. No great reunion, rather underwhelming to be honest."

"Oh, thank God for that. Maybe you'll stop dreaming of him now."

"I hope so, as you know, Jasmine, he's not my favourite man to dream of."

"Do you want to talk about him? About seeing him again?"

I liked the fact Jasmine gave me the opportunity. "No, not really, I don't actually. Tell me about yourself. What are your weekend plans?"

We order wine and nibbles and while away the hours.

14

Evelyn

As I close the menu in the tapas bar we have come to for lunch, Max is staring at me. We have been in Granada three days and I'm craving space. "Evelyn, do you want to tell me what the matter is?"

"I can't listen to it, Max."

"What?"

"I can't listen to your incessant talk of terrorism. I don't want to remember my husband because of the way he died. I can't keep this momentum of anger up."

I do not want to remember Jon because of his death. I do not want to repeatedly unfurl what had happened to him.

I want to imagine how he would have reacted to the Alhambra in the bright sunshine. Last time we were here it had poured with rain, and he had always expressed a desire to come back when it was dry. I wanted to guess his tapas choices, I wanted to share a plate of serrano ham and laugh at the English translations on the menu. I wanted to hold his hand across the table and drink in the atmosphere. I simply just wanted Jon to still be with me. I wanted to argue across the table, like we had last time.

"Sorry if I acknowledge the manner in which he died, Evelyn. I can't just forget. I can't forgive those people."

"It's just not getting us anywhere though. I don't want to think about it."

"You're not the only one who lost him, Evelyn. I lost my brother too."

"Maybe it is best we have some space."

"I think you're right," Max replied. I can see the muscles in his shoulders tighten.

I do not want there to be this level of tension, but I can't help it. "I'll see you back at the apartment sometime."

He leaves me in the restaurant in a side street of Granada and storms off. I breathe a sigh of relief, that I am alone for once.

When Jon and I came here in 2015, we had been at loggerheads for weeks. I had half expected us to begin trying for a child immediately after the wedding. It had not happened, and every time I broached the subject with Jon he rebuffed me. We had been married a year, and although things were still great, I was increasingly frustrated by his lack of want for a family. We had been busy buying the flat and Jon's work had been manic, taking him all over Europe, but it didn't mean I could stop my longing for a baby.

The weekend in Granada was a welcome break from home-buying and the mania of our life in London. I tried to plan our days, but Jon was always much more laissez-faire. We got carried away in the airport and on the plane so by the time we arrived at the hotel, we were both drunk. Jon insisted we made love before dinner and by the time we got to the tapas bar I was exhausted.

"Cheer up, Evie. It may never happen."

"Well, that's the problem, isn't it?"

"What are you talking about now?"

"Children. We never discuss it. It's been a year, Jon, and I'm fed up of you ignoring the subject."

"This again?"

"*This again?* Are you serious, Jon? I'm not getting any younger."

"Evelyn, do we need to discuss this now? We're on holiday, I'm trying to relax."

"If not now, then when, Jon? You can't keep avoiding it."

"If you promise to leave it, I'll talk about it as soon as we get home. I just want some fun, Evie. Just this week, is that too much to ask?" He had smiled across the table and I melted. He always had a way of getting out of these conversations.

Max

He trawls the city by himself, moving from bar to bar. He and Evelyn have decided to have the next two days apart. She clearly needs her space if they are going to continue on this trip.

He cannot help it if he needs to talk about Jon's death, if he needs to process the attack.

He activates his Tinder: there is nothing else to do. Evelyn is holed up in the apartment reading her great-grandparents' letters. They have become part of her routine. He thinks it is unhealthy. He cannot understand why she is spending her evenings immersed in their love story. He spends the evening swiping left and right. He matches easily. Max is dark, tall and brooding and women seem to find him attractive. He never possessed the same charm as Jon: he did not have the energy of his brother. It hadn't halted his success with the opposite sex though.

He chats to a few girls and vaguely suggests a drink with one of them. He is not interested in anything other than company at this point. He wants a distraction, Evelyn is consuming him, and he would just like to switch off for a while. An hour later, an American student arrives to meet him. Max is clearly far too old for her, but he is not deterred.

He does not explain what he is doing in Granada. He brushes off her questions with a lie about a business trip. She babbles on and he wonders if she has made many friends here as she too seems desperate for company. It must be difficult moving to an entirely different city, let alone country. Max has never left London. Jon did for a while in his twenties. He had travelled the world before settling in Montreal for a few years. Max had visited him there and been impressed with how at ease his brother was somewhere entirely new.

Jon had embraced the French-speaking city; he'd loved the Canadian and French combination. He had travelled on the metro there like he would in London, as if he had been there for years. He'd lived in Little Italy. He'd returned to London after three years and Max was relieved – the move had made him feel inadequate.

Max and the American student drink increasingly stronger spirits and as the evening moves on he finds the possibility of going back to her flat more appealing. She is clearly not opposed to this. It is so different now to when he had dated before Nancy. Tinder had not even existed: it was the beginning of dating websites, but it was much more common to meet someone out at a bar, to start conversation organically. When he became single, he had no idea how to manage this new dating game. He'd spent the first week on Tinder swiping the wrong way. He was always very honest that he did not want anything more than an evening or two; after Nancy he was not prepared for commitment.

The girl is pretty enough, and her personality is pleasant. They talked of their pasts and she told him of her hope to move permanently to Spain one day. He thinks her ambition sweet. He wondered what would become of her, if she will ever make it to Europe in the future, or whether she'll return to America and Spain would become a distant memory.

He ends up staying at hers. She provides him with the escape he needs. When he wakes the next morning, he feels bad that he hasn't contacted Evelyn, but he needed space too.

The girl is still dozing when he leaves. "I have a meeting," he says kissing her forehead goodbye.

She murmurs something; he tells her he'll ring later, they'll meet up again.

He is lying, of course: he never meets these females again.

Amy

University for me was like an unfurling flower. I had sprung to life, emerging from what felt like the winter of my youth. I hadn't expected it, it was difficult, up until that point I had been a bit nerdy: isolated. My head had always been in books and then suddenly there were all these new experiences to enjoy. There were boys, friends, alcohol and parties.

My flatmates, Jasmine and Aisha, introduced me to a world I'd been blind to. It felt exciting and dangerous. I couldn't quash the guilt though, the pressure from my family to adhere to a certain set of rules when it came to my behaviour. I knew my father would struggle with me dating men, so I found it easier to remain silent on the matter. As far as my family knew I continued to bury my head in books, university was just an extension of my urge to study, to succeed.

I did succeed for all intents and purposes. As far as they were concerned, I was accomplished. They knew of Jasper but thought I had remained celibate since.

I never felt successful enough. I don't think the need to prove myself has ever disintegrated. Even today whilst I prepare a case, I still question my ability to represent my client.

Our case load is varied and I struggle to switch off. We are representing parents accused of sending money to their son who was residing in Syria, knowing he would use it for terrorist purposes. The parents had no reason to believe their son was involved in terrorist activity.

There is a hearing shortly regarding a man we are defending: he was accused of planning a terrorist plot because he was found to be in possession of an al-Qaeda handbook. It was for the purposes of his PhD study.

We work to protect those who have been penalised by the counterterrorism measures. They have the potential to stigmatise whole communities, especially when it comes to Schedule 7 of the Terrorism Act. Ordinary British Muslims are under the same threat as every UK citizen, yet counterterrorist measures mean all Muslims are under suspicion.

These policies have helped contribute to hostility towards Muslims, by creating a climate of fear and suspicion towards them. Schedule 7 means stop and search at airports can be carried out without suspicion. For some people, these stops have become part of their normal travel routines. They are pulled over and asked questions about how many times they pray; what they understand about jihads; how many mosques they attend. It is rare to be a Muslim and know someone who hasn't experienced these stops at an airport.

15

Evelyn

I spend the afternoon at the apartment. I doze by the pool occasionally taking the letters out to the terrace to read them.

1917

Dear Jack,
My heart is heavy. I feel like my goodbye was simply horrible, I did not say anything I wished. I was trying, my darling, to be strong. I did not want to add to your troubles and break in front of you, but now I fear you misread my behaviour for lack of compassion. I cannot bear it when we part, but yet the very fact we are parting means we have met.
I can only imagine how dreadful it is for you, as we have no idea of the horrors and discomfort you must endure, but I am finding it frightfully hard to stay cheerful. It is two years of this terror now, and I cannot contain my longing. I wish, sweetheart, we could just go to a dance, or I could cook your supper, draw you a

*bath. I wish I could do all the things a proper wife is meant
to do.*

*It is glorious today, the garden is willing me outside, but I just feel
such a terrible sadness. I hope you can still see beauty where you are. I
fear that you are in hell and there is no glimpse of how pretty this
curious world can be.*

Yours always,
Olive

Dear Olive,

*The longest goodbye is also the hardest, for tomorrow I do not know
whether I will see another night in this lifetime. I do not know if I will
ever stare up at the stars again and dream of a future I so hoped to
have. I do not know if these hands will ever grasp a pen again and tell
my love what she means to me. I do not know if life is about to leave
me: I so hope it won't, but, my sweet love, as I lie here I do not know.
It is a terrifying battle we are about to enter into, and I do not know
how much luck will be in my favour: I do hope it is. Guard our
memories, they may be all we have. And know, my darling, that my
last thoughts were always of you.*

Jack

I lie back on the sun lounger and close my eyes. The image of
them both in separate countries, desperate for one another's
company, is so very vivid. I cannot imagine the conditions my
great-grandfather had to live through. Jon would have loved
their story, he was such a romantic. I close my eyes and imagine
him lying next to me. I would do anything to reach out my hand
and intertwine my fingers through his. I lie on my back, the sun

beating down on me. Spanish conversation filters up from the street below occasionally as I doze.

The daylight is drawing to a close when I sit up. It is nearly seven o'clock.

I take two more letters to read – I savour their words. I read them over and over again.

1917

Dear Jack,
I can hear the birdsong, Jack: a chorus of chatter floating across the lawn from the hedgerow. I wonder if the birds occupy the battlefields, or whether they have taken flight to safer surroundings. Such a simple pleasure listening to birdsong, but I wonder if even that has been taken from you.
I know you told me to write to you of all that you miss and can only now imagine out there, but I feel so very terrible telling you these things when you won't enjoy them for a while yet.
Yours always,
Olive

～

Dear Olive,
It will be you I carry deep down in my heart to the front line, in a bid to ease my great loneliness. I will take you everywhere in my heart. I cannot tell you much about the scenery, my dear, it is practically all the same. My thoughts begin and end with you. How sweet it is to kiss you in my imagination.
A world full of love I send to you.
Jack

～

Max did not come home last night. I did not fall sleep until the early hours of the morning, thoughts of Olive and Jack swirling around in my head.

I half expected him to come stumbling through the door to our apartment, just like when he and Jon had been out in the city and arrived home inebriated. I had found it infuriating at the time, but I wistfully look back at those evenings now. I had hoped he would come back because I wanted to clear the air. My anxiety levels were also through the roof and I needed to know he was okay.

I messaged him when I woke up at eight. He replies an hour later, apologising for not letting me know he was staying out. There has obviously been a woman involved. This was never Max's style. It is not in his nature. But he seems to think it is now. Since his ex-wife he has been trying to mask his sorrow. I could easily point out that the beds of other women are not working.

I used to speak to Jon about it. He was of the opinion that Max was entitled to a good time – I did not like that side of Jon when we discussed other women. It was as if I was married to someone I didn't know. There was an edge of misogyny that I hadn't noticed when I first met him.

I decide to have breakfast out. It is sunny today. Jon wanted nothing more than to come here when the sun shone and I may as well make the most of it for him.

Max

He enters the apartment and discovers Evelyn is out. He tries to call her, but her phone is off. He is hung-over, the heat is rising and his dehydration from excess alcohol becomes clear. He finds some paracetamol and drinks a pint of water.

The pool looks so welcoming. He throws on his swim shorts

and enters the water to swim mechanically, his mind switching off with each stroke. He does not know how long he has been in the water, but when he emerges Evelyn is sitting on the terrace smiling.

"Good night?"

He coughs a brief "Um hum".

"You remind me of Jon when you swim. You have the same style."

He had forgotten how much Jon used to love the water. He would swim after every gym session. "What have you been doing?"

"Walking, I had a nice breakfast out – tomatoes on bread of all things, who knew *pan con tomate* was so popular here. Simple and delicious."

"Do you still want time on your own today?"

Evelyn is still smiling and she seems softer. "No. No, it's okay. Let's do something together. Let's go scatter Jon at the Alhambra in the sun: he always wanted to come back when it was sunny."

With that he rises from the pool and grabs the nearest towel. "Yes. Yes, let's go do that."

It is his favourite day yet: they immerse themselves in being tourists. They spend hours exploring the Alhambra palace and the surrounding fortress and gardens. They come to a viewpoint, a panoramic of the city around dusk, the Alhambra behind them. The light is a warm red and the quiet chatter of foreign language surrounds them.

Without saying a word Evelyn passes a small tin to Max. He opens the lid and lets the ashes escape so they roll down the hill on the wind. Evelyn places a hand on his shoulder and they stand in silence remembering his brother.

Amy

I cannot sleep. I have been awake since 4am thinking about work. I have been restless all week, all too aware how lucky I am as I lie in bed each night. I am haunted by the people I am representing or have represented. The sadness of so many humans' lives and experiences, which as a white woman in Britain I will never have to suffer. I boil the kettle and make myself coffee. The flat is extremely cold for autumn.

I turn the news on and Trump fills the screen. I sigh at the state of the world.

When we have leaders who behave like terrorists, what do we expect? When they encourage polarisation and division? No good can ever come from this. We are all warned of the wrong enemy. If we elect global leaders who don't protect refugee children, who rip their parents away, who are racist, prejudiced, who incite hatred and fear in nations, we are inciting terrorism. If we give power to a man who continues to behave as if he were a god with no recourse. A man who is inhumane, intolerant and dangerous. He should be our biggest fear. The man who has made permissible white supremacy through his rhetoric.

16

Evelyn

The rest of Granada is very pleasant. There are moments of great sadness, my legs buckled underneath me one night: grief occasionally floors me. I find myself laughing one afternoon and then the guilt I felt in the aftermath of a moment of happiness is suffocating. I still cry myself to sleep, and it is during the last night that Max comforts me.

It is in the early hours of the morning and my sobs have not subsided since I came to bed at midnight. Max quietly knocks on the door. He comes to me on the bed and lying on top of the duvet he wraps his arms around me and for the first time since Jon died I allow myself to be held like this. He rocks me to sleep, stroking my hair until the next thing I know it is light and I have slept through the night for the first time in weeks.

Max

He knew when he suggested they share a bed it was selfish. He had seen how vulnerable she was. He just wanted to hold her, to offer her some comfort. He half expected her to say no, but she had relented quickly. She had curled into a ball on the bed and he had wrapped himself around her, his arms protecting her from the outside world. He could faintly feel her quiet sobs and her quivering body, he had stroked her hair until she fell asleep. In the morning neither of them had said a word about it. It certainly wasn't an arrangement arising from sexual tension for Evelyn, but rather one of comfort.

It had been their last night in Granada. They hadn't spoken about it the following day and she had retreated from him in the morning as the sun rose. He had reconciled with the pain when she did this.

He wonders if she imagined he was Jon when the room was shrouded in darkness. These feelings confuse him. He tries not to overthink. He wanted to help her through the pain and that seems to be exactly what he is doing.

17

Evelyn

The red, orange and yellow hues of Bologna's buildings basked in the last of the sunshine for the day, illuminated by the dimming sun. The sound of mopeds and youths' laughter filled the narrow streets. Jon and I spent those afternoons in May 2019 napping, the curtains billowing through the window as the afternoon breeze drew them lightly outside.

In the evening we walked under the pillared streets to the nearest trattoria for platters of meats and cheeses. Our bellies were full of the abundance of produce we had already consumed that day, but we were content with the anticipation of more.

We spent the six days we had there replenishing our souls, not only with food and drink but beauty and passion. Jon had been morose for weeks, what with work deadlines and the daily stresses of existence in London, but the time in Bologna pacified him. We were both so happy.

Our relationship had been strained recently, but I did not know what had been bothering Jon of late. He had started visiting the gym far more than usual – he always increased his workouts when he was stressed – and we had been like passing ships in the night. I had begun to worry, until he suggested this trip. It had felt like we were drifting, but I couldn't pull us back.

It is hard, because it feels like yesterday that we were here together. Bologna was one of our last trips. Jon had been a big lover of food – Bologna, known as the stomach of Italy, was his idea of heaven. I have lost my appetite of late so the thought of eating our way around the city is less appealing than the last time I was here. You could get lost in the tangle of medieval alleys that sit east of the main square, Piazza Maggiore. A maze of delis, bars, restaurants and typical Italian grocery stores.

Max is excited and researches restaurants on the plane. Jon preferred atmosphere: he never liked eateries that were quiet. He'd taken me to Osteria Dell'Orsa on our final evening. It was typical Jon – loud, boisterous and exciting. It was full of university students and Jon had embraced the hustle and bustle.

I have fond memories of our time here: things had been off kilter, but Jon was back to his usual engaged self. He had been distant in the prevailing months. I'm not sure what the shift was, maybe work had been stressful: he tended not to talk to me about things like that. He had always kept his worries to himself, he only really shared the positives when it came to work. I didn't have any idea what went on in his office from one day to the next.

As Max and I walk through Piazza Maggiore I remember our last night here. Jon had seemed so content, so present in the moment. I always knew this is where I would scatter him. It had been such a perfect evening. I remember the kiss during our final drinks of the evening. The sweet tenderness he had shown. It had felt like he was kissing me for the first time, as if he was remembering what we had, rediscovering us. I had felt so happy, like all our worries would drift away. With Jon by my side anything seemed possible. I want to sit at the same table, order the same drink and wistfully remember that evening as I look up at the stars, before I scatter him across the Piazza, a little bit of him therefore remaining here forever.

Max

Max had been unsure whether to include Bologna as one of their destinations. He knew that when Jon and Evelyn had come here, their marriage had hit a stumbling block. Jon did not tell Max the reasons: it was apparent there was something going on. Evelyn has never discussed with him any of the problems in her marriage and Max does not want to ask her directly.

But now as they sit in the square Evelyn seems content. Max has extensive plans for the next five days: the city is known for its food and he cannot wait to sample all it has to offer. Wheels of cheese and ham hocks hang from the ceilings as they walk the busy side streets – it is culinary heaven.

There is an energy to the city, home to Europe's oldest university, Max can feel the anticipation of youthful hope in his surroundings. Max marvels at its very own leaning towers – Torre Degli Asinelli. He looks in wonder at *la rossa* (the red) city and he almost forgets his grief for a moment.

18

Evelyn

Max and I continue to share a bed in Bologna, which should have felt strange but was oddly comforting. I have not spoken to him about this arrangement: we just silently enter the same bed each evening. As soon as the lights are out he cocoons me in his arms. It is the only time I sleep, maybe because it feels like it is Jon. Maybe because I am so terribly lonely with grief. Being held by someone who knew him so well alleviates my distress.

In the morning we both withdraw physically and go about our days without mentioning our nightly hugs.

Since Jon's death I've heard so many empty platitudes. *It'll get easier with time. Time is a healer. Day by day, step by step.* I have listened to these words of wisdom, these snippets of advice people scatter around me, and I knew they were just trying to help, but it made me want to scream.

I watch as life goes on city to city, as people continue the daily routine of existence, and I cannot fathom how I am meant to wade through this torrent of sadness when this journey comes to an end. Although you cannot see my scars it does not mean they are not there. Although you can see me smile it does not mean that there aren't a thousand tears hidden behind that moment of brief happiness. The heart broken is the hardest thing to heal.

There is a life before the terror attack and my life now. I do not even recognise the woman who existed prior to that day. She is a stranger in a memory I struggle to identify with: a woman with a lightness that has long since been weighed down. So, a few hugs from a man who also loved my husband seems like a small comfort right now.

Max has gone to the bar to order coffee so I decide to fill my time reading another letter. I know it infuriates him, but it is a distraction.

~

Dear Jack,
I know you are tired, and it must seem pointless but please know that for your sacrifice the future will be brighter; years from now our children and their children will enjoy the beauty that there is to behold in this world. Just think of all the places they'll travel, all the things they'll see. You are making that possible, my darling. Their adventures will be possible because of you and all the men there with you now. Please know you are making a difference; you may not see it yet, but I believe you are all helping to change the face of their future, my love – goodness will prevail.
Stay brave, you'll be home soon.
Yours always,
Olive

~

I sit back and think of all the worries they must have endured during the war.

I myself had learnt life is not linear, my expectations of our marriage were different to the reality just like Olive and Jack. After we were married, and spent a year avoiding pregnancy and the thought of babies, I suddenly became desperate to have a family. I downloaded all the apps, I began to eat healthier, I stopped drinking, I increased my exercise. I knew it could take months, even years, but I had assumed that it would be pretty straightforward with me and Jon.

I had not expected we'd be trying for a whole year before we conceived. The disappointment I had felt every month when I came on my period was getting harder to bear. So, finally in the January when I was late I was overjoyed. We took a test two weeks later, fearful to jinx it. I had not let myself get too carried away, but when the two blue lines developed I could not stop sobbing with relief. We were going to have a family.

In those first few weeks my level of excitement shocked me. I scrolled endlessly through parenting websites. I designed the nursery. I researched the best car seats, beds and bouncers. I could not wait to be a mum. Jon was equally excited, if not a little bit stressed with the financial implications of the new arrival. As an independent wedding planner, I was self-employed, and statutory maternity pay was a joke.

I had not realised there was anything wrong. I'd had symptoms: I'd been nauseous until eight weeks; my limbs exhausted. I felt run-down and drained, but I'd been told to expect this. The first trimester is always the worst for illness, and my friends had explained it would begin to clear around twelve weeks, if not before. So, when my symptoms eased I was certain it was because I was inching nearer to the second trimester.

Jon and I could not contain our anticipation when we arrived at the hospital for the scan. I was twelve weeks and four days pregnant. I had worked out the due date myself and was certain it would fall on November 11 or near enough.

I was trying not to wet myself when we entered the room for the scan: I had drunk far too much water to contain any longer. Jon grasped my hand as I lay on the bed and the nurse applied the gel to my bare stomach. It was a strange sensation. She moved the stick around on my stomach, we fixated on the screen ready to see the first glimpse of our baby. She continued to move the stick around, pressing harder now so I thought my bladder was going to burst.

I felt Jon's grip increase, I knew my hands had begun to shake too.

"I'm just going to fetch a doctor, won't be a sec." The nurse smiled and left the room. She seemed jovial, but I could sense her anxiety. I knew something was wrong. When she came back in her smile was still plastered on her face, but the doctor beside her looked stern.

"Evelyn, I'm just going to take a look, if you don't mind. I'm Dr Green." He had kind eyes.

I couldn't bring myself to respond. I shut my eyes and waited for him to press down on my belly. It seemed an eternity before he spoke. Jon was leant over the bed, kissing my forehead, stroking my arm.

"I'm very sorry, Evelyn and Jon, but we can't detect a heartbeat. Judging by my measurements it looks like the foetus passed away four weeks ago."

The night that followed was profoundly sad. It felt like our future had just been wiped out, or the future I'd spent the past three months planning. I had never understood the sorrow that comes with the loss of a baby. I had never realised the pain of a miscarriage.

Jon was silent, he quietly drove us home, where he cooked me pasta with copious amounts of cheese. He'd bought wine, not to celebrate now, but to drown our sorrows. It was rosé wine, I don't like rosé, but then I wasn't meant to be drinking it.

The following morning, we returned to hospital, the journey so very different to the previous day. The doctors explained it was best to allow the pregnancy to end naturally. We were sent home with leaflets and advice on what to expect. When I got home I read thread after thread on Mumsnet, desperate to hear from other women who had experienced a miscarriage. There was this silent void when it came to miscarriage, a taboo no one talks about.

The bleeding didn't start for one more week. Every day I would dread what lay ahead. When I began bleeding, it wasn't spotting or a little amount: it flowed and flowed. Thankfully I was at home, I lay on the bathroom floor as I crumpled over in agony, the contractions coming in waves. I expelled everything, my physical and emotional pain became one. I called Jon home, he rushed back from work and held me, leant against the bathtub sobbing as we lost our baby. That was the first time.

Max

Max is waiting at the bar in the departure lounge trying to fetch them some coffees. Evelyn is already engrossed in her letters. She hasn't read them for a little while, so he has decided to remain silent on the matter.

Max is ravenous, so he purchases two overpriced prosciutto ciabattas alongside their coffee. Their next stop is Paris. It has been a long time since he'd been, the last time had actually been with Jon, back in their unjaded youth, when Jon had been extravagant and wild.

He makes his way back to Evelyn and watches as a tear streams down her face, he wishes she wasn't so sad.

He thought she had relaxed in Bologna, he had seen hints of the person she used to be but then grief would eclipse her again. He had continued to hold her in the night-time. He hoped the trips were making a difference, but then occasionally it just seemed nonsensical, a bizarre idea dreamt up by Jon that Max was responsible for making a reality.

Amy

I'm distracted when Zahera enters my office. I've been searching for holidays online – my female friends from university try to arrange a trip every year. I have missed it the past few years, but now I can't help but be tempted when I look at the picture of infinity pools – the idea of cocktails and sunshine is very appealing.

As I greet her, I think she looks tired. "How are you, Zahera?"

"Not great. I'm struggling."

"It sounds like you need a holiday." She glances at my computer screen, a luxury hotel still in view. "I've been looking at escaping myself."

"Airports terrify me, they didn't as a child, but they do now. I avoid holidays."

"Sorry, Zahera. I didn't think. Holidays are the last thing on your mind." How had I been so thoughtless?

"No, it's not that. It's what it is like when I'm in an airport."

I thought back to the research I'd done on the impact of Schedule 7 of the Terrorism Act and the reality of stop and search. "Do you want to talk about it?"

"It's just normal now. I dread the two hours of waiting before the flight. Two hours where everyone stares at me, as if I am about to blow them up. I know that I should keep my anxiety under wraps: it will only make security warier of me if I am shaking. But, I am anxious. I am anxious they'll search my bag, I'm anxious they'll question me, I'm anxious passengers will fear me. I am also anxious because I'm scared of flying.

"Only last year my friends were dragged off a plane and accused of being terrorists. I have known Ahmed for years. He'd been travelling with his sister and her white boyfriend. They were going to Prague for the weekend, a congratulatory trip for completing his degree. The plane was still on the tarmac, their bags stowed away. They were reading the in-flight magazine and discussing what bars they were going to in Prague, when the flight attendant demanded Ahmed and his sister follow her off the plane.

"He did not understand at first. He did not know there was a problem. As he exited the plane he was greeted by armed police. Of course he was terrified and confused. There'd been a complaint by a passenger on the plane, an accusation they were terrorists, that she'd seen Arabic on his phone. For a start, the Quran is written in Arabic, it is our religious text. But it does not imply we are terrorists.

"However, there had been no Arabic, no text seen by a passenger. The complaint was based purely on how they looked: their colour, their dress. The police asked Ahmed and his sister about their jobs, their parents, addresses, jobs, workplaces, their social media presence. They asked him to talk through his passport stamps. He had to explain and justify his previous holidays. The police told him they'd already run a background check, they told him it was clear, but they had to be certain.

"After discovering Ahmed's sister worked for the NHS and they were travelling with a white male, they eased. They apologised for the inconvenience, they told them they must respond to threats when everyone is 'on the edge'. They explained the passenger who reported them was very frightened. The passenger who was not dragged off the plane for false accusations and wasting police time. The passenger who reported someone because of their 'look', who was blatantly prejudiced and racist. That passenger was frightened. Ahmed and his sister had been petrified, their rights were not mentioned, their fear was not acknowledged. They were allowed back on the plane in the end. That was the beginning of their holiday. That is why I hate airports."

"That is awful, Zahera. I'm so sorry." I have so much to learn from this girl who visits my office, her experiences in the city are something I can only ever imagine, her reality will never become my experience as a white female. I realise she has not finished. "Go on..."

"I understand why people fear me. They have been taught to. I am perceived as an enemy; a threat. People have been taught that Muslims want to overthrow their way of life. I understand why people think I'm dangerous: they are told I am. I am not. I hate radicals. Their actions arguably have impacted my everyday more than most. I fear the possibility of attack; I worry about terrorism, yet at the same time I have to endure torment, abuse and reassure people they need not be scared of me.

"The 'us and them' has created a distinction when there needn't be one. I am just like you. I go to bars and clubs. My dress is mainly jeans and tops. Sometimes I wear the hijab; I like it, it looks nice, plus it is a reference to my beliefs. Beliefs I should not feel ashamed of. The Muslim faith has been distorted, used by a few extremists and then paraded in the press as the norm."

19

Evelyn

I have dreamt of sitting outside Parisian cafés, smoking Gauloises cigarettes and drinking black coffee since I was seventeen. The city of romance and style had always called to me. In 2014, Jon booked us into a hotel for the night, a surprise snap visit after our wedding before we fly on to America.

The trees were shedding their coats for the winter, the streets were covered in a blanket of orange and red; the city even managed to make autumn a fashion. Lovers crowded the corners; the city was laden with them. Paris sizzled sex.

Jon wistfully took my hand and we walked through the streets absorbing all the city had to offer. Paris consumed us for the evening. We ate at Chartier in Montmartre, with its high ceilings and substantial mirrors. The building, once a railway station, oozed Frenchness. I was in heaven. The Art Deco style and uniformed waiters were a charming cliché.

Jon smiled at me across the table and reached for my hand. "Think of all the adventures that are yet to come, darling. Think of all the adventures."

The next day we were flying to New York for the first part of our honeymoon, before Barbados. I lifted his hand to my mouth and kissed it. The rest of our lives stretched out before us.

~

"Pass me the tin, Evelyn. I'll do it," Max whispers across the table.

I keep my grip firmly on the tin. "I'm not throwing Jon on the floor here, Max!" I cannot bear the thought of his ashes being swept up at the end of the evening.

"But this is what he wanted. He wouldn't stop talking about this restaurant."

"It doesn't feel right. I don't want to be here, Max. I can't keep rehashing the past."

"Tell me about your meal with Jon here. I want to know."

I was fed up of spoiling our beautiful, precious moments with Max. They were our experiences: mine and Jon's. And, now Max was intruding on them, asking me personal questions, making me share the intimate details of our relationship. I certainly didn't want to scatter Jon here. A restaurant of all places, but he'd apparently talked to Max about this restaurant endlessly.

"I don't want to talk about it, Max. Please just leave it for tonight. Can we just enjoy the meal."

"Of course, I just thought you may want to tell me what it was like when you came here with Jon."

"Not at the moment, Max. I'm tired. Can we just eat, please."

We both order steaks, I remain mute as Max relays the order. The waiters in their waistcoats and dicky bows seem too jovial. What I embraced previously as the epitome of Parisian cuisine and tradition, now seems crass. The tourists that fill the restaurant annoy me. How had I not noticed them before on our last visit? It is too cramped. I am too close to the other table. I do not want to share intimacies with them. The waiter writes our order on the tablecloth: I had forgotten they did this. Four years ago, I had found it wildly endearing, Jon and I had laughed as if we'd entered some other world. Today I find it lazy.

"So, what shall we do tomorrow?" I know Max is trying to cheer me, but it is fruitless. I do not want to be cheered. In the end, I cannot bring myself to do it. I refuse to throw a bit of Jon on the floor here. The staff will only sweep it up at the end of the night. I consider flushing a handful down the toilets, but it seems crude and distasteful.

"Evelyn, I know you don't want to scatter Jon here, but it's what he would have wanted. Please just pass the tin here, I promise I'll pick the right moment."

"Not on the floor here."

"Not on the floor."

I passed him the tin and took small mouthfuls of steak. I couldn't wait to finish and leave the restaurant.

After an interminable meal where I fight back tears and Max tries to cajole me, we pay and leave. As we leave the restaurant, coming into a small cloistered walkway, I am suddenly taken aback.

Jon and I had left the restaurant drunk on wine and romance. He had grabbed my waist, and as we reached the road he twirled me around before kissing me in front of the crowds queuing to eat here.

I close my eyes and lift my face to the sky. I desperately want to relive the moment. When I open them, Max is smiling. He lifts his hand in the air and a plume of dust escapes, Jon is carried on the wind down the 9th Arrondissement and I am left remembering our kiss. A silent tear rolls down my cheek.

I return to the hotel that night and pack, ready to leave tomorrow. Once all my clothes are neatly folded I reach for the letters. I cannot help but delve into my great-grandparents' love story at any given opportunity.

≈

Dear Olive,

I'm so sorry it has been so long. It has been a funny old time. There has been trench deadlock for three weeks now. The boredom is impenetrable, but the only interruption promised is that of pure terror. Our beds and clothes are infected with lice. I know the men worry about picking up venereal diseases. We lost a soldier this week to illness. I held him as he died. I held him in my arms – I saw the light leave his eyes, I saw him go. He was in my arms until the end; a pittance of comfort that he felt the touch of human affection as his soul slipped away.

I dreamt of you last night, of our lost youthful happiness before this all began. I pray to see you in my dreams tonight.

Jack

≈

Dear Jack,

I have heard of this shell shock from Kitty. She said that it causes headaches, memory loss and breakdown. I worry about you experiencing this terror, I pray that you do not succumb to it, Jack. It sounds frightful. They have even set up specialist hospitals for all the men who are falling victim to it.

Some of the women are so blissfully ignorant to what you are all having to endure. Violet has asked Robert to omit the details of the reality of war. In her little mind I think she envisages you all at some cheery boy camp, singing songs and sitting by the campfire.

Whereas Kitty is increasingly concerned about Maurice's peculiar behaviour. He appears quite unstable. His behaviour, I fear, has been affected by the war and I fear he is still experiencing the horror in his head.

Oh, won't it be grand when we can see each other next, Jack. I can only imagine our next reunion and what a happy day it will be when this is all over.

Yours always,

Olive

Max

The meal in Paris is one of the most difficult yet. Evelyn is immersed in her thoughts, she barely engages with any of his efforts to maintain the conversation. He remembers a different trip to Paris with Jon, one interspersed with nightclubs and late nights.

Jon had just won a contract at work when he had rung Max. It had been a mundane weekend in November, the temperature had suddenly dropped and all he had wanted to do was hibernate. He'd been ready for a weekend of TV and the pub, but Jon had different ideas. He'd already booked them tickets on the Eurostar and a hotel. It was typical of Jon and no matter how much Max had resisted, he already knew it was pointless. Twelve hours later they were seated in a French restaurant, with Jon searching his phone for bars and nightclubs to drink in.

Jon had an energy to him that Max could never rival. He was the first buying shots at the bar, the one around the table who always ordered champagne and paid for it. He would suggest Ibiza on a Thursday and be there by Saturday. He was the last at the party, the first at the pub. He had a thirst for life Max tried to emulate but never quite could. They'd ended up in multiple taxis across the city – flitting from bars to clubs; Jon was always searching for the next best place to go.

They'd stayed in Hotel Lutetia, in Saint Germain, where they'd spent most their time drinking expensive cocktails in the bar. Jon had taken Max to Café de Flore and recited its history of poets, literary greats and the actors who had haunted its doors. He was alive with knowledge and excitement for the city.

Max does not remember the names of the other places they had visited – there had been so many. They'd ended up on their last night in Buddha Bar, located on Faubourg St Honore. Its opulent red interior reminded Max of a world of luxury he was a stranger to. Jon had relished it. He'd lost his brother whilst trying to get served at an over-crowded bar, only to find him half an hour later entangled with a French model. Max had left and returned to their hotel. Jon appeared the next morning two hours before their flight, full of stories.

He considers how very different the memories he and Evelyn hold of Jon in the city. How their experiences of him were wildly different.

He told Evelyn about the bars as they walked back to their hotel, omitting the model and the extent of Jon's partying. Evelyn needn't know the man he was before he met her.

Amy

After Zahera left my office I could not stop thinking of her experiences. I cannot help but compare my experiences of airports and holidays with Zahera's. Tonight is very much needed. It's so easy to match on Tinder in the city, especially when it is for one thing only. I don't have the inclination for a relationship, so I couldn't comment on its success rate in that sense, but it serves its purpose for me.

I had not made many friends in London, outside of work it was hard to socialise. I did not have the energy to force friendships, to actively seek them out. By the time I'd finished in the office, my head often hurt too much. Exhausted from the cases, research and papers I'd pored through, I found I wanted nothing more than *I'm a Celebrity Get me out of here*, with a pizza on my lap. I kept in touch with a select few of the university girls though. We met up wherever life allowed us and our weekly WhatsApp chats seemed enough interaction.

Making friends in a city full of people is surprisingly hard. My girls had suggested I joined a group: a running club or cookery class. I found their suggestions patronising. I knew they were trying to help, but I did not want to meet friends that did not arise organically. I had never realised that the city could be such a lonely place, but I have got used to it. I am well versed in spending time on my own.

My job is exhausting enough. The report on experiences of Muslim women in London is taking its toll: the interviews made harrowing listening. By the time I got back every day I barely had any energy to speak to anyone else. This week I'd spoken to women who have suffered at the hands of other Londoners.

The woman who was shopping with her daughter when a group of young, white males threw a lit cigarette at her headscarf. The police discouraged her from pressing charges.

The woman who recalled her experience in an airport: the man in front of her was asked to take his shoes off. He pointed back at her and said, "Shouldn't she be asked too? She looks like someone who would blow up a plane."

I do not deny the absolute devastation waged by terrorists or the impact of these attacks on families, friends and the wider community. However, these women weren't terrorists. The impact on their lives because of the casual discrimination and racism fed to us in the media and by world leaders frightened me.

I think back to the day in August 2017 when I purchased a certain newspaper. I remember leaning up against the wall on my way to the office to digest the article. The newspaper had run with the term "The Muslim Problem". The writer argued Islam was the "one unspoken fear uniting Britain and wider Europe". The initial capitalisation of "The Muslim Problem" was later retracted and replaced with lowercases. There is a normalisation of hate by some of these so-called journalists. One of them referred to "cockroach" refugees and tweeted about the final solution.

After the Manchester Bombing a paper printed a cartoon which depicted refugees coming ashore with rats. People have slowly but surely come to equate refugees, immigrants, terrorists and Muslims in the same context, because so many headlines link all of them in one sentence – inferences are drawn, it is human nature. But, these inferences are dangerous. They put people at risk, they are scary.

The Syrian refugee schoolboy who was assaulted in school, dragged to the floor by his neck and told by his sixteen-year-old attacker, "I will drown you," as he had water forced into his mouth. This is the reality of these messages – human suffering.

20

Evelyn

When Jon and I went to Florence towards the end of 2018, work had been getting us down. Jon was working every hour in the week and I was consumed by weddings on the weekend. We'd been having those little incessant arguments that gradually wear you down, which eventually accumulate into something much more cumbersome.

Jon suggested Florence last minute in an attempt to get things back on track. It wasn't that we'd fallen out of love, we'd just hit a bump in the road. As much as I wanted things to work, we just didn't seem to align: our needs and wants are different. I hoped it was only momentary, and thought that maybe he suggested the city of renaissance because he believed that is what our relationship needed.

The city was a magnificent wonder to both of us. Florence is a shrine to beauty and all things marvellous the human hand can create.

Now Max is quiet. He had been so animated, so positive when we arrived in every other city. But here in Florence, I cannot reach him. We caught the train here this morning from Paris. This morning signalled the beginning of December. He has been perfectly pleasant, but every time I try to initiate a plan he is distinctly distant.

We eat breakfast together, but the silence is unbearable. I wonder if it is best we have some space today. We have been living so inside each other's pockets since Granada, I'm sure it would not harm us. I suggest that we make separate plans for the day, that we can meet up later this evening for dinner. He mumbles a "yes", but I still cannot read him. I love Florence, so a day of aimlessly wandering the streets here alone sounds perfect to me.

When Jon and I had visited the city, we had been strained. A shame, as Florence is one of my greatest joys. I had wanted our relationship to reflect the city of renaissance and enjoy a rebirth of its own. We had momentarily forgotten our worries; the thought of babies and the reality of my miscarriages had been playing heavy on my mind.

Jon had been distant for weeks; he had to stay late in the office most Fridays and I had grown frustrated, especially as it was winter and there were fewer weddings. I wanted us to spend more time together, but whenever I asked him if he could leave early or stay late another night he had been elusive and told me it was important it was Friday.

He'd suggested the trip on a whim, and before I knew it, we were flying the following week. Jon did things like that. He was spontaneous, he wasn't tied to plans. I had used to think it was irresponsible, but now looking back it was the most sensible thing in the world; it was if he had known that time was precious, and we mustn't delay until tomorrow – because there may never be one.

He had booked the Savoy off Piazza del Republica. He never discussed finances and cost. I never questioned. He booked me half a day of spa treatments. I had wondered if this was his way of saying sorry for the distance between us. He often threw money and presents at things that he was worried he couldn't fix.

I tried to relax, to appreciate the surroundings, but I had been consumed by our most recent loss. I had thought it impossible I would lose the third baby. I'd heard of friends who had two miscarriages, but three? I had begun to worry there was something seriously wrong with me and the more I thought about it the more the worry swelled. I had tried to promise myself I wouldn't say anything, I'd let it lie, but wine had loosened my tongue and I could not help but bring it up.

I had seen his face descend as I had changed the subject that afternoon. We had been drinking wine outside Gubbe Rosse in Piazza Della Republica, watching the children on the old-fashioned carousel twirl around and around. There was something magical about carousels that always mesmerised me. The sun had been setting and there was a chill in the air, but also that hopeful hint of springtime.

I had only wanted to broach the subject of fertility treatment, but Jon had exploded. I did not think IVF was such a dreadful idea: maybe if we had a strong embryo I would carry to full term. It would give us a better chance of creating our family.

He told me to leave it. I suppose I should have, but I am not one to let things go, especially when it came to us having a baby.

It was the bitterness that escaped his lips, the scorn for me as he relayed how IVF would not work. The implied connotations of his words – the reality that he thought it was all my fault we could not have children. I should have stayed and talked it through with him, but I could feel anger surging to the surface. I had stood up and left. I had no idea where I was going, and it was hours later before I returned to the hotel. Jon was not there when I returned.

The next morning, we woke and packed our things quietly. We never talked about what happened that evening. Upon our return, I had hoped things would be different between us, but he had drifted further from me.

I had forgotten how far apart we had felt – Florence with Max reminds me that things weren't always perfect with Jon.

Max

He had not realised the emotions it would ignite. When the train pulled in at Florence, all he could think about was getting to the hotel. It was a perfectly functional hotel he had booked in the centre and only a short walk away. Evelyn had gone straight to bed: she was tired he could tell.

But Max had a surge of adrenaline that you sometimes experience after travel – the relief of arriving at your destination – and he had decided to have a drink in the hotel bar.

Inevitably it had led to another and then another and he had found himself maudlin at the memories of Nancy. He had not imagined coming back here would trigger such feelings, but this trip seemed to be flooring him when he least expected it. He had promised himself after Bordeaux that he would not allow her to plague these travels any further, but as the alcohol descended he remembered what had happened, what it had been like, all over again.

It had been his dream for years to travel around Italy on the trains. He'd heard Jon talk of trips to Florence and Rome and he had been desperate to experience the food and the culture too. Nancy had been non-committal: she did not specify where she wanted to honeymoon, and Max had assumed she'd be happy for him to take the reins as she appeared to have no preference.

He had organised it all: the destinations; the dates; their

itinerary; the accommodation. He had booked all their trains in advance, so there was no stress when they arrived. He had it all planned. They had married three months previous but had delayed the honeymoon due to his leave with the police.

Nancy had been temperamental on the plane, angered when the steward had taken too long to serve her a drink, impatient when she had tried to call them back for another. He had told her to calm down... he realised his mistake immediately. She did not take well to being told what to do. She had been snapping very quickly of late.

Nancy had seemed so carefree when he met her, but the happy-go-lucky woman he had married appeared to be slipping.

They'd arrived in the hotel too late for dinner: his first mistake. He'd spoken to the receptionist who had said the bar was still open for drinks and snacks: his second mistake. He had stood up for himself when she had told him his efforts at a honeymoon were pathetic: his third mistake. He had never been hit by a woman before. When they'd gone back to their room, it was apparent she'd drunk too much and she was seething.

He had tried to calm her, put his hands on either side of her arms, but she had exploded. After she repeatedly punched him, he tried to restrain her, but the kicks came next. He could have easily fought back, but it seemed so wrong. He'd fallen asleep with her telling him, "It is all your fault. If you were a real man, it wouldn't have happened. You are a poor excuse for a husband."

The next morning Nancy had showered him with love and apologies. He was confused but put it aside. She'd been stressed at work – overwhelmed – before they'd come away.

At that point, he had thought the first time would be the last time.

Amy

I stayed over at my date's house. I always knew I was going to; that was my intention with any of my Tinder dates. I left as the sun rose this morning: I never stayed for long. I hated the awkward, uncomfortable mornings where we both pretended we'd call, when in actual fact our meeting had just been a beneficial transaction that needn't be repeated.

The man had been pleasant enough, handsome in a boring kind of way, a face that could merge into a thousand others in the city's bars on a Friday night. We'd exchanged the usual information: our jobs, where we came from, where we lived as if these facts defined us. I never tell these men my real job. I prefer to remain anonymous. There is no reason for them to have any insight into my life.

I have the weekend off. I realise that I have not looked into Zahera's brother's case properly as promised, what with work and the research paper there never seemed enough hours. I had promised her, though, so I would. I just needed to find the time.

21

Evelyn

I did not read my great-grandparents' letters for days. I was simply too sad to read of anyone else's grief. But, there is a strange comfort tonight in their correspondence. I do not feel so lonely, just knowing that grief like this existed between other couples diminishes the isolation I sometimes feel. I packed some of the letters in my bag this morning. I had been hoping for a moment of my own without Max suffocating me with his worry. I had slept as soon as we got here, but today I plan on exploring.

I walk to the Boboli gardens, where I find a spot in the afternoon sun. I lie on the grass and retrieve the papers from my bag. Florence is laid before me in all its glory.

Dear Jack,
I have news. It must have happened on your last visit, but I've been so

preoccupied I failed to notice. I am with child. It came as an awful
shock...
I so wished you'd have received leave again by now, so I could have
shared the news with you in person. I do hope you're happy with the
news. The doctor has said we should expect the baby in the spring. It
is something to look forward to, my love.
Something pure within all of the horror.
Yours always,
Olive

Tears stream down my cheek. The news I had forever longed to receive, my great-grandmother had, but she couldn't share it with her husband. I cannot bear to read any more. I am overcome with anguish. The heartache that I will never carry Jon's child is devastatingly confronting.

Towards the end of his life, we had stopped trying. Jon was adamant that it was too much, that he couldn't go through it any longer. I had appeased him, but ultimately, I was certain he'd change his mind. He couldn't give up on our child that easily.

It had been hard, but it was not his body that had expelled the babies. It wasn't him who had to acknowledge their body was a failure month after month. It was not him who had to say goodbye physically to their baby every time it happened.

Maybe motherhood was my purpose and that is why I'd felt so unfulfilled of late, because it was the one thing I could not seemingly do. The hardest thing was the questions, the endless questions from friends, acquaintances and even strangers about my situation when it came to children. *Do you want children? Are you going to start trying soon? I wouldn't leave it too late; it's never the right time. I'd do it sooner rather than later. What are you waiting for? If you're hesitating, maybe it's because you're with the wrong person.* So much presumption and unwelcome interference.

Had they known I'm sure they wouldn't have commented, but I didn't feel I should have to disclose our grief to them. Perhaps I should have told them. It may have been easier, but then I could not cope with their pity.

I walk back to my hotel hours later, my cheeks still wet with tears, after a day crying across the squares of the city. I have just enough time to shower and change.

Max is in the lobby when I walk through reception. "Evelyn, where have you been?"

"Sorry, Max. I lost track of time."

"I've been worried. I couldn't find you."

"I'm fine, Max." I make my way to the elevator. "I'll be back in fifteen for dinner."

Max just sighs and informs me he'll meet me in the bar. I know he worries, but I find his worry unwelcome. I initiated some space for his sake and now I am met with an avalanche of concern. I do not know how to please him.

Max

He was trying as hard as he possibly could to do what was best for Evelyn, but she seemed to forget that it was hard for him too. She was not the only person who had lost someone. Over breakfast this morning he had arranged to meet her in the hotel lobby for dinner. She had been late. She did not seem to understand that he worried, he had no idea where she was, what she'd been doing in the city.

He needs to snap out of the memories he ignited yesterday. It is a waste of time reliving what happened between him and Nancy. It is just a part of the past.

The meal with Evelyn is delicious, in the sense the quality and taste of the produce spoke for themselves. Evelyn is quiet, but he does not push her tonight: he knows when to let her be with the conversation.

They have four more days here and they plan their excursions. They'll visit the Uffizi tomorrow and delight in the greatness of the art. Max can't wait to admire the Duomo and Giorgio Vasari's and Domenico di Michelino's artwork. Evelyn suggested they hire mopeds and have a day in the Tuscan countryside too. There is so much to look forward, yet everything feels so forced – their happiness only pretend in the vain hope it will become real.

~

"Let me take your bags, Evelyn."

"If you're sure."

As they leave the hotel four days later, Max thinks that the rest of the trip has been a success. They were so enamoured with the city and all it had to offer, they had almost forgotten themselves. The day in the Tuscan countryside had felt like a tonic and Evelyn had appeared carefree and joyful. He could picture Jon riding alongside them, a massive smile on his face: he had loved experiences like that.

"Max, before we head to the airport there is one more place I want to go."

"Where?"

"Follow me."

"Just tell me where we're going, Evelyn. I don't want to be traipsing around the city with all the bags."

"It's not far, give me the bags back then, Max. We'll share the load." Evelyn had removed them from his clutches and set off ahead.

"Wait for me." He watches her weave through the people ahead before she stops at what appears to be a small market close to the Pont Vecchio bridge, the Mercato Nuovo: leather belts, bags, knitted ponchos and scarves being the wares on sale.

"I don't understand, Evelyn. You want to do some shopping? Could you not have done this before we were leaving?"

"No, I don't want to shop. You'll see now, it is just around the corner."

He does not understand. It is only as they walk around the back of the market he sees why they are here. The large gold boar takes centre stage, the Porcellino of Florence has a crowd gathered around it, each person vying to get to the front.

"They say if you stroke its nose, it is a guarantee you'll return to the city. If you put a coin in its mouth and it falls through the grate underneath, it is thought to bring you luck. Jon made me do it last time we were here." Max does not believe in superstitions, but he doesn't voice his opinion to Evelyn.

It is only when it is her turn with the boar, he realises what she is doing as she releases Jon's ashes into the boar's mouth whilst rubbing its nose – it is for Jon, in the vain hope he'll come back in another lifetime.

Amy

My guilt is amplified when Zahera arrives in my office on Monday for her final interviews. I try and concentrate on the subject in hand, avoiding the fact I have yet to uncover anything to help Mohammed's case.

"I don't have much time today, Zahera, sorry. So, I'll begin straight away. I'm looking into Muslim's childhood experiences in London since 9/11, could you tell me a bit about yours."

"Okay, that's fine." Zahera smiles. It is a sad smile, one that doesn't reach her eyes. "Amy, when I was in school there were innocent questions, such as, 'Do you speak Muslim?' I'd point out tactfully that you cannot speak a religion. The innocent naivety has disappeared. The climate towards Islam is now arctic. I can't see it warming soon."

"Can you tell me any other experiences of your childhood and discrimination?"

"My brother and I weren't allowed to go to the park alone. My parents feared we would be targeted and beaten up. Islamophobia in real life is terrifying: twice when I was growing up the back door of our house was kicked in; twice the police did not turn up. It has been stressful, scary and my anxiety has suffered as a consequence. Sometimes I imagine that wearing a headscarf is similar to how the Jews were made to feel when they wore the star. The headscarf is my choice, I know, but I did not choose the stigma, the vilification. Why should I be made to feel the guilt of a terrorist when all I am is a young girl going about my business not harming anyone?"

"Did you ever feel protected in the city? That the public were looking out for you?"

"Sometimes, but generally I learnt from an early age that no one defended me from the abuse, if someone shouted 'terrorist' at me everyone suddenly lost their ability to hear. I remember one incident, shortly after Boris Johnson had described women who wear a burka as looking like 'letter boxes' and 'bank robbers', that I was pushed to the ground for wearing the hijab."

"I remember reading other Muslim women had been attacked that week, Zahera. There is a monitoring group called 'Tell Mama' that records anti-Muslim attacks. After Boris Johnson's comments they recorded five attacks on Muslim women the following week. Did you report your attack?"

Zahera tells me she did not report her incident: she did not see the point. It makes me overwhelmingly sad.

We continue with the interview and I furiously write notes. As we are coming to the end of the meeting, she remembers one more incident.

"It was the 3rd of April 2018. I remember the day clearly. The first time I was made aware of the letter that was doing the rounds was when my friend WhatsApped me and told me to read the news. I made my way to the tube station immediately: I needed to get home fast; I knew better than to risk my safety by staying in the city. I stood on the tube shaking as I scrolled through the BBC news.

"A letter titled 'Punish a Muslim Day' had been distributed around London. The letter began: *They hurt you, they have made your loved ones suffer. They have caused you pain and heartache. What are you going to do about it?* What followed was a list of rewards based on the encouraged actions taken, these actions included: *Verbally abuse a Muslim; pull the headscarf off a Muslim; beat up a Muslim; torture a Muslim using electrocution; skinning or use of a rack; butcher a Muslim using gun, knife, vehicle or otherwise; burn a Muslim or burn a mosque.* There was a sliding scale of points. I'd shuddered. I'd stood in the carriage on the tube as I let this level of hatred towards me sink in, and I shook violently. I was terrified, all I could focus on was getting home. I needed to get home, Amy.

"A lady saw how visibly distressed I was. It is unusual to approach someone on the tube, but she did. She asked me if I was all right. I tried to explain my panic. She stood with me for the journey and even offered to walk me home. What stands out to me about that day was the realisation that there is still kindness. London is littered with lovely people willing to help, to offer compassion and assistance. It can be easy to forget."

22

Evelyn

We are waiting on the plane. We have been delayed. I do not mind. I am used to prolonged periods in an aeroplane seat now. Sometimes, it feels like all Max and I are ever doing is flying to the next city. Max idly flicks through the online food and beverage catalogue. I do not know why he does this on every flight. He knows all too well the contents and price of all the items – I know he'll order a Heineken and a tube of Pringles: he is so predictable. I never knew what Jon would order when we flew. They are... they were so different.

I prepare for take-off. I put my headphones in. I'm not listening to anything, but it means I can avoid conversation with Max for the duration. I pull some letters from my bag.

1916

Jack,
Your letters have been rare, which makes them ever the more precious.
My imagination runs wild some days. I imagine there are plenty of

distractions there: I hope not in the form of little French women. I know, sweetheart, you would never be tempted, but the mind plays funny tricks when time together is so elusive. I hope you have received my news by now. I try not to be fearful that I haven't heard from you since.

I hate to think of you so chilled, with nothing but masculine companionship to keep you warm. I wish I could be there if only briefly, just to warm you. I am sure you will learn to love the camaraderie again. It is understandable you find it weary for it is all your waking hours at present.

Yours always,

Olive

Dear Olive,

You are very much in my thoughts right now, not that you aren't always, but tonight it seems more pertinent. I still remember the first time I saw you, darling. I said to Teddy, as clear as day it was, 'There goes my wife.' Teddy laughed, but I knew. I just knew from the moment my eyes locked on you that there was nobody else. I still remember the red dress you were wearing, your hair was swept to one side, your lips pursed so beautifully. I could not believe my eyes. You always have been a stunner, my love. When I lie here in the night I think back to that day, more than you can imagine, I think back to that moment when our future unfurled before us. Little did we know of the heart-wrench and pain we'd have to endure.

It was a hard day today. I lost more men. I sometimes feel like I'm on the edge of eternity here: it feels like this horror and grief will never end. Frankie was badly wounded, for his sake I hope the recovery is longer than this bloody war. The best I can hope for that young lad is he falls in love with a VAD, and he spends the rest of these war days

*being taken care of. What I would do to not be here right now, my
love? What I would do?*
Goodnight, sweetheart, from somewhere in France.
Jack

~

Olive,
*I have just received your letter – what a shock! A delightful shock, it is
just such a surprise. I am going to be a father! A smile has lingered on
my lips all day. How are you feeling? I hope you do not have sickness. I
do hope I am home soon. I just want to be with you and our little bean.*
Jack

~

I must have fallen asleep; the next I know I am woken with a
thud as the plane hits the runaway. My dreams of children I
could not reach are still swimming through my thoughts.

It is days before I have the energy to read any more of the
letters. The news of my great-grandmother's pregnancy in such
dreadful circumstances shook me. It has taken me back to a
place I have desperately tried to close the door on.

So far, I have spent a long time in my room on this trip. Max
seems happy to explore Venice by himself. I am lonely though,
so very lonely as I lie here night after night, Max sleeping beside
me alleviates my suffering somewhat. I do not understand the
point of this anymore. I have not left the room today, I cannot
bring myself to. I reach for my bag and pull the next letters free
from the knotted pile.

1917

Jack,

Elsbeth's son has joined up. She is beside herself, Jack – he is only fourteen. She is doing her best to send word to the War Office and get him home, but she said he is a stubborn mule.

A girl approached him in the street and handed him a white feather. Why he didn't tell her then and there that he wasn't a coward and that he was just too young to fight, I don't know. Instead he took himself straight to the army office.

He didn't even tell Elsbeth he was leaving, or what he had done. Just left a note on the table telling her he was fulfilling his duty. He is only a child: war is no place for our children. I'm praying for his safe passage home, Jack. I can't bear the thought of a young boy exposed to what you are having to see.

Yours always,

Olive

I think of all the sacrifices these young boys and men made. Of all the days, they endured so we could live in the world we do now. Our... my neighbour in London has a fourteen-year-old son. It is so terribly young. I cannot imagine a boy so young leaving home to fight. He is still a child. I wonder what happened to Elsbeth's son? I wonder if he got home?

1917

Olive,

Everything here is ugly beyond imagination, it is inescapable and unforgettable. Everything here repels me. I washed in stagnant water gathered in a shell crater today. It was my only means to feel remotely clean. This place is becoming more and more dull and cold by the day,

the air dank with misery. I not only see death here now – I feel it: I
feel it in the darkness. Death penetrates my every pore.
Jack

~

Dear Olive,
The darkies have arrived. I have never seen anything quite like it. We
had heard that they were very savage, but the chap I met seemed far
from it; he was very well spoken and educated. I must admit I'm
grateful for their presence: we need as many men as we can get out
here. They talk of protecting the "Mother country", which seems
rather daft as they have never lived there; but we mustn't complain.
One chap even told me he'd paid his way here from the Caribbean.
Can you imagine, my darling, how much that cost the poor man?
Jack

~

Dear Jack,
I wondered if you had met any of the darkies yet. Ivy was sure you'd
be fighting alongside them. They are quite exotic, aren't they? I cannot
help but stare when I see one. Ivy heard the first recruits had arrived
at a camp near Seaford. She only went and took the train there! She
said she quite fancies the look of them. We heard there are more
coming too, not just from the Caribbean, but from Africa too. To think
of you fighting next to a negro.
Yours always,
Olive

~

Dear Olive,

One of the men has been court martialled for, how shall I say it, well
for a deplorable offence. They say he is suffering with a sexual
perversion and it is quite unnatural to have these afflictions. No one
talks of it because it is against the law, but I have witnessed a few of
the men seeking affection where they should not. One of which I
certainly would not have down as a Nancy boy, as he is very brave in
fire.
I'll be home soon.
Jack

Dear Jack,
Tonight, I am full on beautiful memories of your last visit. The dance.
How I loved the dance. The music, the lightness of your touch, I felt
like you could lift me into the heavens of happiness, and in that
moment, I just knew that everything would work out for us.
The swing of your hips, your lips as they smiled down upon me. I
could have simply melted when you gently kissed my forehead to the
sound of swing.
I could dance with you to the end of this earth my love. I will fall
asleep dreaming of dancing with you tonight. The baby is kicking as I
pen this letter to you. It is as if they know.
Yours always,
Olive

So much has changed in terms of people's attitudes towards
sexuality and race since those days, but I cannot help but think,
not enough. I lie on my bed in this canalled piece of heaven and
contemplate 2016 when Jon brought me to Venice.

I had wanted to relocate to Italy, but Jon was too driven, he had too much of a thirst for London, for the endless momentum. I would have been happy with a slower, simpler life, but Jon thrived on the fast pace of the city. It was as if he was trying to cram years of his life into days. Jon had arrived home drunk. He was slightly manic, his words running away with him. He often became too intense when he was in one of these moods. I wished for the solitude of his quiet moods, for the peace of the mornings when the effects of alcohol had faded.

He'd booked us flights for the weekend. I found his spontaneity endearing and frustrating in equal measure. This week I did not want the rigmarole of airports, I did not want to pack a bag and walk endlessly exploring. I wanted to be still, but then that was not a word in Jon's vocabulary, not recently anyway. I wasn't in the mood for Venice.

It had rained, an impenetrable wetness was all that prevailed in my memory of that weekend. Piazza San Marco was flooded knee-deep. Its architecture had both devastated me with wonder and left me unsatisfied. The trip seemed to be masking our overall disappointment with life. We had just lost our second baby, and Jon was losing himself in alcohol to mask his bereavement: his joviality a charade.

We were in the midst of an existential crisis, neither of us willing to admit our grief that we could not fulfil what we saw as life's main purpose – to procreate. The timelessness of the square, the heart of the city was too busy for me, the mass of pigeons overwhelming. I found the gondolas a cliché, the Venetian masks tacky. I just wanted to sleep. Jon and I had argued, monotonous arguments about nothing in particular. My temper was shredded, I felt unfulfilled. The smell of stagnant water was putrid. I found beauty nowhere.

Today, for my visit with Max, the city is awake. The maze of canals and bridges is busy, its infinitive beauty reflected in the water. It is splendid. I realise now that the definition and perception of beauty changes over time. I could not identify the wonder of Venice last time I was here, but now it is so abundantly clear. I had not wanted to return here, but Max had insisted: apparently Jon loved our visit here. Maybe it is a false memory, maybe it is testament to how distant we were at that time.

Strangely, I appreciate remembering the negative. It makes our story more real, more lifelike. I have the propensity to idolise what we had, where we had been and hoped to go. It was not always perfect: I was not, he was not, we were not. We had struggled, we'd argued. Some weeks during that period I felt shrouded in sadness, a fog loomed that I was terrified wouldn't lift.

Max does not speak much today as we peruse the narrow streets. He is distracted with his food, and I feel like he has slipped away whilst we've been here. I don't ask him to air his troubles; I respect his silence. I cannot begin to imagine any of Max's struggles – his divorce, the loss of his brother; complicated, sorrowful Max.

Max

Today the trip resembles madness. The quest to honour Jon's life, value his memories, seems so entirely pointless. Jon is no longer here. This perpetual country hopping and throwing the remainder of him in the air feels self-indulgent and contrived. Max wonders what they are doing. How could this be serving Jon, this sitting in opulent squares eating rich pastries.

Max feels he is intruding on a life Jon and Evelyn have already lived. He worried that he was making Evelyn rehash moments that he had no right to share. *They are hers*, he thought, *hers and his, not mine to steal.*

Max has always known they were different. Jon was the effervescent younger brother, the larger-than-life energy. He remembered a holiday from their childhood. The family seated around a table in a Spanish harbour – his brother acting up: loud, dramatic and full of his magnetic charm. Max had sat quietly as Jon held court, his parents enraptured. A lady on the next table had caught Max's eye and smiled: a knowing smile that understood his position. Her eyes recognised the shadow he would grow up in. He would never compare to Jon: no one ever did.

He wonders if his parents would have secretly preferred him to be the deceased. Jon was sparky, he was special – he saw how people responded to him; the friends who flocked to his side.

Max could never emulate the same level of charisma, which resulted in Jon's popularity. He'd always been the less attractive brother, not that Max wasn't handsome, but Jon was distinguished. He'd stopped women in his tracks when they were younger, before Evelyn.

Amy

Nothing shocks me anymore, but today I am taken aback with a development in the Met Police. I am getting ready for a night out with Jasmine and Aisha, attempting to decide between a dress and heels or jeans and top. The TV is blaring in the background when the news comes on screen.

"On tonight's news, how did a Met Police officer go undetected as a former member of a banned neo-Nazi group? The arrest of a serving Metropolitan Police officer has sent shockwaves through the police force tonight. Now it faces questions about institutional racism and white supremacist ideology within the force."

I sit down, dumbfounded the police who are meant to protect the public against such extremism have failed to identify a domestic terrorist in their own ranks. As I watch on I learn that the police officer in question had failed to reveal that he was a former member of a banned far-right group. Upon his arrest he was found to have material that detailed knife combat and how to make explosive devices.

I can feel my anger rising.

The police officer was only discovered after an anonymous hacker leaked details and the IP addresses of every account on a white supremacist message board. The police officer was a member of the same group that was banned for celebrating the murder of the Labour MP Jo Cox, the same group that plotted to kill another MP.

I sit in silence contemplating how corrupt and unjust the world is when there is a knock at the door. Aisha and Jasmine are early. They will be a pleasant distraction from the realisation that when it comes to race and those in power, not much has changed.

23

Evelyn

Jon and I had not realised how cold Bruges would be when we visited in January 2017. For some inexplicable reason, I did not pack a warm coat. Jon always teased me for my lack of forethought when it came to my packing. He was surprisingly jovial considering we spent the first day of the holiday traipsing around the shops trying to find me a coat.

Bruges is such a pretty city, like a fairy tale that has been bought to life, that we spent hours exploring the streets.

Max has not been to Bruges before. His excitement is palpable. We'd left Venice after days spent walking the canals, we'd scattered Jon's ashes standing on one of the bridges on the last night. Our trips are drawing to a close now and Max seems far too cheerful. It is irritating me. I want to walk quietly through the streets remembering the titbits of my time here with Jon. I suppose I should be pleased Max has cheered up since Florence, but my patience is wearing.

We enter the square and I see a signpost for a virtual reality experience of medieval Bruges. I turn to Max and begin to laugh. I hold on to his arm as I try to explain how funny we'd found this attraction. Max stares at me mutely. I realise that it is only Jon who would understand. I know this is where I'll scatter Jon's ashes before we leave. The memory is now only mine, I cannot share it with him like I used to. I will not relive it with him in the future. We will not look back and laugh like we once did. I am the only carrier of these memories and moments now.

Max realises his mistake and tries his hardest to question me about the day. He feigns interest and attempts laughter, but it is not the same. He is not Jon. He cannot understand. It is not his fault, yet I resent him: I resent Max being here with me when his brother cannot.

I am grateful for the end of the day when I can retire to the hotel room to read my great-grandparents' letters. There are not many left and I have been trying to spread them out, so I can savour their story.

1917

Dear Olive,

Your letters do alleviate the beastly length of time here. Do not worry, my sweet, I think we have endured the worst. I long for the murmur of a quiet river, the simple pleasure of running water, meandering its way through the lush green valleys I long to see. I pray for this, and I pray for home.

Instead my days are filled with sweet pleading souls staring up at me, their eyes hollow from such horror they have had to bear. Tell me of the beauty in the world, paint me a picture of what you are doing right now, Olive. I wish to be there with you.

Your love is a sea of happiness where I could quite easily dissolve right now.

Jack

Dear Jack,
It is a beautiful spring evening here. I am drinking water out on the
lawn. The baby has begun to kick more – it is a giddy feeling, like
hiccups but in my stomach. I forget how enchanting nature is as I lie
here and watch the sunset. The bluebells have bloomed, the air feels
hopeful. If only you were laid by my side.
Yours always,
Olive

Olive,
I know most of all that we are all fighting our own battles and suffering
our own sorrows here – it is not just the greater cause we fight on for, I
have seen the fractures in my men's minds appearing. I hope Maurice is
recovering. I have seen their devastation, their longing and distress –
the war does not make a man: it does everything it can to break him.
I am full of the dead, Olive. The dead occupy my senses: my sight, my
smell, my touch – my mind is macabre. War is insatiable, there is a
greed given to killing like no other.
Jack

Olive,
The snow is beautiful: like a thousand faded stars floating towards us
from the inky deep sky, so delicate and otherworldly. Time seems to
stand still as I watch them fall from above me, a welcome alternative
to the shells that aim at us daily.
Jack

Jack,

I had terrible news. Maurice went back to the front, Kitty had not heard from him for weeks and today she received her letters to him back through the door. "Killed in action" were scrawled across the envelopes and all subsequent correspondence. How frightful, I do not know how the telegram did not arrive, how the regiment did not write to inform her. Kitty had no wire, nothing, darling – she just had her letters returned with "Killed in action" in big, fat, red ink.

I cannot imagine her shock, or sorrow, of knowing her messages of love never even reached her sweetheart. And, Maurice shouldn't have gone back to the land you occupy. His mind was still unwell.

Yours always,

Olive

Max

He is growing increasingly tired of Evelyn's grief since Florence. She is so consumed by her feelings she has totally forgotten that she is not the only one working through this. She has retired early again tonight to read the letters that seem to be the only method of communication that penetrates her walls right now.

Max is not tired. He roams the small back lanes of Bruges and lost in the city he stumbles across a gin bar.

It is intimate, and it seems like the perfect place to while away the hours. Once he sits down, he feels restless. He doesn't know what to do so he logs on to Tinder – he had not been on since Granada, but he was bored and lonely. He'd had a brief stint on Tinder after Nancy, but he'd never really got on board with it until recently. He'd struggled with the idea that it was purely a transaction without any meaning.

Tonight, it seems much easier. He does not care for conversation and the idea of a one-night stand to take his mind off everything is welcome.

He wonders if Nancy is on these apps. He has not heard from her since Jon's funeral. He was shocked when she came; but then maybe he didn't give her enough credit – regardless of her mental illness, there was an element of kindness; of unforgotten love towards him. She sat at the back of the church, out of respect he hoped; the last thing he needed was her close to him that day. He saw her in the graveyard afterwards, leant against a tree waiting for him.

He approached, out of politeness and curiosity. "Nancy."

"Max, I'm so sorry. I wanted to come. I should have rung, should have checked you were okay, that you didn't mind me being here."

"Yes, you should have."

"He was my family too, for a while."

He saw then she had been crying. He tried to empathise with her, briefly thought about giving her a hug. But then he remembered their relationship, and found himself pulling back and walking away from her. "Bye, Nancy."

They were never going to be the type of couple who could be friends after the break-up. There was too much hurt. The pain inflicted had been irreversible. He knew the ending had ultimately been his fault, but there had been so many incidents that had led him to that point.

Max wonders if Nancy ever felt guilty, ever realised that her behaviour wasn't normal. He wonders if she was sorry. He orders another gin, he wished Nancy didn't interrupt his thoughts like this. He continues to swipe through Tinder, but he has lost interest now. He doesn't have the energy to consider even a casual hook-up. The barman approaches when he has finished his gin and suggests another, they start talking, and before he knows it it's two hours and four expensive gins later, when he finally decides to head back to the hotel.

Amy

The night with Jasmine and Aisha had been nice, but I'd been consumed with anger at the state of the world. They'd noticed I wasn't quite myself. Jasmine had broached my mood first.

"What's up, Amy? You don't seem yourself."

"It's just work, nothing new. I'm just frustrated, it just feels like I'm fighting a losing battle."

"I mean, I get it, I don't understand how you can offer any legal advice to those type of people."

"Sorry, what do you mean by 'those types of people', Jasmine?"

"I'm just saying, I'm not sure I believe the whole sob story. Really were they forced out of their homes? Or do they just want to live off our state?"

I can feel my anger rising.

"Jasmine, imagine that you must leave your house immediately in the middle of the night – you have word ISIS is coming. You have five minutes, you can only take a small bag. You suddenly must go, you no longer have five minutes – they are closer than you thought. You leave with your family, your children. You must flee. You must leave your home, your job, your pets – if you stay you are dead. You use all your money to get out. You risk everything to leave because the only other option is worse than this one, and that is to stay."

"I know what they say, but you've got to wonder, haven't you, if it is true. In my opinion most people come to this country because they want more pay, better lives. I don't believe the choice is out of their hands."

"Jasmine, if you were a mother, could you imagine you must put your children, the most precious things in your world on a boat that is so overloaded that the fear you feel is so crippling, but there is no other choice, you must overcome that fear. It is risking death escaping this or it is ultimate death if you stay. You make the journey, you are cold, scared and hungry. You see people die on board. You listen to families sobbing. You grieve for all you have lost. You do not know where you are going, what life will look like. You do not know if you will make it. You have nothing left. You make it – others do not. You watch your fellow companions on the boat die. You arrive, and this new land is lonely and unwelcoming. You are not allowed to work, you are mistreated, seen as a threat. One day someone screams at you in the street to 'go home' – you only wish you could. Nobody leaves their home, their whole life, easily. They have no other choice."

"I know what you're saying, Amy, but I also know that you only see the best in people and I think you're naïve. For all you know you're helping to harbour terrorists."

"Woah, woah, woah. Enough girls!" Aisha interrupted, the energy around the table was charged and I tried desperately to calm down. "Do me a favour, girls, no political talk – I want to have fun."

I'd spent the rest of my night seething, if my best friends didn't understand, how were attitudes ever going to change.

24

Evelyn

Jon and I had eaten copious amounts of fish when we went to Portugal in 2015. I remember the smell of the mackerel on the barbecue in the restaurant, which was busy with the lunch rush. The fisherman had delivered their morning catch, which had been thrown straight over the charcoals.

We caught ferries to the islands and lazed on the beaches all day. The holiday was undemanding, in the sense we did not need to do anything but slowly search the streets for food and drink. We had discovered our future over copious amounts of wine. It took some cajoling, but this was the holiday when Jon agreed to try for a baby.

I had been terrified and excited all at once. I could not help but be apprehensive at such a life-changing commitment.

I have never understood when people say they are trying for a baby, because really what they want is a family, not a little baby, but a family to grow old with: a child that will become an adult.

Back then I hoped it would take a few months to get

pregnant, that I had a bit more time pleasing myself. Of course, Jon was convinced we'd be pregnant before the end of the month.

Looking back now, I think how naïve we were about our fertility; how wildly optimistic our future had seemed. Grief is isolating. It sucks at you and sometimes it manages to pull you down. Today it is a constant struggle to stay standing.

I sit on the beach by myself. I need space away from Max. Portugal was not how I remembered, the charm has disintegrated. Tourism has ploughed away the town's culture, and in its place lies a vulgar reminder of all that is wrong with Britain. There were signs this was happening five years ago, but I had hoped the locals had managed to stave it off.

I got too drunk and sang karaoke last night. I danced melancholy at a bar and Max had to take me to bed. I did not even have the energy to be embarrassed. I hated what the place had become, but I also hated myself. This grief-stricken woman roaming Europe, city to city, trying to cling onto her past and somehow still make it her present. My grief was so embedded now I did not know what else I could talk of. It had become my identity – an unwanted addition, but it was formidable and would not leave me be. Grief was the unwanted friend who stayed too long, clinging to me whilst simultaneously draining me of anything worthy I had left to give.

I lie back on the sand and tears stream down my face. I open my bag and pull out the letters.

1917

Olive,
The sound of the shells arriving is the worst. We all drop to the floor and cover our ears, the only protection we have, which really is none

at all. *Like sacks we fall, some of us rise again, many stay there:*
extinguished by the air artillery.
Why are we fighting? What are we fighting for? The question
consumes me in the depth of the darkness, but it must be for the
greater good, for our children's future. When I am here? I wonder
what will become of this country we occupy, what the future of
France is. All I imagine is slosh and mud right now, but then I have
heard of the splendour of Paris, and the beauty of the poppy fields in
the south, of the gentle river that runs through picturesque villages
and valleys. I heard there is beauty to be had here.
Jack

∾

Olive,
Yesterday was very distressing. The tanks needed to push on, they
needed to move forward, but they could not wait for the men before
them, the injured men lying there helpless. They drove straight over
them, Olive, straight over, my darling, as if they were fodder and not
fellow comrades. That is the thing with war, it forces impossible
choices that we should never have had to consider. I am truly bone-
tired love. Bone-tired. I fear I will never shake this tiredness. There is
no rest here, even when we sleep our bodies are still on high alert as to
our fate.
Jack

∾

Dear Mrs Bates,
I am writing with news of your husband who is currently
incapacitated. Mr Bates appears to be suffering from traumatic
neurosis, and as such he has been granted leave to recover. He is

currently situated at Moss Side Military Hospital in Liverpool where he is receiving treatment.
Yours sincerely,
Charles Myers
Physician

I google Charles Myers. I wonder who this man was, what his involvement was with my great-grandfather's treatment. I discover he was the leading psychologist on shell shock. He'd written the first paper on the condition in 1915. He'd studied this illness of the mind, using hypnosis to treat many soldiers. I wonder if my great-grandfather was one of his subjects, if he'd managed to help him recover.

I lie awake in a room in the Algarve and I read pages and pages on the condition that so many soldiers on the front line suffered. It literally was a physical shock to the nervous system. I had never realised it had affected so many: fifteen per cent of all soldiers. Their symptoms varied but included blindness, deafness, remaining mute and uncontrollable shaking.

I can only imagine the reaction, knowing how far we have come with attitudes towards mental illness. Originally patients who were severely affected were sent back to Britain and at first were treated as incurable. Over time special shell shock hospitals were set up. I look at one such hospital in Hampshire and find a picture of the fields near the hospital covered in tents, full of fallen heroes.

Dear Olive,
It has been an awfully strange time here. The best I can describe to

you of what happened is nothing. There was suddenly nothing, as if my mind had gone totally blank. I just could no longer do anything. I could hear the shells, I could hear my men shouting at me, but I could not move. And then there is nothing. My mind shut down I presume, because the next thing I discover I am in this hospital with all these men, and I am no longer somewhere in France.
Jack

~

Dear Jack,
The letter gave me such a fright. It is so wonderful to hear your words again. I had no idea how long it would be until you were able to communicate. In one sense it is a blessing you are in hospital as I do not fill my days with worrying what injuries you may endure. The baby is awfully big now, I imagine it will be any day before I meet them. I so hope you are well enough to come home soon, to our own little family.
Yours always,
Olive

~

Dear Olive,
I am recovering well. The methods of treatment have not been particularly pleasant, and some days it feels more like punishment, but I have regained my speech, and my shudders are lessening. They have transferred me to Craiglockhart Hospital in Edinburgh. It is more appropriate for officers to receive treatment here, I have been informed. It is really quite a splendid building, rather like an Italian villa they tell me. It is very grand, it is pleasant to be somewhere so easy on the eye. There is a chap in the bed next to me, Wilfred Owen, he keeps me entertained with his musings and poetry.

I await news of the birth with great anticipation.
Jack

Max

Portugal was one of their last trips. Max knew it was coming to
an end and he hated the thought of returning home, of the
reality that lay ahead. At least whilst they were away there was
still a sense of limbo to their grief – life had not yet begun, there
was no need to get used to a new "normal". He did not have to
concentrate on how to really live without his brother.

Albuferia was not what he expected. The Portuguese culture
seemed to have been sucked out of the town and replaced with
British drinkers. The temperature was pleasant considering it
was December and it was perfect for walking.

Evelyn had suggested they take a trip down the coast
tomorrow to a small fishing village, and he welcomed the idea. It
is where they will scatter Jon. He would like to see the real
Portugal, as opposed to this English fairground of pubs.

Evelyn is at the beach today. He has opted to walk further
afield: he wants to find the smaller villages, the places where
tourism hasn't eroded the culture. But when he walked he
thought. It was ironic he had found himself attracted to
someone who possessed similar traits to Jon. It was not lost on
him when he met Nancy how similar she was to his brother. Jon
hadn't warmed to her, and Max had always wondered if it was
because she threatened him.

At twenty-eight he'd felt the pressure to settle down; he'd
never played the field, just gone from one mediocre relationship
to the other over the years. There was the university girlfriend,
Emily: she'd been sweet, but they had both known that their

careers were going to come first. Karen had followed, but it had never progressed past dates, even after a year. Then there had been Cheryl. He had been fond of them all, but there had not been that intoxicating spark he felt when he met Nancy.

He had attended the party at the last moment. His colleague, Paul, had convinced him staying in on his own drinking beer was a sad way to spend a Friday night as a single man in his twenties in London – he knew it was, but he'd been looking forward to the downtime. It had been a dreadful week in work, with an increasing number of stabbings. He had witnessed the reckless loss of too many youths. He had wanted nothing more than his sofa, but Paul had convinced him otherwise.

The party, the thirtieth birthday of a girl Paul knew, was at a three-storey townhouse in Hampstead. He and Jon had always aspired to own houses in Hampstead – it was a race to see which one of them got there first. Max wondered how a woman who was only thirty had managed to buy such a building so young. He had brought her a bottle of wine and flowers, although he didn't know her.

It was busy when they arrived, the celebrations already in full swing. The guests were already spilling over into the garden and he had to squeeze past people on the landing and doorways.

He noted the décor; whoever this girl was she had a unique sense of style. The hallway walls were covered in framed oil paintings, each a portrait. They were quirky in their style, the dark navy wall behind them meant the faces looked even more dramatic. There was a large chandelier hanging down, its crystals spun light over the paintings. He and Paul made it through to the kitchen, where they cracked open a beer. The kitchen was a haven of trinkets, every shelf and surface was filled with egg cups, old saucers, plants and books. It was a household full of life. Max noticed the girl in the corner, her head thrown back, her laughter filling the room.

He watched her as the evening progressed, she was always surrounded by a crowd. She commanded the room. He asked Paul who she was.

"That's Nancy," he'd said. "The birthday girl. Come on, I'd better introduce you."

For the rest of the night Max felt like his whole world was suspended. Nothing seemed more important than this woman. At the end of the night, he had stepped out into the frosty Hampstead night and looked left then right wondering where they would catch the night bus. They had settled on right, but before he had got a hundred yards, he'd heard running feet.

"Max! Max! Aren't you going to give me your number?"

And when he had typed it into her phone, she'd left him with a kiss lingering on his lips.

Nancy had seemed so perfect in that moment. Little did he know.

PART II

TWO YEARS EARLIER

"There is only one good – knowledge; and one evil – ignorance."
— **Socrates**

25

Jon

He thought back to 2012 and one of his first trips with Evelyn as the television played on repeat the footage of the attack in Barcelona. It had only been two months since the attacks in Borough Market. There seemed to be no end to these atrocities.

Now, five years later since their trip to the Spanish city, as he lay on the couch, hung-over from the night before with the boys, he couldn't believe what he was seeing on the news. He felt a strange protectiveness towards the city. He felt an affinity with Barcelona because it represented the beginning of his relationship with Evelyn: the beginning of his and Evelyn's life together. The attack ignited an anger in him. It swelled slowly at first, but by the evening it was a hurricane of rage he could not contain.

At 4.56pm a twenty-two-year-old man had driven 500 metres through a plethora of nationalities: of people. Jon could not believe how in forty-five seconds this man had wreaked such devastation. He watched the footage in which the vehicle zigzagged, ramming into cyclists and pedestrians.

He thinks back to the last time they were in Barcelona. He remembers the cartoonists, the street vendors, the flower stalls, the ice cream kiosks. He remembers the families, couples, groups of friends and children playing that gathered on Las Ramblas, the heart of the city. He'd been enchanted.

It wasn't the first time that year he'd been somewhere in Europe directly affected by these people. Last winter he and Evelyn had visited Brussels, where in March 2016 there had been three co-ordinated suicide bombings. He thought of the terror the city had been plunged into in the months leading up to the attack. The city on lockdown, the people afraid for their lives.

He scrolled the news app on his phone. He read article upon article as the night passed and his hangover eased. He messaged Evelyn, asking her to pick up food on her way home. He was hoping she'd be back from work by around 10pm.

He briefly considered arranging to meet his brother, Max, but he could not fathom the energy to go out.

He cracked open a beer and logged on to his Facebook. His feed was full of news on the unfolding events in Spain. He felt his frustration and resentment swelling. The injustice of these terrorist attacks across Europe infuriated him. Why were these people not excluded? Why were they allowed in the countries? He did not understand how these terrorist cells could go unnoticed.

He thought back to May that year: the Manchester arena bombing. A home-made bomb full of nuts and bolts had been detonated at the end of an Ariana Grande concert, killing twenty-three people and injuring 139. More than half of them were children.

He opened another beer and continued to comment on

social media posts. There was a suggested group for him. He clicked to join. Minutes later admin admitted him. He scrolled down through the posts and was met with numerous political views on race, culture, immigration and identity; he found himself in agreement. He was relieved to see others too, believed the nation was in decay. There were others who also felt their rights were ignored and oppressed.

He hated how people were investigated just for liking a social media post. It seemed like no one could express an opinion any more. It was a relief to meet like-minded people who understood people's liberty must be protected.

Jon was adamant immigration had damaged Britain, this uncontrolled and rapid import of workers who had taken our jobs. The UK was too densely populated. Jon found it ridiculous that the government continued to let these people in. *This uncontrolled immigration must stop*, he thought. It was not hard to solve the problem: stricter border laws, foreign students deported after study. He could not understand how the UK continued to let in and breed terrorists. But Jon felt he could never express these opinions.

He opened another beer and began to comment on the posts. Evelyn had messaged to say she'd be late – again. He ordered a pizza to be delivered. By the time she arrived home that night, he was passed out on the sofa, five empty cans strewn on the coffee table next to him.

Celine

I did not know why I bothered. They never caught my attention and even if they did to begin with, they could never hold it. My staff had set this date up: they were convinced I needed some romance. Something outside of the restaurant I owned. He'd been pleasant enough, but I'd grown bored by the second course and made my excuses. As I walked back through the streets of London, I found myself thinking back to all my memories of this city I had grown up in. My parents were Italian, but I had lived only in the UK. Although my heritage was Italian, I had always felt and identified as British.

My exotic looks ensured I was never short of attention, but I just wasn't interested. When you own a restaurant, or even work as a full-time chef or front of house, there is not much time for anything other than work.

My life revolved around my work. I lived and breathed my business. My staff were my family. We spend up to eighty hours a week together, so we know each other pretty well. There was not much time or energy for anything else.

I knew they would all be disappointed when I arrived back at the restaurant earlier than they expected, but they'll understand. This is not the first time it has happened. I'm hoping I can get back before tonight's close-down. Every evening before and after service we all sit down together and share a meal and wine. It is my favourite part of the day and when I really feel like this is my community – my family.

I know Angelo, the chef, had offcuts of steak tonight too. I love nothing more than his steak rare with parmesan, balsamic vinegar and rocket. I see my bus ahead and break into a jog to ensure I don't miss it. As I take my seat at the back of the bus, I'd be mistaken for thinking I wasn't in London at all. The amalgamation of foreigners is striking, brown faces look back at me, some veiled, others hidden altogether. It is thirty minutes back to the restaurant and I can't wait.

26

Jon

There was something about Evelyn that stood out when he first met her. She was beautiful, not in the sense she would turn everyone's head when she entered the room, but she had an ethereal beauty that became increasingly apparent. She was quieter than most of his exes; her demeanour was charming. He had not been looking for a partner. He was always looking for women, but not because he was looking for a future with any of them.

She was different. Evelyn made him feel safe. When he was with her, he didn't want to leave. He would clock-watch on their dates, aware he only had an hour or so left of her company. He had never done that with a woman before: he had been too busy ripping their clothes off, too consumed by sex to really notice anything other than their bodies. They had merely been a distraction. Evelyn felt like more: she felt like home. Comforting.

He had known he was going to marry her for a long time. He was relieved when he met her. His father had always told him and Max that one day a woman would arrive in each of their lives and she would complete them. Jon had truly believed that woman was Evelyn, and she had completed him for a while. He had grown tired of the constant dating. He had really wanted to settle down.

A wedding was on the cards from very early on in their relationship. He did not see the point in wasting any further time. He'd always thought he'd plan an elaborate, expensive proposal, but with Evelyn, simple seemed enough. He knew she loved picnics, the park, Sundays – there had been no other option.

He had honestly thought he'd changed. He had managed it for years. Evelyn in her white spaghetti-strap dress lying on a blanket in the park had seemed like all he'd ever wanted the moment he had placed that ring on her finger. He could still picture her wide brimming smile, her sparkling eyes: his future wife.

Celine

It had been like every other day. I'd arrived early in the restaurant to bake the pastries for the weekend. My father usually arrived at 10am on Thursday after a quick catch-up with his brother who also owned a restaurant nearby.

He didn't die in the 7/7 terror attack that day in 2005, but he was never the same afterwards. It was the stress, the PTSD that killed him – his heart and head had never recovered after he'd witnessed such atrocity. His gait was that of a man who'd had all his energy sucked out of him. The act of living was more than enough – there was no room for as much cheer. His sadness at what he'd witnessed was too grave. He deteriorated slowly. He would no longer travel on the tube and buses. His daily visits to his brother stopped. His circle became smaller and smaller, until he did not leave the restaurant bar except to retreat upstairs to sleep.

He was devastated by what had occurred in his city; he was also terrified of it happening again. He tried to be happy, but it had consumed him for years. His mind was too disturbed to keep going.

I suppose after his death I'd been desperate for a focus, a purpose. I spent hours online searching for information on the group that had caused my father's death. What I hadn't expected to find was a community with my views and beliefs – a community that understood how I was feeling.

My brothers didn't understand. They'd left the restaurant in their early twenties because they had found the business suffocating. Gianni had fled back to Italy in the hope of sunshine and Italian women, whilst Antonio had gone to business school, his pity on our small business has always been palpable. He'd not visited much since, almost embarrassed at his meagre beginnings. They didn't understand my loss, my developing hatred. I had tried to discuss it on the telephone, but they insisted I drop it and had manoeuvred the conversation towards lighter subjects.

I had to stay on in the restaurant after my father's death. There was no other option. He'd taught me most of his skills, but there was always a little magic missing in my dishes: the seasoning not quite on point, the complexity of flavours just missing the mark.

There was nothing else for me to do, though. Cooking and the restaurant were my family's life. It was what was always intended for me. The customers still came, but the liveliness that had consumed this building previously was missing – an energy evaporated that could never be replaced. A sadness cloaked our door.

Maybe it was sentimentality. I think many people stay in failing businesses for this reason – a misguided commitment to a venture that they should have walked away from years before. But ours was London's oldest family restaurant. How could I close the doors when we alone owned that accolade? It was never really my choice to make. The restaurant was written in our family's history, and it was also understood that it was our family's future.

My father had arrived with his brothers after World War II when there was a labour shortage in the UK. They'd been lured by the opportunity to escape farming life. My father had been trained to cook by his *nonna*, his passion for food a childhood education passed from generation to generation.

He'd worked as a porter in a restaurant, progressing over the years to become a chef. He followed an admirable, honest life. He'd married my mother, saved money and then opened the restaurant. Whenever I open the restaurant doors I'm aware it has been in the family for half a century. My memories were made inside these four walls – crawling around the floors as service was prepared; the hustle; the rush; the love of food; the community; my family – I lived and learnt everything Italians love here. My mother had not appreciated his hard work and sacrifice, she'd left one autumn without so much as a goodbye. I have never understood how she could abandon me and my brothers – what kind of mother does that? She'd only tried to contact me twice since I was fourteen years old, but too much damage had been done. There had apparently been a man; my father never spoke of my mother again, but I'd heard raised voices between him and my *nonna* over the phone. I have tried to fill the gaps in the stories I overheard, but whatever information I have been privy to never portrayed her in a favourable light. It was easier to pretend she did not exist.

27

Jon

He had not been bothered about the day: he had wanted the marriage, so he could call her his wife. It was a surprise how much he enjoyed his wedding, but he had always loved a party. The chateau in Bordeaux had cost more money than he liked to think about. He would check the balance months later and swallow down his horror. Years later he didn't like to think of the cost.

They honeymooned in Paris. Evelyn was in her element: she viewed trips like this as moments on a movie set. She saw the wonder in the landscape that Jon had lost at the end of his childhood.

The manner in which she saw the world was infectious. He could tell from the glee on her face as they turned every corner that Paris for Evelyn was everything she had ever imagined, and the Parisians the epitome of class.

They ate croissants with jam every morning and sipped on cappuccinos. They frequented restaurant after restaurant and stopped in cafés for glasses of wine and patisseries. Jon wished he could have paused that time in Paris with her for an eternity. He had felt satisfied.

He wished he could have seen the surroundings as she had. She didn't see how the world was being eroded – she loved Paris for everything typical to Parisians. She didn't see how these cultures were continuously under threat. She never saw the underbelly of the cities, the immigrants crowding the metro, the poverty that was rippling through the outskirts. She was the same in London. She was proud to be British and of her heritage and history; she just didn't understand that it needed protecting.

Jon had told her what a remarkable country the UK was, he had tried to educate her about leadership, but she didn't seem to understand why the UK must lead the modern world. Jon valued Britishness. He was fed up with the notion that multiculturalism was a positive development. He believed people should integrate into our culture rather than promote theirs.

It was so frustrating when he tried to discuss these views with his wife and over the years he had stopped. She was very forgiving, Evelyn, and far too liberal for her own good.

Celine

I had left London in my mid-twenties to travel. I had a wanderlust in my twenties and every year I tried to deny it I became increasingly unhappy. The restaurant and family life at the time had seemed suffocating. My future was laid out before me and I could not see a way out. I was desperate for new experiences. I began in southern Italy. I knew if I went north to Emilia-Romagna I would be hounded by my extended family, and I just wanted to travel solo.

I took trains around Puglia, staying in cheap B&Bs. I was

enchanted by the small towns dotted around Italy's heel. I stayed in Polignano a Mare for the first week, charmed by its dramatic cliffs and winding streets. I moved on to Ostuni where I got lost in the maze of alleyways in the whitewashed town. Lecce, the Florence of the South, was next. I was only meant to stay a week, but a man happened. It was a love affair with both him and the city that shrivelled as quickly as it had ignited. The thrill of him still haunts me.

I left Puglia after we had parted. I had used Lecce as a base to see all its offerings. The lesser-known part of Italy was littered with hidden wonders: from the picturesque harbour of Monopoli, to the crystal-clear waters of Salento and the charm of the *trulli* huts in Alberobello. I took a bus to Matera and ended up staying a year. Matera is one of this planet's rarities: when you arrive you feel as if you have stepped back hundreds of years. It is breathtakingly beautiful: every night as I looked out from my balcony at the view, I struggled to contemplate the landscape.

I got a job in a restaurant: it was ironic I had left London because I felt stagnant in my job, yet there I was doing the same abroad. I practised my Italian, I made friends. I felt alive. As with travel, it was never meant to last forever, and I returned home the following winter, with tales I would grow old with. I have tried to travel every year since: I have flown to South America and Mexico more times than I can remember, exploring the countries city by city.

Since my dad's passing though, it is harder and harder to get away, the responsibility of the business too great. His death is a burden on me in more ways than one.

28

Jon

September had been a difficult month – *perfect* Max had moved in. Evelyn insisted the moment she heard he had separated from Nancy. Jon loved his brother, but he was constantly reminding him of all his downfalls. Max the protector, the provider, the perfect man. Although Max was the younger brother, people always assumed otherwise. His personality was more serious than Jon's; he portrayed a maturity that Jon did not seem to possess.

But there he was on the doorstep, bags in hand. Max wasn't quite as perfect as he made out. The affair with a younger colleague was a cliché of course, but then Max was a cliché, so Jon wasn't particularly surprised.

Evelyn was disappointed at Max's behaviour, but not surprised given what they suspected. She forgave people's mistakes easily. Jon had always been amazed at her ability to love unconditionally. It was what he'd originally fallen for – this endless capacity to see the best in those closest to her. Her loyalty had afforded Max a bed, no matter how disappointed she was in him. Jon didn't have an opinion one way or another, and he knew far better than to judge Max: his little brother knew all about his past.

It was actually far more confronting than Jon had realised to begin with, seeing Max broken like this. He was used to his brother being the one with his shit together. The one who knew when to call it a day in the pub; who always stopped before he'd reached "one too many". It had irritated Jon to see Max on the sofa, unshaven, in joggers and a stained T-shirt. This was not his role. It was not their position in the family and it made him uncomfortable. Max had always been the reliable brother. The dichotomy between Jon and Max had never been threatened before.

Evelyn had tried to coax Max out of the house. She suggested walks and outings, but in the end, Jon had thought a hard-line approach was necessary. He could not watch Max wallow any longer. Jon and Evelyn had made the joint decision, after much cajoling on Jon's part, that it was best Max move out after a month. He needed to pull himself together. How he was managing his job as a police officer Jon did not know.

Jon had hoped that Nancy's behaviour was temporary. After all, Max had only entered into a temporary fling. There was no need to end a marriage over Max thinking with his dick just momentarily. Jon had always thought Nancy was a bit fitful: she had the tendency to blow hot and cold. He had not been particularly happy when Max met her, all too aware his brother was ticking the boxes of expectation society has you believe you must achieve.

Jon could have told Max it wouldn't work and he had always predicted the demise of their relationship, but he had thought it would be years later, after children and boredom set in. But on his own wedding day he had realised that things weren't as rosy between Max and Nancy. He had seen the scratches on Max's back, noted the bruises. He had thought their relationship rocky, but assumed they'd work it through. He'd suspected Nancy might be the wrong side of wild on occasion; but who was he to interfere?

Celine

My father and I were very close. I spent hours in his restaurant watching him cook. Food was our life, really. It always had been. I had grown up in the kitchen. Cooking was as innate to me as breathing: one of life's basic tasks we must commit to everyday.

My overriding childhood memory of my father was how jolly he was: loud, raucous and generous with his time. He wanted to please people, he wanted to make people smile. His pasta was unrivalled and the simplicity of his dishes surprising upon tasting them. He was well-known, I suppose by default I was too: "Gianni's daughter was never going to sit in the background," he'd tell people when he introduced me. He presented me as a prize, his pride palpable. I could do no wrong.

Of course, I had my moments. When I was nineteen he'd despaired at the flock of boys that would arrive in the restaurant to see me. He hated his only daughter receiving so much attention from the opposite sex. He was fiercely protective. I had never been interested in boys; my father was a substantial enough male: there was never room for anyone else.

His death has left such a monumental void in my life.

It is Tuesday, the restaurant is closed, but I am still in the kitchen preparing food for the week ahead and writing the menus. I have been here all afternoon and I can feel myself tiring. It is getting late and I still need to make the ravioli for the next two days. I make myself an espresso and take it to the kitchen, where I turn the radio on.

The presenter is talking about the investigation into Salman Abedi, the man who killed twenty-two people, including children, in the Manchester terror attack at the end of an Ariana Grande concert in May. Included in the news is segments of interviews of the families affected by this atrocious act. I hear the voices of the mothers who'd lost their children crack with emotion, the friends who talk of their great loss. The tragedy is all too common. I cannot listen any more, it angers me so much that such evil roams our streets unbeknown to even the security services. What kind of world do we live in that this happens?

29

Jon

Max was relentless in his wallowing even after he moved out. Jon could not cope with it: they all had their own problems. He could have foreseen three years ago at their wedding that this would happen. He had noticed the way Max and Nancy had avoided each other all day, Nancy becoming increasingly animated as she drunk more and more, Max seething in the corner at her behaviour. He had not cared for it then and he did not care for it now.

He was angry. Evelyn had miscarried for the third time over the weekend and they were both in a pit of despair. Parenthood seemed to be eluding them, their slight snippets of hope extinguished before they could flourish. He had never even considered the possibility that he wouldn't be able to father children. It had seemed like a given, much like everything else he had achieved in his lifetime so far. Jon had always been lucky in that sense: he didn't need to work excessively to succeed; he'd always had an effortless way with the ladies. His life had just fallen into place.

Work was getting him down too, the relentless commuting, the constant networking: forever people pleasing. The weekends when he was off were a constant reminder of how stagnant his relationship with Evelyn had become, consumed by having a baby. He made excuses to stay out after work, catching the tube later and later, avoiding the inevitable sadness that filled their home.

One night he met Max for a few pints in the pub. He'd listened on as Max detailed his situation with Nancy, bitterness seething from his lips. Jon had learnt to switch off from these endless rants, where Max said the same thing over and over about his ex-wife. He approached the tube and messaged Evelyn, wearily hoping for a quiet carriage and a seat.

He had noticed London changing over the years. The sea of white faces gradually eroding, until the tube carried colours of every description. Today he may as well have been abroad it was so bad.

His rage had inflated gradually. He had no recollection of when the anger had begun, but now it was present every day. He had been quiet about it at first: these beliefs he held weren't necessarily considered politically correct in all of his circles. However, he'd discovered that certain work colleagues shared his feelings – it had taken a few drinks and some disparaging remarks before he'd realised, but he was relieved they were all on the same page.

He was not racist. He was angered. He had always been told to respect other cultures when he was visiting countries abroad: to speak their language; try their cuisine; dress accordingly. Why, then, when foreigners visited Britain, or moved here, was it acceptable for them to not respect British culture?

This is not what my father's father fought for, Jon thought. *He fought to retain our sovereignty, our Britishness, and now, now we are all expected to sit back and watch as it is eroded.* Jon felt that democracy and freedom of speech were at risk. He couldn't express his true views about his country's identity and he felt silenced when all he wanted to do was discuss a very real national threat.

Celine

The community online had provided me with much comfort. It was reassuring to meet a like-minded group of people, who too were touched by grief due to these Muslims. I was fed up at not expressing my views, my opinions, honestly. At least online I could speak to people who were the only ones who seemed to be the voices of reason. Everyone I worked with was far too left-wing, too forgiving. I had learnt quickly to not speak aloud my outlook.

One day we had a table of Muslims dine with us and I had muttered under my breath that they should "go back to where they came from". I saw the look on the chef's face. I had momentarily forgotten that I must be "politically correct".

The group had evolved over time. I'm not sure who was the first to suggest we actually meet up outside our virtual communication. There were quite a few of us from London and it seemed to make sense. It was also more secure: there is no way to trace face-to-face conversations. We were always aware that chatting through our Facebook group carried its risks, not that we were doing anything wrong, but you weren't allowed to speak freely without being policed.

Our first meeting had been in a little pub in Kensington called The Builders Arms. It was a pretty venue, painted mint green, with flowerpots adorning the outside and the interior was warm and cosy. We'd all got drunk, the anticipation of meeting in person spurring us on. There were only six of us then. There are many more of us now, but we tend to keep our numbers low when it comes to public group gatherings. That first night had been such a relief, to finally meet people of the same calibre, to laugh about how ridiculous the city had become, to realise I was part of a group, a family of sorts, where we were safe to speak our minds.

30

Jon

"I've said it before and I'll say it again, we need stricter border control. This country has become a free for all." He could hear Tom, his colleague who'd initially invited him to the meetings, debating with the group as he arrived that evening.

"They'll let anyone in, it's the benefits they want. We pay our taxes for this – it is disgusting."

Jon couldn't agree more, it was nice to finally have an outlet where everyone discussed their collective views. Tom was particularly vocal tonight.

"I just don't think it is safe anymore, they don't vet these people. They could be anyone. Who knows who is roaming our streets."

"Bring back the days when London was the best of British." George entered the conversation. Jon didn't know what to think of him, there was something slightly unhinged about him.

There were nine of them that night who met in The Island Queen, a pub on the backstreet of Islington. Jon liked the high ceilings there. The pub had personality. When they first met, he and Evelyn used to go there on Fridays to watch the live bands they showcased. They didn't tend to go out much together anymore; he realised it had been a while since they'd been away together too. He thought of his work schedule for the rest of the year, he was sure he could book something in – it is what they needed.

The door swung open and two more people entered, they waved towards Tom, and Jon realised they were there to meet them. They had introduced themselves as Celine and Nathan, he assumed they were a couple. Everyone was familiar with them, they must have been long-term members. He thought it was nice they shared the same views: Evelyn was infuriating in her pity of immigrants, she was far too left wing for his liking when it came to politics. She was forever trying to correct him by calling them asylum seekers or refugees. They'd eased into conversation; he couldn't help but notice how attractive Celine was. There was something about her sultry looks that intrigued his interest, she did not speak to him for long, she seemed distant. He wondered what brought her there, what had led her to the group.

Celine

"Nathan, hold on. I'll walk with you." I'd spotted him as I left the tube station on my way to the pub for the meeting. I was glad to see a familiar face, even if it was Nathan's.

"Celine, it has been a while! Where did you go?"

"Work, just work, work, work." I hadn't been to the weekly gatherings for a while: the restaurant had been too busy to get away. That night, we met in one of my favourite pubs, The Island Queen.

"You need to ease up. Why don't you let me take you for that drink this weekend?" Nathan was always trying to instigate a date. He was sweet, but I wasn't interested. This happens a lot: men are forever trying to take me out, but it wasn't what I needed or wanted at the time.

I brushed him off. "Oh, you know me – weekends will never work."

"Newbie tonight you haven't met yet. Tom has brought someone from his work for the past few weeks."

"What's he like?" I assumed it was a male because there were not many females in the group. I was the only one regularly attending the meetings at that time.

"Seems okay, pissed off with the way of the world, like us. That is all I know from my brief encounters with him. Tom said he's sound though, so at least he's been vetted."

We always needed to be careful with new members: you never knew what their intentions were, who they may be working for.

As I entered the pub, I noticed him straight away. He was very handsome, tall with a full mop of sandy blond hair and striking blue eyes. He seemed at ease with the others and I wondered how long he had been attending meetings. Clearly this was not his first week.

I did not interact much with him over the course of the evening. I prefer to observe people first, get the measure of them. I did watch him though: the mirrors that cover the pub's walls are handy for that.

31

Jon

"I looked online yesterday and what do you think of the idea of IVF, Jon?"

"What?"

"Because of the miscarriages, I thought maybe that is something we could try?"

"Evelyn, I'm not talking about this now. I'm late for work." He knew the chasm between him and Evelyn was growing, but he didn't know how to pull them back together.

"It's just a suggestion, if we had a stronger embryo…"

"Enough, Evelyn." He had raised his voice. "I'm not going to say it again. Not now." He hadn't meant to raise his voice so much, but he was tired of the constant fertility conversations.

"Maybe we could talk about it in Florence?"

"Maybe." If he was honest the idea of spending their holiday discussing Evelyn's fertility windows and treatments was the last thing he wanted from their break. What he really craved was the carefree fun they'd had in the early days.

He'd been thinking of Celine too much, he knew he was

playing with fire. Not that anything had happened, but he knew what a dangerous temptation she was. There was an intensity to their friendship that had developed over the weeks, it had taken him by surprise last week when he discovered that Nathan was not her partner. He must admit he'd felt his heart skip a beat when she'd mentioned she was in fact single, he could not fathom how – she was beyond beautiful.

He supposed he felt guilty too, hence why he'd booked this trip. There was an intimacy to his and Celine's relationship that he knew may be crossing the line. He had begun to discuss things with her he didn't even mention to Evelyn. The more he tried to stop it, the harder it became, he seemed to just walk closer and closer to the edge of the cliff with Celine. He had always been a thrill seeker and if he was honest, maybe he'd missed the thrill of the chase.

He hadn't been to Florence for years; last time he'd been here five years ago, it was a business trip with clients. He'd spent the weekend then wining and dining them; trying to win a contract. He'd succeeded, and the clients had become some of the firms most valuable. He had always been very charming when it came to winning people over.

He has booked a hotel just off Piazza della Repubblica, his favourite square. The firm has been doing well, so he has gone all out and they are staying at the Savoy for five nights. He has even made sure to book Evelyn in for half a day of treatments at the spa there. There is tension between them from the moment they arrive, he tries to pacify her, but Evelyn is quiet and brooding. They eat in one of the city's many fine dining restaurants, it costs an arm and a leg, and he immediately regrets it as Evelyn appears to not care one ounce for her surroundings.

The days pass. They enjoy moments of happiness, but there is a layer of sorrow that has descended upon them they can't seem to shake. They spend the last afternoon in one of Florence's many squares drinking wine and eating pizza. For a brief period, they laugh. They hold hands, it is as if all their troubles have evaporated – they are back to when they first met, when the only thing that was important was getting to know one another. It is blissful.

It doesn't last. He should have known it wouldn't last, as time passed it became more likely the conversation would be swayed to the one topic he wanted to avoid. The thing about Evelyn was she became stuck, she could not leave it, she had to keep pushing his buttons. There was no point in IVF he'd told her before, it wasn't that she couldn't get pregnant, it was that she couldn't stay pregnant. She was adamant they go for fertility tests, embark on hormone therapy. He had gently tried to tell her it clearly wasn't him who was posing the barrier to them having a family – he knew as soon as he said it, he shouldn't have, but it had already slipped through his lips. She stormed off. He would have followed but he no longer had the energy. Instead, he wandered the Florentine streets as the sun fell down on Italy for the night.

Celine

I could tell something wasn't right when Jon arrived at the group the next week.

His façade suggested he was his usual vibrant self, but when the others weren't looking, or the attention wasn't focused on him, he stared into the distance, the weight of the world on his shoulders.

It was not unusual for Jon and me to stay on for another drink: it had become our little habit. Week by week I could feel us getting closer. That night, we stayed right until last orders. We discussed everything, not only our common views, but travel, his past, my hopes for the future.

I told him about my father. It wasn't that I kept my reasons for being there a secret, but I had never felt confident enough to share my story with another member of the group. We all had our reasons for attending and I just preferred to keep mine quiet.

"Tell me about him," Jon said.

I relayed stories about my father. I laughed. At one point I discovered I was crying. It was the first time it had felt similar to a date. There was a shift in Jon. He was trying to fight it, but we both knew what was inevitable between us.

As I got increasingly drunk and found myself with an urgent need to express my desire for him. It was as we were leaving that I plucked up the courage. I leant on him for support, aware I'd had too many wines.

"Come on, you. Let's get you home, Celine."

"I don't want to go home."

"Well, I think it's time. The pub is shut and we've all had quite a bit to drink, I think." He laughed then and put his hands on both my shoulders. "We will share an Uber. I'll drop you first."

He booked a taxi mechanically on the app and then placed an arm around my waist to stop me swaying. It felt so nice that I leaned into him, aware I was crossing boundaries, but hoping I could just pass it off as being too drunk. The car eventually came, and I slid into one of the back seats. I couldn't help but place one of my hands on his thigh playfully.

He didn't stop me. He smiled shyly to himself. I knew I was right, I knew it was more than friendship. It did not take us long – the car came to a stop outside my restaurant.

"Night then, Celine. Here is your stop."

"Or, you could come in and stay?" I was brazen. A boldness overcame me.

He faltered. I didn't know if it was shock or temptation or both. He looked down as he replied, unable to make eye contact. "We both know I can't." He closed the door quickly and said something to the driver. The car sped off, leaving me crimson with embarrassment.

Jon was different. There was something pure about him: unjaded. He had a hunger for the cause that was more positive than most. He didn't rant angrily; he discussed change rationally. He had an urgency in his manner, but it also seemed thought out – considered. I have never warmed to people quickly, I'm wary, almost distrusting some would say, but Jon... Jon was different.

I understood him, no matter what he said about his wife, I knew their relationship was flawed from the beginning. If it was as *perfect* as he described, I couldn't understand why he wasn't honest with his wife about our meetings. I assumed *she* had similar values to Jon, but then he had never confirmed this. I have never had a man turn me down before, so when Jon rebutted my initial seduction I was enraged. I was surprised he was so willing to stay faithful to his wife. I'd seen the way he looked at me.

32

Jon

Turning her down had made it all the more exciting. It was dangerous and exhilarating, this beautiful young woman staring at him across the table, knowing she wanted him. God, he found it difficult. He started to justify the possibility of a one-off, just to get it out of his system. If she wasn't just a fantasy, he could banish these thoughts about her.

It wasn't just about a sexual attraction with Celine. He enjoyed their conversations. They didn't always talk about their mutual views; often they'd spend their Friday nights discussing their favourite films, where they'd travelled. Celine used to love to travel and Jon soaked up her stories of south America and Mexico. He had lived in Montreal in his twenties, but never got to go further south.

Evelyn worked every weekend during the summer and it was easy to get lonely. He'd return home for the weekend, spent from work, just as she was beginning to work spilt shifts all the way through until Monday. He did not know how she managed to deal with so many weddings. He imagined it must be incredibly boring after the first few: a conveyor belt of declarations of love.

Celine became a friend. He should have known it was wrong, he should have known something would give. He omitted to tell Evelyn about Celine. Maybe that was deceit in itself. He knew that if Evelyn saw Celine she'd be threatened. He couldn't fathom how Celine didn't have a partner: there was so much to find attractive about her.

The issue of conception had weighed heavy on both him and Evelyn for months. They had shut down their communication, but he could tell Evelyn was sinking deeper into herself, withdrawing from their relationship and even her friends. He had noted that in the past few weeks the friends she'd normally meet in between work appointments had waned.

"It's too difficult, Jon," she'd said when he asked. "I'm the only one without children, and I can't sit there while they harp on about their offspring."

He found it difficult she was so consumed by a child. It had become central to their relationship. He yearned for some fun. He wanted to holiday like they had when they first met. He'd become disillusioned with his life – not just his relationship, but the state of the country too. It all compounded to add to his frustration and he sensed he was losing control.

Celine

I avoided the meetings for two weeks. I was too mortified by Jon's rejection to see him.

But then I started hearing about the influx of immigrants posing as refugees, when the real worry was they were in fact

Islamic terrorists. It disgusted me and I could not understand why there wasn't national outrage. It disgusted me so much that I had to go to the meeting. I was too angry at this country to stay away. I felt the urge to take a stand, to start a movement. I told them across that pub table: "There is a nation below a nation forming here. A nation based on hatred and Islam's preachings. The police turn a blind eye as they don't want to be seen as discriminating against these people from Syria and Iraq."

Jon was watching me as I talked, and I shuddered as I remembered him shutting me down.

Until that point, all we could do was post material online, in the hope that it would stop the rising of jihad terrorists. We were inspired by a man slightly older than us, who was not afraid to speak up for white people – the emerging minority.

I read his tweets daily and his calls for support. His freedom of speech was quashed and we were told he had been radicalised. But we believed that maybe it was the other way around: Britain had been so radicalised by a new wave of races and religions, so blinded by integration, that we had not realised we were quickly losing our identity.

I saw this man addressing the crowds, thronged with journalists and police, at Speakers' Corner in the spring of that year. Those who were on the right side proudly held the Union Jack aloft. Our American friends joined us with their stars and stripes.

But it was a shambolic affair: liberals and Muslims turned up to disrupt the event. Above the chants and boos I could not hear a thing. It was clearly a police conspiracy: they didn't want us to hear what this man had to say. He had wanted to express his views on immigration, integration, the war in Iraq, Islam, Brexit and grooming gangs, but all of this was stopped. The police were too threatened by the reality of this divide, so they suppressed us before we had even begun.

I was enraged by this breach of my civil right to freedom of speech. We discuss a rally, a protest, a sit-in. I told them, "There must be something in our power to stop the erosion of our culture and this threat that swells daily."

33

Jon

Celine had not meant to be anything. He had left that side of him behind when he met Evelyn. He'd sworn he wouldn't retreat to his old habits. He had so desperately wanted things to be different this time around, he had so desperately wanted to *be* different. He never actively sought it out; he didn't have to, never had.

But he had been drawn to her instantly. He was only human: she oozed sex. He had tried to avoid intimate situations with her, afraid his willpower may be tested in a moment of weakness. It had worked – initially. In the Uber on their way home he'd been so close to succumbing to temptation, but he had stopped himself.

There had only been one woman before her. It had been a one-off. Well, a one-off that lasted a few months, but he had quickly realised his mistake. He'd called it off, then booked a trip to Venice with Evelyn to banish his guilt. He was manic in his need to put things right with her. The woman was a consequence, he knew that now. The months of trying and failing for a baby had taken its toll on him too. He had just needed a release from the stress, a reminder of simpler, happier times. The affair hadn't been about Evelyn, it was about him. Just him. His needs, what he needed in that moment. And, it had worked, it had worked for a while, Evelyn had been enough, more than enough – his beautiful, radiant wife he was so lucky to have. But, then Celine had entered his life and although he hoped otherwise, he already knew he wouldn't be able to avoid the danger of her.

Before the other woman, there had only been the occasional one-night stand, but there was nothing to them. They didn't mean anything. It was just a simple transaction. He had felt limited guilt over those interludes. They'd mainly occurred on stag dos; part of the fun. But, Jon did not believe that was cheating.

The last meeting he'd seen Celine at, she spoke with such passion, such authority, he could not help but fall under her spell. He had waited outside for her as she left and pulled her aside. "Celine, can we talk?"

"Look, if it's about what happened before, ignore me. I'd drunk too much. It won't happen again. It was inappropriate."

He could tell she was embarrassed. He imagined she was not used to rejection; not many men could resist her. "What if I wanted it to happen, though?" He hadn't realised he was going to say it until he did. He could feel his mind whirling: he knew exactly what he was embarking on, but he was reckless. He wanted her so much in that moment, all thought processes about his marriage were abandoned as he looked at Celine's sultry eyes and full lips.

He placed his hand on the back of her head and guided her towards him, he felt the softness of her lips immediately and it needed everything in his power not to take her right there.

The months of tension and sexual attraction imploded. He

no longer believed he had a choice as they rode in a taxi back to her flat. It was written in the stars.

Celine

Men could never resist me for long, and Jon's desires were far too obvious. He had remained strong for longer than I thought. I admired him for that. However, our chemistry was undeniable: neither of us could fight it any longer.

After our initial kiss, he had come back to my flat. I had not had a man in my flat for as long as I could remember, and he seemed alien amongst all my belongings. I fetched wine from the restaurant and returned upstairs to find Jon surveying his surroundings. I hoarded trinkets, plane tickets, train stubs. Everything pinned to walls or in my frames told a story. I hate houses where you cannot decipher the personality or life of the occupant – I wanted my house to tell a story. Jon was drawn to all the pictures of my travels, I quietly watched him before re-entering the room with two glasses of red wine.

I could tell he was nervous. I could sense his conundrum, but we both knew at this stage there was nothing we could do to stop what was happening between us. I broached the subject of him staying over, he said he'd like to. I wondered what his wife thought when he didn't return home. I briefly sat with the idea that I may not be the first or the last, before pushing it to the back of my mind.

We'd finished the bottle of wine before he leant in and kissed me again. Tenderly to begin, but his kisses quickly became more passionate; an urgency to them. The desire to have him was so great, we didn't make it to the bedroom. We spent the rest of the night barely sleeping, our lust for one another keeping us awake.

He left early in the morning. "When will I see you again?" I asked.

He hesitated, then said, "I'll call you."

I was not sure what to believe. I was not sure whether what happened between us held as much meaning for him as it did me. But I had a busy day ahead in the restaurant, so I compartmentalised Jon until later and got ready for a Saturday shift.

34

Jon

He had tried his hardest. He had rejected Celine's advances for as long as he could. But then she'd leant into him and in that moment he couldn't bear it. He had tried to remain strong for Evelyn, but it was no use.

Once he was back at Celine's apartment he knew he was at the point of no return. The wine had helped ease his guilt about what they were about to do. She was irresistible. As soon as they begun kissing he was taken over by animal instinct. He'd spent the night with her. He knew Evelyn would question where he'd been, but he often stayed over one of the lad's houses if he was on the other side of the city and missed the last tube.

He left at sunrise. As the light emerged so did his intense feelings of guilt. He had betrayed Evelyn in a sense before, but not at an emotional level – not with another woman who actually meant something to him.

Evelyn was still asleep when he let himself into their home. It was Saturday and she'd had a wedding of over 200 guests yesterday, so he imagined she hadn't finished until late.

He showered and did the remaining dishes on the side before making her a coffee that he took to her in bed. She stirred gently, as he looked down at her in bed.

It won't happen again, he promised himself. He would not betray his wife for a second time. He gently kissed her on the lips, rousing her from her slumber, before they made love in their marital bed.

Celine

I did not hear from him that weekend, or for the following week. I had messaged in the group about our meeting on Friday, but he had not replied. I had not had him down as a coward, but I decided I would not waste another breath on him. If he was there on Friday so be it, but I promised myself I'd avoid him.

I hated how he'd made me feel with his lack of contact. I thought he would have the decency to not let me feel so used.

I arrived early at that Friday's meeting: I did not want to walk in and see Jon all cosy and confident, and I wanted to position myself so he could sit nowhere near me.

Some of the members are growing increasingly passionate – Nathan and George discuss the need for definite action. They are tired of us just talking. I am still wary of something so public. I worry that it would have ramifications on my business and the lives of other members who also must keep up public appearances.

The letters are an ingenious ploy. They will create enough fear, whilst growing momentum across the city. I can't remember who floated the idea, but we spend the evening discussing the logistics of the campaign. We settle on 10,000 letters to print, which we will distribute across London, the Midlands and Yorkshire. Our chosen date is 3rd April 2018. We chose the headline "Punish a Muslim Day". It is a tonic to finally put our ideology into practice.

It is Tom who suggests the points system for action taken. We all laugh as we suggest ways to humiliate and harm them, the way they have our friends and family. The way they have spread fear and hatred through our communities. Now it is their turn. I think adding as one of the tasks "Burn or bomb a mosque" is a bit extreme, but all the others are fair in my eyes. If you can pull a headscarf off a Muslim woman, then so be it: they should respect our fashions, our culture.

We all leave the meeting elated at our plan. It is nice we share the same humour and there is a sense of unity amongst us. We are regaining control. Jon arrived late, and I've done my best to avoid him. As I rise to leave he tries to gain my attention, I blank him. He walks towards the door with me, but I raise my hand.

"No, Jon. Just no." I walk out and the door swings behind me. He does not follow me.

35

Jon

He did not understand this country. There were veterans who were homeless. Men who have fought for their country, yet they can't access support. Men who were principled, who deserved more. He thought of George, a member of their group; he had fought hard for his country and been deserted after the war. Jon could see George was troubled, if not slightly aggressive at times but he was afforded no support after everything he had sacrificed. Yet, the government lets these illegals invade our land. It sickened him. He did not wish to support this far-left Marxist rubbish. There were plans to turn military camps into houses for these immigrants: a house for rapists from Iran and Iraq. He wondered what Churchill would think of such madness: he longed for a leader who kept Britain British.

Evelyn had watched with empathy as these men were interviewed on the news. He'd had to leave the room because he could not cope with it. He hadn't always felt this way, but the country had spiralled out of control. It wasn't something that had concerned him so much in his early twenties, but now he recognised the extent of the problem, and he'd seen it first-hand, he could not deny what was happening.

Tom's idea to distribute the letters was a start. There was obviously more that needed to be done though. He'd tried to speak to Celine at the meeting last night, but she had just blanked him. He supposed it was for the best: he could do without the complication of their relationship.

He had been for a swim with Max that morning. He was trying to convince his brother to date again, but Max was ambivalent. His brother had never been a lady's man. He had always despaired at Jon's way with women when they were younger. Max needed to loosen up in Jon's opinion.

He had briefly considered telling Max about his dalliance with Celine, but he couldn't face the judgement. He and his brother possessed very different moral compasses.

Celine

I had tried to avoid Jon for weeks, but there was something magnetic pulling us together. He had kept his distance too, but then after one of the meetings we'd drunk too much. Evelyn was away for the week at a wedding abroad and Jon was clearly bored. I hadn't thought it through, but there was something about our chemistry I couldn't resist.

The pub was closing, and Nathan had suggested we all go for a curry. I knew I should retire home: tomorrow was Saturday and it was always busy, but it was nice to be out around people. At the end of the night, Jon and I were the last to leave, both waiting for separate cars. My Uber cancelled at the last minute and I was infuriated that I had to wait any longer.

"You can come in my car, Celine. I'll drop you."

"If you're sure?" It was late and although I didn't want to necessarily put myself in temptation's way, there was no other option.

Ten minutes later we were travelling across the city. I could feel the weight of Jon's leg against mine. I could tell he was drunk. Our hands mingled next to each other on the seat, his finger brushed against my hand. The electricity between us was intense. We both knew it shouldn't happen again, we understood that we shouldn't allow this any more traction.

But, I have never been good with temptation and nor for that matter was Jon. We had begun kissing before the taxi came to a halt. I didn't need to invite him, he had just followed me to the door. It wasn't all about sex that night. We talked into the small hours. I questioned him about his wife, but he would not talk of her to me.

Jon did not leave the next morning, or the next, or even on Monday. He stayed in my flat for four nights, popping home to get some clothes. Evelyn was away so he took the opportunity to spend more time with me. Maybe it was easier as he wasn't exposed to his guilt daily.

We lazed in the evenings watching films and eating pizza. On the third night, he had run the bath for me when I arrived upstairs from my shift and had cooked us steaks, which he served at a candlelit table. Jon had not warned me he was an awful cook, the food was terrible, but it was the effort that mattered. I did not tell anyone in the restaurant about my visitor. I wanted Jon to remain private. It was a necessary secret.

36

AUTUMN 2018

Jon

He had told himself he wouldn't allow it to happen again, but then she had arrived on that Friday night and he could not take his eyes off her. She was warmer than she'd been a few weeks ago. She had softened. He understood why she was mad at him. He had not meant to use her, he just couldn't help himself. He had tried to do the right thing.

He knew as soon as he offered Celine a lift in his Uber that he couldn't resist. Evelyn was abroad – an extravagant wedding had taken her to Santorini for the week. She had rung him briefly on Friday morning and explained how busy she would be over the weekend and said she wouldn't be able to call him. It made his deceit all the easier knowing he was nnot going to be reminded of his wife's voice.

It had been exhilarating living a different life for a few days. He rung into work sick and stayed at Celine's. If he had spent one more night with her, a few more wouldn't make a difference. Once he'd compartmentalised his wife it had frightened him how easy it was to switch off any feelings of remorse.

It was an insight into a life he could live. Celine was at work in the days and the Saturday evening, but they managed to spend Sunday night and Monday together. He had pampered her on the Sunday, aware she had been on her feet all day and night this week. He found himself wanting to look after her. There was a vulnerability to Celine: she was not as independent and fierce as he had first assumed.

On the Tuesday, he had left. He had to get back to the flat before Evelyn arrived home the following night. He needed to wash off his infidelity. He could not expel Celine from his thoughts.

He tried so hard to stop: time and time again he promised himself it was the last time, but she was so appealing. When he was with her, all his feelings of dissatisfaction disappeared.

Celine

I had never been the other woman. I tried my hardest not to be jealous, to quash the thoughts of them together. When I was with Jon I could not understand how he could feel anything towards another woman. He was so attentive, so passionate. I wondered if Evelyn ever wondered where he was, ever thought to check his phone, his Facebook, his Instagram.

I did not understand how Jon could manage his multiple lives. It must have been exhausting, this constant deceit. We took things slowly to begin with. We booked a weekend in a country hotel closer to Christmas. Jon told Evelyn he had a business meeting with some clients they were trying to win. I was looking forward to a weekend of relaxing with him. It would be a relief not to be on tenterhooks, always looking over our shoulders, worrying who may see us.

I never thought I'd be this type of woman. I hadn't

understood being the other woman before, but I could not help my feelings. It was comfortable when we were together. It felt like I didn't even have a choice when it came to Jon.

37

Jon

He found the affair strangely easy. Occasionally he was alarmed that he could carry it all out so perfunctorily. Evelyn didn't seem to suspect a thing, but he supposed they had been taking it slowly these past few months. He did not want to mislead her.

It was the escapism he needed, the slight thrill that broke up his working week and things with his wife. He didn't tell anyone, he had toyed with the idea of speaking to Max again, but despite his own infidelity, he knew Max would make him end the affair or tell Evelyn.

He didn't think anyone in the group noticed – the conversations never veered off their mission at meetings; there was no time to talk of personal matters.

Their following had been slowly growing online, which pleased Jon. The online space is a place for them to unite: an echo chamber where like-minded people can discuss their views safe in the knowledge they are all just as disgruntled as the other. Jon liked that there was an uprising, that people had begun to wake up to what was happening and fight back.

He had taken Celine away for the weekend. They arrived at the country hotel around 10pm, exhausted from driving on the motorway. He was glad he had booked the cottage suite; the fire was lit, the bed turned down, the minibar full, a bottle of champagne on ice. He could not wait to spend the next three nights out of London. He needed to rejuvenate and Celine's company was easy. There was none of the emotion and intensity of his marriage – none of the guilt or pressure about children.

They spent the next few days exploring the coast of West Wales, eating in small pubs and lazing in the suite. Celine is more relaxed than usual: he almost forgets they are having an affair – it just feels natural. He forgets about work, about the group; about the babies; his wife; London; his anger. In this cocoon in Narberth he stops properly for the first time since he can remember – he escapes.

Celine

The temperature had dropped so dramatically the week we went away. It seemed likely that it would snow over Christmas and I'd been really worried that our trip would be cancelled due to the weather. I bought new underwear, two dresses to wear in the evening and some other treats for Jon. I cannot wait to have a weekend off work, to drink wine, take long baths and lounge in our dressing gowns. I did not intend leaving the bedroom much, except for dinner.

Jon picked me up just after six on the Friday evening. I'd managed to finish the lunch service by 4pm, so I'd had time to shower and pack. I met him around the corner from the restaurant, so no one saw me. His car has blacked out windows in the back, so I climbed into there, but I moved to the front seat once were outside London and on the M4.

He had booked a hotel four hours' drive away. We knew we'd arrive too late to eat at the hotel on the first night, so we got food on the way. I'd booked us in at the hotel's two restaurants for the second and third nights. We stayed in the Master Cottage Suite of the small, intimate hotel set in beautiful gardens. It appeared to be the height of luxury. I never discussed finances with Jon, but he insisted on paying. Money never seemed to be a problem for him: he never questioned the cost of anything.

38

Jon

He saw Celine sporadically throughout the holidays. Office Christmas parties, drinks with various friends and family obligations meant there was little time for anything else. Christmas for Jon was always a marathon metaphorically and physically. He had to travel across the country, trying to fit all their family in, as well as attending a plethora of social events. Evelyn had insisted they visit her family this year. He had convinced her to wait until Boxing Day: selfishly he much preferred the day at his parents' house.

They had floated the idea of Christmas in the flat together; but they were aware it would be Max's first proper Christmas without Nancy. Although they had already split up last year, Max had left the country to fill the void. Evelyn had understood when Jon explained Max's situation. Secretly, Jon preferred the routine of his family home, the ease of helping himself to beer and food from the fridge. He did not like the way Evelyn's family spoke in platitudes. He was always on his best behaviour and therefore couldn't properly relax.

This year they'd spent Christmas Eve with friends, playing board games in the pub. Celine had tried to ring him several times in the day to see if he could visit her. He had grown rapidly tired of her neediness. A little time apart would not be such a bad thing. The weekend in West Wales had been nice enough; he'd indulged the escapism, but it was becoming more and more difficult to juggle. He could manage a fling, but Celine seemed to want more lately. He'd address it in the New Year, in 2019.

Jon and Evelyn drove to Eastbourne on Christmas morning. Jon's parents lived in a red-brick Victorian house with all its original features, four bedrooms, a study, dining room, lounge, a large hallway – it was beautiful. A swimming pool took over the immaculate lawn; he and his brother had spent their summers reclining on the sun loungers surrounded by friends and Jon's many admirers. He had wanted for nothing.

Christmas Day began with smoked salmon and scrambled egg on toasted sourdough, followed by presents. He and Max still sat in their parents' lounge to open each other's gifts. He remembers the year Max had saved his pocket money to buy him a leather jacket, he was very thoughtful like that. Jon usually stopped at John Lewis on Christmas Eve and visited the "gifts for him" section. Before lunch, Jon had insisted they all played cards. He loved card games but hated losing. He didn't cheat per se, he just used certain tactics to win.

Lunch was a three-bird affair. Evelyn and his mother camped out in the kitchen for most the day whilst he, his brother and father drank copious amounts of expensive wine. They were traditionalists and always sat to watch the Queen's Speech, still bought the *Radio Times* to see what was on TV, even though it was all listed on Sky. His parents insisted on crackers and party hats: prawn cocktail to start, Christmas pudding for dessert – they followed all of Britain's traditions.

He'd bought Evelyn diamond earrings: she appreciated the classic gifts that would last a lifetime. To Celine he had posted underwear. He supposed his choice of gifts said a lot about how he viewed both relationships and what their purpose was. Evelyn had been sweet all day, the perfect daughter-in-law and wife. She had showered him with gifts and he had struggled with his guilt.

They'd watched the film *Elf* before he fell asleep, Evelyn's head on his lap, content with his love and food.

Celine

Some of the staff who did not have family in London came to the restaurant for dinner on Christmas Day. I invited some regular customers to join us. My brothers did not return from Italy – they never do. It is as if they have forgotten their place of birth and only remembered their heritage.

There were ten of us in total and I had volunteered to cook, an amalgamation of family traditions. I served up food exactly as my father would have, my eyes misty with the memories of him at the table with us. An absent chair is never as profoundly missed as it is on Christmas Day, the greatest reminder that someone so important is missing from our world.

The restaurant was open Christmas Eve, although we always finished slightly earlier so we could sit down together for dinner. Traditionally in Italy on Christmas Eve, we eat *La Vigilia*: a meat-free dish understood to purify the body before a religious holiday. We feast on seafood: octopus, shellfish and anchovies with *salsa verde*. I have so many oysters I'm surprised we manage them all. It is accompanied by sides of artichokes, zucchini and broccoli.

I have barely managed to clear everything from the night before I have to start cooking Christmas Day dinner. I had hoped to see Jon at some point today, but he has made it clear it won't be possible. He is swamped with family engagements. I try my hardest not to think of him and Evelyn on Christmas Day; what their little traditions may be.

I begin by making the *gnocco fritto* to serve with an antipasti board to start. These little balls of dough fried in lard are delicious with a selection of meats and cheeses. They'd been my father's favourite snack. For our first course, we had *tortelloni in brodo*, which is meat-stuffed pasta in a clear soup. It is the dish my family has cooked since I can remember, so instilled in the hills my father came from.

The main course was incredibly rich, although I've also made turkey, as I know it is nice to keep with British traditions for everyone. *Cotechino in galera* is a cured sausage famous in Emilia Romagna, wrapped in prosciutto and flattened beef rump, then braised in wine before being sliced and served with mashed potatoes or lentils.

By the time we finished these dishes the table was determined they couldn't eat any more, but I insist. It is not Christmas Day without *panettone*, Italian sweet bread and my *nonna's zuppa inglese*. I describe it to most my customers as trifle, but it is more than that: sponge fingers soaked in *Alchermes* (an Italian liquor) layered with custard cream and chocolate.

The day passed in a lively mass of chatter, cooking, eating and laughter. The mixture of people at the table helps alleviate thoughts of Jon. We do not clear the table until gone eleven at night and by then the chefs and I have drunk so much, there is not much to do other than go to bed.

I tried not to think of Christmases past and how different they were when I was growing up. I have tried to keep up the same traditions, but it is not the same. Not one person around the table was a blood relative, yes family, but of a different sense. I thought of my mother momentarily, but then I banished her. She did not deserve my thoughts: she lost that right when she abandoned us all those years ago.

39

Jon

Christmas week had been a whirlwind: he was always jealous of those who returned to work and discussed how relaxing the week between Christmas and New Year had been. For Jon, it had been exhausting.

He and Evelyn had attended so many social engagements that he longed for a night in their flat and a takeaway. He loved socialising, but he felt the urge to just stop momentarily and recuperate.

Celine did not seem to understand: she sent him message after message demanding his attention, questioning when she'd see him again. It was not that he didn't want to engage with her, but the group wasn't meeting up over Christmas and he was too busy with other commitments. He'd see her next week and smooth everything over.

On New Year's Eve they were going to a French restaurant with friends. Evelyn was not a fan of New Year's Eve, but Jon loves the excitement, the buzz and the energy in the air. To him, there was nothing like London on New Year's Eve. It was his favourite place to be.

It was Evelyn's idea to eat out. He would have preferred a bar, but she insisted they all go somewhere more civilised.

They left the flat just after 6pm. Evelyn in minimal make-up and wearing a simple black dress, her hair wavy and natural. She looked beautiful and he had the sudden urge to kiss her. It was as they crossed the road that he saw Celine in the bar opposite. She was staring straight at them, a glass of wine in front of her. It took him a moment to register that his lover was in his environment. He stiffened, then veered off to the left, his arm around Evelyn. He looked back at Celine, mouthing: "What the hell are you doing?"

She looked sheepish: he had caught her in the act. He could not have her just turning up at his house.

Celine

I knew I shouldn't follow him, but things had been different since Christmas, his messages few and far between. I could feel him pulling away from me.

I understood it had only been a week, but it was the fact he had not wanted to see me at all that riled me. *Surely*, I thought, *Christmas is the week you want to be around those you care about, those who are special to you.*

I suppose I wanted to see what his other life looked like. I'd asked Tom, his work colleague, for the address of Jon's flat in Hampstead – I feigned it was to send a Christmas card. There was a bar opposite, so I could sit in the window and spy out of sight. I managed two drinks while I waited.

It was 5:30pm on New Year's Eve and the bar was filling up. I noted the Edwardian building their flat is housed in. It would not have been cheap. I wondered what the interior looked like. Modern and expensive, I imagined. I can't picture it with another woman in, though. I ordered another glass of wine.

They appeared together at the door twenty minutes later. She was not what I expected. I had imagined high glamour, like a model. She was pretty, don't get me wrong, but she was more girl-next-door. There was a sweetness and vulnerability to her appearance – nothing like me. I am far more exotic. She wore a simple dress, her hair loose on her shoulders. She looked relaxed, not a woman who knows her husband is cheating on her.

She laughed at something he said. He leaned down and kissed her, a smile on his lips, then clasped her hand as they crossed the road towards me.

I tried to pull my hair across my face as they neared the bar, but it was clear he had clocked me through the window.

He tensed and immediately steered his wife in the opposite direction. He turned back and mouthed something at me. He appeared pissed off. I realised he was extremely threatened by my presence. He would not be comfortable with me being so close to Evelyn. I imagined he was worried at what I may do. I enjoyed the power momentarily. I wasn't even sure what I was hoping to achieve that night, what my objective was. Was I just torturing myself?

40

Celine

Whats App became particularly useful as the group grew. We could have up to 256 of us chatting all at once. We could share information really easily, and it helped it was all encrypted too. Our group title is "Modern-Day Crusaders". It was tongue in cheek, but we were helping to save the free world to some extent. At least we realised the threat.

Our online community is transnational: people all over the world support our cause. I watched the attacks in Christchurch live on Facebook. I am the first to say I was shocked, but not surprised. What did they expect if they silenced people for so long; seeking the recognition of the community, his crime was almost a performance. He was promoting himself, his act, our cause.

He was acting on behalf of our community. His international recognition would surely propel other members of our community to commit similar acts. Our WhatsApp group had exploded with messages. We had some people leave: they were sympathetic to our cause, but they turned away as soon as it got too messy: real.

ISIS has spent years producing propaganda footage for their cause. They've self-filmed violent acts. Why is it so alarming that some people have shown them the shoe can fit on the other foot? Certain world leaders knew these people were fighting back; they understood about the greater good. To us, one particular leader represented a symbol of our identity, a renewed sense of common purpose – he understood that there were people invading our lands. He recognised that we should fear an entire cultural and racial replacement in the West.

When I was with these people in our WhatsApp group, I felt like I finally belonged. I felt as I had before my father died, when the world had purpose, when I could identify with my surroundings. They were akin to me; I had spent so long feeling lost, frustrated at what had happened to our family and now I identified with these people's anger. I felt part of something – united.

Jon

"I just think he took it too far, Celine. I'm all for action, but that reflects badly on our cause."

"It's about the message, Jon. Without crusaders like him nothing will change. When are you going to wake up? I question your commitment sometimes."

"I am committed, Celine. I just think there are better ways of going about things."

After the Christchurch incident he began to worry about what the group was evolving into. It had equally united and divided them in the group. He noted the number of members who had left their WhatsApp group and he too felt tempted.

Their intentions suddenly felt too certain, too solid. He had always sympathised with their views, but he was not an extremist. He thought these lone wolves that murdered people in mosques threatened their integrity. It would not help to be associated with people who were unhinged.

He and Celine had begun to increasingly argue about the matter. He could not understand how she supported these people. Surely, they were carrying out exactly the same kind of attacks that had enraged them against Muslims in the first place. It made no sense to him. He did not think you could fight this political war, which would affect their cultural landscapes, with such brutalism.

Celine accused Jon of not being committed to their cause, she sees his lack of communication in the WhatsApp group as a direct slur.

He longed for the early days when the group just discussed their views over a few drinks, laughter interspersed with jokes that some would consider too close to the bone. He missed the nights spent with Celine when they idled the hours away exploring each other's bodies. He longed for those evenings when they had first met, the explosive lust when they were so consumed with each other, he could momentarily forget that it was wrong.

His doubts had been bubbling to the surface for a little while. They always did when it came to women. As with the other women, he had begun to realise that the grass wasn't always greener. He thought of Evelyn more and more when he was with Celine. He longed for her sweet naivety and loving attitude. He identified with the anger of the group and Celine, but not the intense hatred.

He knew he was withdrawing from her, maybe he always knew he would. It was in his nature to take risks and then grow bored quickly. His distance had been amplified by her turning up on New Year's Eve.

Celine insisted they go for dinner tomorrow night, he has agreed, purely to pacify her. He doesn't want to tip her over the edge, he needs to appease her. He knows the conversation will happen soon, the one he is dreading. He has been contemplating a trip with Evelyn and he is on the verge of booking.

It came to him with such clarity in the middle of the night, how foolish he was being, how reckless he had been with their marriage. He promised himself it would stop. He would put distance between them.

41

Celine

Our relationship progressed slowly, and by the spring I'd thought we'd be spending more than one night a week together.

Jon always insisted he was too busy for anything else. I didn't ask him what his life entailed the rest of the week. He was always cagey about his life beyond me. I was aware I wouldn't be invited to meet his friends or family. It is the nature of an affair. Those in our group weren't even aware of our relationship, and Jon doesn't want his colleagues to know anything.

He did not like us going out in public, though when we did, he was nothing but a gentleman. He didn't touch me; you would barely know that we were friends.

At dinner that night I could tell he was agitated. I tried to reach his hand across the table and he flinched. I do not cope with rejection well. I longed for another weekend away where we could pretend things are different between us. We had not been away since that weekend in Wales.

I tried to explain how I felt, but Jon dismissed me. As the

evening progressed I quietly seethed. By the time we reached my apartment I was ready to explode. Jon seemed to have no sympathy. He tried to kiss me. He clearly just wanted sex tonight. It frustrated me that though we were in private, he was not as attentive as usual. I did not want to feel like second best all the time. I also didn't like the fact he seemed to be withdrawing, not just from me, but the group too.

"I could tell her, Jon. I could tell her and then it'd all be out in the open and we could be together."

"It's not as simple as that. You know that, Celine. You know I can't leave her, what with the babies."

"There is always an excuse, Jon. Always a reason – you're never going to leave, are you?"

"I don't want to discuss this, Celine. It's not the right time to talk about it."

"Why? Why isn't it the time?"

"Because I want a nice night with you. I want to enjoy myself, before I go away."

"Go away?"

"I was going to say. I'm going away next weekend, so I can't see you for two weeks."

"Where? Where are you going?"

"Italy. We're going to Bologna for a long weekend."

"WE?"

"Yes, we."

"As in... you and your WIFE."

"Yes, Celine. She is still my wife."

I exploded. I could not help but lose it. *How can he be here with me one minute, and then flying to Italy for a romantic weekend the next?* My body began to violently shake with rage. My face felt on fire. I clenched my fists and tried to control my anger, but it was too late.

"This is a joke, Jon. An absolute joke." I spat the words at him. "You need to get out. GET OUT. GET OUT. GET OUT." I screamed at him as he gathered his things and left. I pummelled his back with my limp punches. They did not seem to penetrate him emotionally or physically. I could not believe how detached he seemed when he told me: it is as if we mean nothing to him. It will be weeks before I next see him now, and even then, I'm not sure I'll want to.

Jon

Celine had proved more problematic than he realised. The fiery side of her personality had presented itself a few times. He found it difficult to pacify her, and he did worry she may reveal herself to Evelyn. He needed to get away for the weekend. A trip abroad was called for. He often booked flights on a whim when the pressure of work, the affair and his extra-curricular activities got too much. Evelyn enjoyed travel and never questioned his intense need to leave London.

He'd booked Bologna as an escape because he'd been so distracted and agitated at home. He made the decision to stop communication with Celine for the duration of that break. Evelyn deserved more. He'd thought he may be able to separate himself from Celine on his return. Their last meeting had not gone well.

Those days with his wife, where they'd idly eaten copious amounts of food then dozed together later in the afternoons, had been a tonic. It'd been pleasant to distinguish his two lives with physical distance.

The group meetings had increased in their intensity. Anger was predominately the emotion he came away feeling afterwards: hopeless and angry. He realised it was on the verge of getting out of hand.

He knew Evelyn deserved more and in the moments of pure relaxation, he really thought he could make it work. He considered suggesting they move, but he wasn't sure he really wanted to leave London. Life in Bologna seemed simple though, in a moment of clarity he understood that when he returned home he must end it with Celine. He should never have re-ignited it after that first night – he'd known since that night he lay in bed, his thoughts swimming, but he realised that time was not on his side.

He saw with clarity now that he had been confused. He'd got caught up in the moment. He didn't want Celine, he still loved Evelyn. He was just looking for escapism. Instead of facing head-on the problems with his wife, he had run away. He had run straight into the arms of another woman. He was weak, it was cowardly. As soon as he got home, he'd tell Celine that it was over, and he'd stop communicating with the group.

Jon did not feel the relief he first had when he'd met everyone. Of late, he found that the group's views had taken on a darker narrative. It wasn't that he didn't believe in the cause; but he had become uncomfortable with the level of racism – it wasn't just towards Muslims and immigrants now, there were new members of the group who believed in Hitler's manifesto. He didn't want to exterminate races; he just didn't think it was healthy when they mixed. He wanted to preserve cultures.

On their last night in Bologna, he had booked Osteria Dell'Orsa. It was exactly like described: lively, loud and full of atmosphere. He wasn't sure if Evelyn would have preferred something quieter, but he had wanted the buzz of a typical Italian restaurant.

They were led downstairs, to a small table in the corner. They had packed in as many people as possible. It was full of students drinking beer, eating cheap, generous dishes. The ravioli was divine, the tiramisu he could have eaten three times.

Evelyn wore a pale blue dress and it brought out her eyes. As he stared across at her, he thought how beautiful she looked tonight. He felt like such a fool for jeopardising their marriage, for betraying her. Maybe they would look into adoption when they got home. Maybe he would broach it in a few weeks. He knew she wanted to try for a few more months. He didn't think he could bear for her to suffer another miscarriage though. He didn't know whether he could witness her pain.

They polished off a small carafe of red wine and decided to head to one of the bars in Piazza Maggiore for a cocktail. They sat overlooking the Church of San Pietro, enjoying the breathtaking contrast between the bottom and the top of the building with marble that seems to shine below the dark bricks.

He looked across at Evelyn admiring the view, and was overwhelmed with gratitude that he had a second chance to put everything right. "I love you, Evelyn. You do know that."

"I love you too." She had smiled at him underneath the beautiful Italian starry sky and he had smiled back, before he kissed her. Everything was going to be all right.

42

Celine

"What the hell is this? This is not tortellini," I snapped at my staff. My father had prided himself on his tortellini. His *nonna*, who had grown up in the hills surrounding Bologna where the dish was a staple, had taught him to make it, and he had spent hours teaching me the intricate folding, his hands moving masterfully quick. It had looked so simple, but not one of my staff could master it.

I did not have time to work the kitchen and the front of house, and I'd had to hand over the making of the tortellini to one of the chefs. I could see the standards slipping. I long for my father's steady manner, his ability to bring stability to the business.

I was meant to be meeting Jon after work. I tended to take Friday nights off and it was when we spent our time together. I understood that my mood was due to the message he had sent me the previous day, but my fiery temper reacted without thought so I took my feelings out on others. I still could not believe he had taken a trip to Italy for the weekend. And of all places Bologna.

Maybe that was what heightened my sensitivity to our pasta tonight: I was aware he was eating the same dish in its country of birth. I imagined him and his wife strolling through the city, hand in hand, stopping for glasses of wine. It took everything to stop myself from going mad.

He had never promised me a future, but he had also not once implied that there was one with his wife. I had assumed that as he was conducting an affair it was inevitable we would end up together. I tried to gather myself for service, but I caught my reflection in the mirror. My skin looked sallow, my eyes sported deep dark rings and my hair was thrown on top of my head like a dishevelled bird's nest.

The evening passed. Tables were turned over again and again and I found it difficult to keep up with the orders. I shouted rapidly at the kitchen, animated in my approach. The young waitresses I employed were also of Italian heritage – I liked the restaurant to feel authentic.

Once we had cleared down and the chefs had served the staff all the leftover ragu with spaghetti, I told them they could all leave for the night.

I locked the doors and then found myself an expensive bottle of red. I sat on one of the wooden benches and poured myself a large glass. I opened my Instagram and searched for Jon: I follow him so I can see what his movements are. The first photos were platters of meats and cheeses; there were a few more of the architecture, but the latest image was of her. She was tilting her head slightly to one side, the afternoon light dancing on her face. She looked happy. I had seen her before of course, but it was still a punch in the gut to be greeted with the reality of her existence. It was a reminder of his other life, the woman he must have loved dearly enough to marry.

I shut down my phone and reached for the bottle. I sat in the restaurant until gone 2am drowning my sorrows, progressively getting more and more angry.

I fired off texts to Jon without thinking, before I retreated to my flat upstairs and dreamed of Jon and his wife in Italy.

Jon

He had ignored her text messages, a torrent of abuse, whilst he was away. He knew she was frustrated, but he couldn't give her what she wanted. He had met with the group on Friday and had a few drinks afterwards.

He and Celine were civil. He knew he could do this. He could keep the relationship platonic, it needn't escalate.

He was, of course, avoiding the inevitable, but he had managed to avoid an intimate exchange with Celine – especially with the possibility of a baby now, they could not continue. Evelyn was only a week late and they knew it was too early to get excited given her history of miscarriages.

He always found this time the most difficult. He couldn't allow himself the possibility of joy at the news, all the while trying not to dread Evelyn losing another baby. He was sick of being helpless every time it happened, exhausted of putting on a brave face. Their grief was so compounded after every loss, and there was an expectation they should just recover and try again – Jon found it frustrating – the pressure to be parents was everywhere and so was the idea that you're a failure if you're not.

43

Celine

Our movement was growing on both sides of the Atlantic. George had been in contact with other groups who understood our struggle. Tonight, at the meeting he told us of the Proud Boys, a group that formed in America during the 2016 Presidential elections. I tried to explain to George that these groups went back decades. It was just that they had only recently started vocalising their views in the public domain, but he really believed it was a new uprising.

George did not understand that I had studied our narrative, our joint history. In the late 1970s there was the white power movement in America, formed of Klansmen, Neo-Nazis, a white religious group known as Christian Identity, and many other white warriors – they had been fighting the cause for much longer than George realised. The Proud Boys group was just an extension of this fight, but they also demonstrated their beliefs with militant power.

At one of our meetings, I told Jon about Britain First, a group similar to ours. "This country needs a patriotic political movement that puts our people first. Britain First is trying, but the police and the government continue to silence them for their own agenda."

From his expression, I could tell he thought I was too stringent. More and more I was starting to doubt whether he leant to the left too much on some matters. He was not tolerant, but he certainly needed to be increasingly intolerant if we were going to achieve change.

Jon

After the trip to Bologna with Evelyn, he tried to avoid moments alone with Celine but found himself increasingly drawn to her. At least she could laugh with him. He looked forward to alcohol-fuelled Friday nights with Celine, when Evelyn thought he was at the gym. Her job meant she was busy with weddings most weekends, so the situation suited their circumstances.

He never took Celine to their apartment: he wasn't that disrespectful. No, Celine was more partial to public displays of affection since they had got back together. It had concerned him at first, but now it was a matter of course. There was an urgency to Celine, the way her life manifested. She was forever trying to fit three things in at once, no matter how inappropriate.

He couldn't help himself: home life had become increasingly tense. Evelyn was obsessed with her pregnancy and their evenings were spent talking about the child they may never have. He had tried. For Jon life wasn't fun anymore, it wasn't the marriage he envisaged. He wanted to travel the world, he wanted them to indulge themselves, live the lifestyle they could afford. But Evelyn was a home bird: he often thought she'd be far more content in a cottage in the country.

At the beginning they had been perfect. He could still

remember the excitement laced with lust, the joy he felt every time he saw Evelyn. But more and more he was questioning if they were too different, too far apart.

44

Jon

"What's this?" Jon pointed to the pale blue shopping bag, his heart sinking.

Evelyn looked away. "For the baby."

Her obsessive shopping had reared its head again. Every pregnancy she bought clothes for the unborn child and it worried him. There was a wardrobe in their flat full of clothes for children who are yet to exist. He couldn't help himself. "Don't you think it's a bit early–"

She exploded, threw the bag down and stormed from the room.

He understood it was a manifestation of her yearning, but it only pushed them further apart and amplified their losses. He was glad to leave the apartment that night and go to the meeting where it was safe for him to air his views.

He was not a fan of the far, far right. He did not believe there was a need for guerrilla warfare, this desire to push their beliefs on the masses by organising attacks. He believed there was a place for protests and sharing information with the right people.

He knew there was a need to reignite Christianity in Britain. The prevailing religion seemed to be Islam and it didn't sit right with him. Islam had infiltrated the country's history and culture. He understood the fear – Britain's way of life being eroded. He did not believe in conspiracies, he did not see a white genocide happening, but he could understand why some people believed in it.

Jon thought there were identity issues with a culture that is too different; and that a strong sense of identity was crucial to happiness. There was something unsettling to him about multicultural societies. He thought this diversity could be quite toxic if it wasn't controlled appropriately.

From Max he has heard what happens on the front lines of policing when the white working class are oppressed. Max has told him about the number of call-outs involving unemployed white males.

"And I bet they'd have been working if it wasn't for eastern Europeans taking their jobs," Jon had commented.

"It's a bit more complicated than that," Max said, staunchly disagreeing with him. But then his brother had always been too forgiving. If he'd been more cut-throat, stronger in his convictions, maybe he wouldn't have ended up alone so young – he needed a backbone.

Celine

Jon arrived at the meeting looking despondent. He was normally so sharply dressed, but he looked dishevelled. I'd approached him before the meeting began.

"What is the matter, Jon? You don't look yourself."

"Just home stuff." He shuffled his feet but wouldn't make eye contact with me.

"Well, it looks like more than stuff."

"It's Evelyn, look I don't want to talk about it, Celine." She could hear the exasperation in his voice. "It's been a long week. She's just fragile at the moment, what with her desperate want for a child. I'm finding it all a bit much."

"Do you want to go for a drink and talk about it after?"

"No. No, Celine. I don't actually. I don't want to talk about it all."

I knew Jon's wife had had miscarriages, but Jon never opened up about his wife's desperate need for a child except to remark about his wife being fragile. I'd never wanted children. The maternal urge had never arisen. I'd waited for it, then came to think it absurd that this biological clock would kick in.

We'd sat down then, the conversation ended. We're in a hall again tonight, the group has inflated so it seemed necessary to hire a private venue; hopping from pub to pub to avoid being noticed had become impossible with our increase in numbers. I leant towards Jon in a final attempt to speak with him.

"We could just go for a drink, no need to talk about anything."

Jon was about to respond when George launched into a scathing attack on the group.

"Where is your courage? I can't sit here any longer and listen to everyone chat, but not putting words into action." I wasn't sure who George was aiming his dialogue at.

"What do you suggest we do, George?" Jon retorted, he realised he disliked him.

"Force, we need brute force. Make them understand what it has been like for us. If they are going to kill our people, I think we have every right to kill theirs. An eye for an eye."

"I don't think killing people is the answer, George! I think we'd all agree we need to be a little more intelligent than that."

"See, this is what I mean – no courage in your conviction. You're not willing to sacrifice for the cause."

Jon had stood and walked towards the toilets, ending the conversation between them. I agreed with George, not with his extremities, I thought murdering people was too far.

"I know what you're saying, George." I tried to pacify him. "I'm sure there is a way we could inflict some harm to get the message across without being so extreme."

George smiled back at me: "I knew I could trust you to agree, Celine."

"Let's just leave Jon out of these plans though."

I knew he would have disagreed, it seemed logical to exclude him given his state tonight too.

45

Jon

By the summer he could not be in the house with Evelyn. Grief permeated the walls. There was a curtain of sadness shrouding the door to every room. This had to be the last attempt at having a baby. The doctors had said, too. They could not go on like this. She was destroying herself with every loss. He'd tried to convince her to get out of bed, but there was nothing he could do this time. It was as if she had shut down entirely.

He had only meant to go out for one or two to drown his sorrows, but he couldn't cope with the reality of what he'd return to at home. Evelyn's devastation repelled him. He hadn't meant to ring Celine, but he couldn't get hold of Max and all the boys were away. She'd picked up on the third ring. He didn't say much, but she seemed to sense there was something wrong.

She was flustered as she entered the pub, her hair swept across her face. The weather was atrocious for July. He'd explained slowly about everything they'd been going through, how upset his wife was. This felt like the ultimate betrayal, discussing Evelyn's emotional state with his lover. He felt like a shit. He was a shit. He'd wanted Celine to help him forget, but she'd just made him remember why he was here and what a bad husband he was.

He knew what he needed: a release. They went outside for a cigarette. He pressed her up against the wall, urgently pushing into her. She was more hesitant than usual. She normally had no issues with public displays. He dragged her around the side of the building – it was dark. He fumbled with her tights, ripping at them, he pushed her skirt up. It was over quickly. Celine seemed disorientated. He hadn't been as engaged in the moment, he knew, but he couldn't help it. He didn't feel engaged at all today.

Celine

He was clearly upset. We normally used protection, but there was an urgency to Jon today. I knew I was in love with him. I'd tried to avoid it happening, but he was addictive. Time with him was like a drug – intoxicating. Tonight, he had talked about Evelyn. He never talked about his wife, his last shred of loyalty towards her.

I did not know how hard they had been trying for a baby over the years. I felt sick to the stomach. I realised I'd been naively living in the hope it was only a matter of time before he left her. I realised with sudden clarity where I stood in Jon's world – another secret. I did not speak much as he relayed their problems. It was both upsetting and fascinating to discover more about this man – I wondered if anyone ever knew the true man behind the façade or whether he was so multi-faceted he needed to maintain the separate acts – impossible to be his one true self with all members of his life.

46

Jon

He could hear George talking about his big plan; he thought he was a bit full of it. He always made out he was the most committed of the group, but as far as Jon was aware he just ranted. He tried to conceal a laugh as George continued.

"Something funny, Jon?"

"I'm just thinking, you always go on about the need for action, but what have you actually done?"

"I can assure you, more than you. I bet you've never even had a fight."

Jon thought back to when his anger really began shortly after the 2017 London attacks. He could not believe it when he'd turned on the news that morning. Him and Evelyn had enjoyed a date night on the Saturday evening – all devices, phones and televisions had been turned off. It was the only time he ever did, and he welcomed the simplicity of not being stuck in front of a screen.

As the news reporter's voice filled the room he stood in

disbelief staring at the television. Evelyn plodded into their living room still sleepy and in her pyjamas.

"What's happened?"

"A terrorist attack again."

They both watched the footage of the white van ploughing through pedestrians at Borough Market before the men launched a knife attack; they were silent.

"It's got to stop now." Jon was angry. He'd had enough of the state of affairs. Why were these men and women even allowed in his country? What exactly were the police doing to keep them safe? Not that'd he'd bring it up with Max, he was too defensive.

"You think you know me so well, George."

"Prove me wrong then."

"It was two years ago, just after the London attacks. I'd had enough of it. The boys had asked me for beers. That's when I first spoke to Tom about issues, I'd realised we held the same views. Finally, someone who thought like me."

Tom had patted Jon on the back, he knew Tom had already heard the story, so understood what was coming.

"That's when Tom first told me about the group. I was so buoyed up to finally find like-minded people. Tom had riled me up, I felt invigorated." Jon could see the group was transfixed.

"I saw her get on at Oxford Circus. I had stared at her. Her veil covered the majority of her face. I could only see her eyes, unblinking undeterred. She would have grown up alongside these monsters. I could feel my anger rising, I clenched my fists. How dare she stand on the tube, indignant in her hijab as if she belonged here, especially after what they had done in the city that weekend. I did not even think about it, it was time for action

– if people weren't going to stand up against this threat I'd have to."

It had began slowly at first, but with each word Jon became more and more vicious: "Go home, you terrorist bitch. Standing there in your terrorist headscarf. No one wants you people here – you're scum."

"I could see her retreat, she didn't like it now, not now she was called out. I could see my stop approaching. I headed to the doors to exit, but as I did I made sure to pull her hijab down before spitting in her face."

Jon remembered the feeling so well. For the first time in a long time he felt powerful as he walked back to their flat, like he was finally taking control of the situation – making a difference. That was just before he joined the group, in the beginning.

He saw George slouch down in his seat, defeated; Jon was not a coward at all as the other members gave him a round of applause.

Celine

The group was tame to begin. They didn't do anything too risky: it was a quiet rising, harmless and amusing in the early days. They'd laughed uncontrollably the day the "Punish a Muslim Day" letters went all over the city. I could only imagine the brown terrorists scared – well, that's how we felt every day in our own city. They should be scared and then they should go home.

George had become a bit of a hero in their group, his courage to speak out about what mattered in the UK made me proud. I know that if people were entirely honest with themselves, they'd admit they preferred Britain when ethnic diversity wasn't so prevalent. It is normal to want to be amongst your tribe: it is simply nature's way. I am not racist, but I don't want my way of life corroded. I don't want to be the only white face in a sea of turbans, hijabs and blacks. It had already started with terrorism and the epidemic of knife crime – none of these are "white" crimes: facts are facts.

That meeting was particularly fraught. George had been threatened with imprisonment. Ridiculous! All he was doing was exposing rapists who had no right to be in our country. The group was angry. I was angry. What was the world coming to when he was imprisoned for exposing a Huddersfield grooming gang? How could that be considered wrong?

I never believed all these people were really that desperate to come into Britain. How can it be reasonable to allow all these immigrants with no documentation, no proof of their identity, into this country? How can they police them, when they don't even know who they are? I agree we should help people, but there was already a housing crisis in Britain. We need to help our own first. Instead, the government gives free healthcare and education to strangers.

Jon had disengaged from the group since Bologna, retreating as more and more people joined the cause. I'd questioned his commitment, although he was more engaged tonight. He preferred the group when it was more talk than action. But talk won't change anything. We need a call to arms, to tackle this from the ground up. Our group numbers are increasing week by week. It just shows the unease, the dissatisfaction with what Britain is becoming.

Some of the new members were desperate to make a difference. I liked them, but Jon thought them too extreme. But maybe that is what we need: those who are willing to be brave, to hammer home how dangerous these people are. How many more attacks must there be before they take notice, before the security services protect British citizens from overseas threats, from Islam, from these terrorist Muslims?

We'll attack them. If they think they can infiltrate our city, we'll prove them wrong. Not many of our group were informed of the plan. It was better that way. George was willing to sacrifice himself for our cause, and we needed more people like him, more who would give up their lives. Our ancestors had sacrificed their lives in the wars to protect our country; now it was our turn.

47

Jon

The room fell silent as he arrived. There were even more people here tonight, including the men from Luton who had joined recently. He hadn't liked their talk last time. It went down paths he considered too extreme. They were so incensed with the lack of white people in their community that they pushed for increased violent action. George rallied them.

The underbelly of the group frightened him now. What had begun as a place to voice his opinions now felt different. The air was charged.

He wanted change as much as the next person, but he was not willing to use force to achieve this. Celine seemed to agree with the more extreme members in a way he hadn't expected. He thought she was slightly more considered.

She was more distant these days, but that he didn't mind: it would make what he had to do easier. He needed to break it to her that the affair was over. He needed to tell her that he can no longer carry on as they have been going. He did not want to lose Evelyn.

As he sat listening to the men discuss the need for violence, he understood that he could no longer meet with these people. He wanted to preserve British culture as much as other people in the group, but not at the risk of his reputation, his job.

If he is serious about his marriage, he must break all ties with Celine. He did not want to do it over drinks, so he decided to ask her for lunch on Monday. It would be easier to do it somewhere public. He would make sure it was brief, he'd be courteous, but also firm. He knew what her temper could be like and he didn't want to risk a big, dramatic showdown.

He waited outside the hall for her; she takes forever to come out. He had no idea what she was doing, but he briefly thought she had been crying. "Celine, are you okay?"

"Yes, yeah. I'm fine. What are you doing?"

"I was waiting for you. I was hoping we could meet Monday for lunch?"

"Yes, sure. What time?"

"Twelve? I'll see you then, I'll text you the restaurant." He turns and leaves her with a small wave.

PART III

"As long as people believe in absurdities they will continue to commit atrocities."
— **Voltaire**

48

Evelyn

I'd been aware that looming at the end of the trip was reality and included with that was Christmas. Max had repeatedly asked me what I was planning, but I'd avoided making any plans up until the last minute. I could not help but think back to the Christmas before. I am so glad we had gone to Jon's family: at least they all had that lasting memory.

In the end Max and I spent the day together. He could not face his parents and the gaping hole in their home. I couldn't face anyone. I spent the majority of the day staring blankly at a wall. I could not cope with the gulf of sadness that encompassed me. Max seemed equally despondent. We ordered pizza in and lay on the sofas in mine and Jon's flat. I can't remember what we watched on TV; I was detached.

Amy

I'd had one last meeting with Zahera on the Monday before Christmas. We have built a relationship of sorts, although I know she is impatient as I am yet to properly look into her brother's case. I find I'm increasingly intrigued as to her experiences.

As I catch the train back to my parents on Christmas Eve, I can't help but think of her experiences on public transport and how much something as simple as our appearance could alter how we are treated in life.

My brother and his wife are staying for Christmas too, an unwelcome reminder of everything I have yet to achieve. They make marriage look so easy, and I wonder how I got it so wrong with Jasper. I suppose I'd got caught up in the image of him in university, rather than the reality: he was "cool", other girls wanted his attention, something he was sure to make me aware of.

I'd confused the toxicity for a challenge. I'd been blinded to what was really going on. I think back to the Christmases we spent together. They'd not been too bad: Jasper's large family masked any problems. The energy of the household meant everyone was swept up in jovialities and it was easier to ignore the fact he'd not put any thought into my presents and paid me little attention.

This year it is nice to get out of the city, away from the sad realities of the world I work in daily. I take long walks, wear pyjamas for days on end and eat far too much – everything you are meant to do at Christmas.

Celine

I don't mourn the Christmases I had with Jon because there weren't any. Last Christmas had been spent frustrated that I couldn't see him. I'd tormented myself with what he was doing with his wife, annoyed that he continued the pretence when he clearly wasn't happy.

How could he keep up such a façade? Did he find it difficult to mask his true feelings, his real beliefs?

His life with Evelyn was the one he needed for the outside world, whereas when he was with me he got what he wanted, not just in a one-dimensional way, but he could talk to me about his true feelings, his values, what frustrated him. He didn't have to hide who he really was.

Max

Max had repeatedly asked Evelyn what she was doing for Christmas. He'd brought it up several times during their trips, but she was evasive and reluctant. He could not imagine being at his parents' home now as a single child.

He texted her on Christmas Eve but she didn't reply. So he knocked on her door. He wasn't giving her the choice. "Hey..."

"Max, come in. What are you doing here?"

"I did text, Evelyn. I've come for Christmas. I'll take the spare room. Before you start, I don't expect dinner. I thought we could just hang out together. Order pizza in, pretend it's not Christmas at all."

She raised a small smile. "Okay, Max. That sounds... okay."

He hadn't expected to feel so deflated but come Christmas Day he was floored by absolute exhaustion – even the idea of Christmas without Jon too tiring.

49

Evelyn

It has been difficult since Christmas. I have begun grief counselling, but it only irritates me. I do not want to sit in a room whilst this woman asks me how I'm feeling. This morning during my one-hour session I had felt a surge of rage towards her as I relayed the thoughts in my head.

"I'm just haunting myself with 'what ifs'. What if I'd rung him, what if I'd woken up that morning? What if I'd made him breakfast, he may have left the house earlier? I'm just swimming through various 'what ifs' that would mean he wouldn't have got THAT tube, and he'd still be here and that would mean I wouldn't have to be in this room."

"And, how does that make you feel?"

I swallowed down tears and remained mute – it is obvious how I felt. I regained composure before speaking again. "I sometimes enter the flat and shout his name. Not because I forget he isn't there, but because I miss calling his name. I miss shouting for him when I arrive home. I worry I will forget I used to do this if I stop. I worry I'll forget what life with Jon used to be like. What no one understands is the only person I want to speak to about Jon dying *is* Jon. He is the only one who would understand. I don't have the words for anyone else."

The counsellor tilts her head to the side and asks me again, "And, how does that make you feel?"

I realise that it is not going to work, not counselling per se, but me and this woman, and I know how important it is to find the right counsellor – I've been here many times before with the miscarriages.

When I return to the flat, a package has been left in the hallway. It is from either Max or his mother: neither of them have offered to relinquish their keys. I know they worry about me. It is Jon's memorial plaque. His mother commissioned it: she wants it for the house where they all grew up. We saved some of his ashes for his parents' garden.

I stare at the square tile. I hate it. How is it possible Jon has a start and a finish date? How can a person suddenly expire? How is that fair?

I've realised that there will never be a day of dawning, a final realisation – it will just forever feel like something so fundamental to my core is missing: him. I want to speak to my twenty-year-old self who knew not of the grief that was to come, the irreplaceable loss I would experience once my youth had vanished. I thought we were all invincible then, the lessons I have learnt about death in my thirties has left me feeling hopelessly empty for the pointless worries of my twenties. If only I'd just enjoyed living in the moment and not fretting for our future so much.

I wrap the plaque back up and go to the kitchen table where I have laid out the last of the letters in order. I pick up the first one and allow myself to be transported back to another world, another love story, where my great-grandmother had longed for the same as me.

≈

1918

Olive,
Oh, darling, if only you could delve into my dreams here, because I am sure in some realm they are real. We are dancing with joy and the world is at peace, you, my love, are in my arms, a smile dancing on your perfect lips. We are so happy. At least in my sleep I am sharing moments with you.
Jack

≈

Dear Jack,
She has arrived, our beautiful little daughter; I have named her Rosa. She is perfect. I cannot wait for you to meet her. Do not worry about us, we are doing quite all right here. They've introduced rationing this week on most food essentials not just sugar; food has been so short and not everyone was getting their fair share; the German U-boats have been attacking the ships bringing the food supplies. I queued for so long outside Tom's groceries on Monday and there wasn't a scrap of butter or milk left by the time I got to the front of queue.
They have started printing posters too, telling us to save food. I suppose it is fair, now we will all have the same amount of flour, margarine, butter, milk, sugar and meat. Kitty's mum has started growing her own fruit and vegetables, I might try too, every little helps they say, darling.
Yours always,

Olive

Max

He hadn't intended to develop feelings for her.

Max felt a huge amount of guilt as he battled the emotions that seemed to be taking over him. He hadn't realised at first. He thought he was just concerned about her well-being; he was being the dutiful brother-in-law ensuring she was looked after. But. But, then he had started to think of her when he did simple everyday things: he'd order a coffee and note what Evelyn would have if she was there. He saw things on the street and was instantly reminded of her. He thought of things he must tell her. He started to notice her little quirks: how her nose would twitch when she was nervous, or how she wound her hair around her finger when she wanted to go home.

Of course, it was impossible. It was wrong. He felt disloyal to Jon. She was Jon's wife. He should not have these feelings. It was inappropriate. The more he fought the feelings though, the stronger they seemed to get. He had begun to imagine undressing her, slipping her dress from her shoulders and kissing her neck. He knew it was madness, but he couldn't stop it. He just wanted to look after her.

Amy

I caught the train back to London shortly after New Year. I hate New Year's celebrations in the city: it is just a reminder I am not surrounded by lots of people. I had enjoyed the tradition of my family home, watching Jools Holland and falling asleep shortly after midnight on the sofa.

As I travelled back to the city I flicked through my Tinder, mindlessly swiping right or left. I did not care that much: I was just looking for a casual outlet after the suffocation of being with my family for over a week in one house.

It amazes me what men think women want on some of these sites. The topless pictures; the more explicit pictures; gym selfies; the obligatory travel snap – usually at the top of a mountain. These dating platforms required you to market yourself, though. It's a necessary evil of the modern-day dating scene.

As I pull into Paddington train station my phone pings – I have a match. He is handsome enough. I fire away a quick message and see if he wants to meet tonight.

50

Evelyn

As I sit on the roof terrace watching the sun setting over the island, I cannot help but think about the significance of the day, the plans we already had in place, where we would both be right now – had the universe played out differently for us.

We had booked a week in Santorini. Jon had always wanted to visit Oia, with its beautiful whitewashed dome buildings. I couldn't wait to enjoy the Greek paradise with him. I have been here once before, for work. It was the summer of 2018 and I'd been working for a bride who had booked a wedding venue overlooking Oia. She had spared no expenses on her wedding, a week-long affair, with rehearsals, pre-wedding photo shoots, multiple meetings and disasters with local suppliers who could not understand English.

I had loved the island, but I couldn't wait to get back and enjoy it properly, without the stress of a wedding to organise. It was the kind of place that was even more spectacular than it looked in the photos. I had it all planned out, fresh fish, wine tasting, excursions, I couldn't wait.

We had booked for January, winter: we already had the rest of 2020 all planned out, and it was the only time we could fit it in. Plus, I thought we'd avoid the crowds. We weren't particularly fussed on it being hot. Both our schedules for the rest of the year were incredibly hectic and it was tiring just thinking about it. It is still a shock I am on here on my own.

I have the last of Jon's ashes with me. His final resting place will be somewhere he always wanted to go – here. I order two drinks: one for me, one for Jon. I'm not sure why, it is silly I know, but I somehow feel like he is here with me. We had discussed it so many times and I had described to him exactly how beautiful the view is. It is quiet, I am glad of this. Tourists tend to flock here from April onwards.

I sit in silence for a long time thinking about the week ahead, I will still go to all the excursions we had booked. He would want me to continue living. Jon would have told me to enjoy myself, plus I needed to get used to being on my own. It has been five-months now. It is still surreal. I am still struggling to come to terms with the loss of him. I don't think I ever will.

I have brought some of the last letters with me. It seems fitting that my great-grandmother's journey begins to finish at the same time as mine.

Jack,
The rationing has become harder: they have dropped our weekly
allowance. I tell you though Jack, I am becoming quite resourceful, I
make the food last far longer than I could ever have thought. Of
course, Rosa knows no different and she is such a bright, cheery little
thing I doubt she'd complain even if she did. How I aspire to have the

resilience of our child sometimes. We are so blessed to have her. She is
all that keeps me going some days without you.
Yours always,
Olive

Dear Jack,
I did not want to work in one of the factories. I've heard some
dreadfully scary things about the chemicals they use there. There is a
job in a café I can take, plus they'll allow me a meal each day, which
would be very welcome. I long to hear from you.
Your always,
Olive

Dear Jack,
The Spanish Lady is upon us, after all the anguish how is it now fair
that we may lose one another to illness. It has taken people so quickly,
and they are young, Jack, so very young – not children but men, men
and women in their prime. I will not burden you with the names as
you have had too much death thrust upon you for a lifetime already. I
pray for us, I pray this flu passes us by.
The children have a new song in the streets that they sing over and
over:
"I had a little bird,
Its name was Enza,
I opened the window,
And in-flu-enza."
It is frightful, I shudder as I hear their sweet little voices skipping over
rope, singing of death.
Yours always,

Olive

∾

Dear Jack,
I do not know as I pen this letter why I am writing. I know now I can
no longer reach you. They came this morning with the letter. The men
so smartly dressed, delivering the news of death. I collapsed of course.
Kitty tried to lift me, but it took the two men to carry me inside. I have
taken to bed now; a numbness has overcome me – I cannot fathom
that this is it – that war has taken my darling from me. I will not tell
anyone of your true fate. You were no coward. You were the bravest
man.
I am all out of love stories now. The war has surrendered us to misery,
the latent loves of our future incinerated by the bombs.
Yours always,
Olive

∾

Max

He supposed he thought it would eliminate Evelyn. If he could fill his bed with another woman he may banish the thoughts of her that consumed him. She was just the distraction that he needed now their trips were over.

He was still hurt Evelyn insisted on the last trip by herself. He'd been quite taken aback by Amy's messages – forthright and blunt in their delivery, she had made it very clear what type of relations she was looking for. Since Bruges he'd struggled to connect with anyone on Tinder and it was refreshing to find someone looking for a similar situation. He admired her boldness, and he liked how certain she was that apart from tonight it would lead nowhere. There would be no future meetings, no stolen kisses shared, no messages relayed: it was just sex.

She was attractive, slimmer than her profile suggested. Her limbs were lithe and toned, she was wearing a simple black dress that hugged in all the right places. She'd already ordered when he arrived and was drinking a Martini. There was a surety to her manner that he guessed may not have always been there. He wondered what had led her to this lifestyle? What men had gone before him? If she too had been scorned hence why she kept even the possibility of emotions coming into play at arms' length, setting out her guidelines before they'd even met.

He had been on Tinder on and off for three years now. It served its purpose, but he never really felt comfortable with the interactions online. It was so difficult to continue these conversations online, when he had little or no interest in anything other than casual meet-ups. He ordered a pint at the bar, before approaching her table. She stood to greet him, leant over the table and shook his hand. Formal, businesslike, assured.

The evening went as he expected. The usual pleasantries before they came to leave. She had insisted they head to his house, she preferred to keep her address private. He wondered how many men she needed to keep it private from. They'd taken a taxi back to his where they had spent the rest of the night in bed, before she insisted on leaving a little before one in the morning. There was no offer of another date, no talk of seeing him again. She had thanked him and left abruptly.

51

Amy

I didn't intentionally set out to ghost these men, but it was far easier than having to explain to them I wasn't interested. I always made it clear to begin with what I was after, I never led them on. But, inevitably there was always one or two who thought they could change my mind, who considered themselves such charmers that I would fall at their feet. I didn't. I always replied politely at first if they insisted on messaging after the date, but after the third message I simply blocked and deleted.

These men were not important to me. Why should I have to entertain their communication? It was just the nature of Tinder, Bumble and Hinge. I saw my dates as transactions – nothing less, nothing more. I was not invested in them, I did not remotely listen to their conversations, in my memory their voices were all just a monotonous dull hum. Before I began ghosting I used to politely tell them all the same nonsense: "I'm not ready for a relationship so soon after my ex-boyfriend". It was clearly a line, but I still received replies, questions. It was too much hard work.

I never told them what I did: they needn't know, and I only ever vaguely asked them about their professions. I was not particularly interested in anything other than the physical element of the date. Tonight's was tall, dark and brooding: he emitted no warmth. If I hadn't known better I would have guessed he'd been forced into coming on this date, but I had already made it clear what I was after, and he was more willing to provide it given the messages he'd sent. He'd also made it clear he was here for one reason only.

We had shared a few drinks before I had invited myself back to his. I did not need the date to last longer than necessary. We both knew what we were here for. His apartment was anonymous, the type of home where you cannot decipher anything about who inhabits it. It told me nothing about this man, Max, but then I was only really interested in one thing.

There was an urgency to him in the bedroom that I had not encountered before. His eye contact was intense, as if he was searching for something I could not offer. There was a hunger to him, a forceful urge. He was definitely only there for sex. It was the first time I had recognised my needs reflected in another. For the first time since I split with Jasper I was intrigued.

52

Evelyn

I attempted to return to work, but everything seemed so trivial: the bride's dress, the cake, the flowers. I used to think a wedding was an event for these women to express their creativity. A moment when they could be artistic. Now, I just see narcissism and pretence. I see brides who are trying to prove a point, who want to outdo other brides. Everything has lost its meaning: weddings don't appear to be an act of love any longer, but rather a statement of wealth.

It had been a job I loved for years; I suddenly felt no passion for it. I cannot stand the questions, the endless emails. The small enquiries about the colour of ribbon, as if anyone will actually care. I do not recognise myself in my job. I do not understand how I had managed to work in this industry for so many years.

Of course those that know me, who know what happened, are sensitive. They ask me how I am, tilt their head to the side and show me their sympathy smiles. It is unbearable. I feel like I am on a conveyor belt. Every wedding resembles the next.

Max is concerned. He rings incessantly. It is suffocating. I have still not really spoken to him since I arrived home from Santorini. I needed some space. I need to get used to being on my own, I cannot rely on Max to hold my hand all the time, I need to find my independence.

Amy

I always felt I was playing at being a grown-up. My brother seamlessly entered the world of careers and relationships. He married young, bought a beautiful detached house and increased his wealth and family in unison annually. I just felt like I had never really got there. I was behind in the race, trying to catch up, just hoping the others may trip so I could make up the distance: children and marriage seemed so far from my reach.

I knew it was down to my life choices. I had chosen to focus on my job; I had left Jasper; I had left my friends and moved to a city to be anonymous; I chose men that were emotionally unavailable; I made sure nothing could ever come of these men. If I was married to my job, if I was successful at my career, it made it easier to avoid everything that was missing.

The end of my thirties is rushing towards me, I know I should settle down, buy a house – but if I am honest, I do not want to. The predictable future I had always scheduled for next year, just has never seemed that appealing. As I entered the office the receptionist signalled that Zahera was waiting for me. We did not have a meeting this morning.

"Zahera, I wasn't expecting you. I didn't realise we had a meeting."

"We don't."

"Okay, how can I help?"

"You said you'd help me with my brother."

"I did."

"And, have you even looked into his case."

"I'm sorry, Zahera. I've just been so busy–"

She interrupts me before I can continue. "You promised you'd help."

"I will."

"When?" Her eyes are pleading.

I cannot help but feel guilty it has taken me this long. "This week, I promise."

Celine

It'd taken me a while to track Max down. I had avoided the funeral, my grief too immense to even consider a goodbye. I would also have to see his grieving widow, and I couldn't cope with the façade. The Jon I knew and the Jon his friends and family knew were worlds apart. I would not have been welcome there if they discovered who I was.

Guilt surged through me as I reached his door. Jon had told me bits about Max, namely immaterial facts such as his age and that he was divorced. We never shared a great deal about our "normal" lives in the group – it was safer that way. The man who answered the door was handsome – chiselled. He was familiar, but straighter than Jon, smarter. He smelt of musk and had an air of authority. Jon had always called it arrogant, but now I wasn't so sure, there was a sadness behind his eyes that did not portray any hint of cockiness.

I had no idea what I was thinking once I was in his living room. Straight lines, sleek, grey granite: it screamed masculinity. Now I was faced with Jon's brother, why I had come here seemed impossible. I could see Max was wary. He frowned like Jon. I had promised myself I wouldn't tell Max why I was really there. It was still too hard.

Max

She identified herself as Celine. Spanish or Italian he initially thought: her colouring suggested the Mediterranean. He invited her in; he opened the door and was again struck by how clinical his flat was. It hadn't always been like this. His marital home had been warm – one ready for a family. He'd possessed teapots, eggcups, letter racks, blankets, cushions – well, his ex-wife had. They'd all been left with her. His previous life had been discarded for this minimalist future.

Celine hesitated, before he told her to take a seat. He studied her. She was very beautiful, that was undeniable. He could see why Jon had been involved with her – she had "Jon" written all over her: exotic and dangerous.

"So, how did you know Jon?"

"Through friends."

Max had never heard of her, but then he didn't know all of Jon's friends. He didn't recollect her from the funeral though. He hadn't seen her before, he was sure of it.

"Why are you here? Sorry, Celine, but I'm not entirely certain what this is about?"

"It's about Jon. He wasn't meant to be on the tube."

"I'm not sure what you mean."

"He wasn't meant to be on that tube, it's not the tube he catches. He always gets the earlier one."

"I know, I know, but he must have been running late. We can't haunt ourselves with 'what ifs'."

Max was used to pacifying Evelyn when she was distressed, he was used to pacifying his parents, but he didn't know who this woman was. He didn't understand why he was having to discuss his brother's fatal tube journey with this woman; a stranger.

"That's not what I mean. He wasn't meant to be on *that* tube."

"I'm not sure what you mean, Celine."

"I just wanted to say sorry."

"Sorry?" Max paused. "Which friends?"

"What?"

"Which friends did you know Jon through? He has never mentioned you."

"Just friends."

Max can see she is cagey. Her guard rises very quickly. The conversation has confused him. He does not understand her apology. A standard apology over his brother's death he has come to expect, but this woman... There is something specific about her apology that irritates him.

She rises suddenly, obviously eager to leave. He stands and blocks her way. "Why have you come here, Celine?"

"I just wanted to say *sorry*."

"I don't think I understand your apology, though."

Celine barges past him then, tears threatening to spill. He shouts after her, but he doesn't have the energy to chase her. After the woman left he could not quash his feelings of unease. Why had she turned up on his doorstep now, months after the event? Her apology was genuine, but he felt there was more to it than he knew. He was aware that Jon had secrets: he had always known his brother kept things aside that he wasn't aware of.

He is meeting Amy, the girl from the dating app tonight. She is proving to be more than adequate at distracting Max. He hopes she can help him forget the visit from Celine. They still don't know a huge amount about each other – snippets. Their dates, if you can call them that, haven't developed past drinks and sex, but they often talk afterwards. He likes her. He enjoys the fact she is not Evelyn and she doesn't know anything about Jon. She is his escapism.

He still doesn't know what she does, and she doesn't know what he does. There is something freeing about only sharing certain amounts of information with her. His life can just be how he describes it: there are no grey areas – no grief. He knows elements of her past, knows she lived on the Welsh coast, knows she went to university there, imagines there was a boyfriend – maybe not such a pleasant one.

She never wants to discuss where they are going, what their future plans are, or if what is happening is anything more material than it is in the moment. It is both refreshing and unnerving. Max has not met many women like Amy. He imagines her job, he tries to place her in the real world, but she is so full of mystery it is impossible.

Evelyn

I cannot help but spend the week thinking of my great-grandparents and what fate had in store for them. I had not realised how fundamental letter writing was in wartime. I pore over the internet searching for historical correspondence from this time.

I had a few letters still to read, but Jack had died so I did not understand why Olive went on writing. I discovered it was common for wives and sweethearts to continue to write to their men, those killed in battle. These letters remained unposted. I suppose it was a way of continuing contact.

I did not understand the last letters I read. Jack's last correspondence said he had been in hospital. How did he end up back at the front line? I sit in the flat, and weep for my great-grandmother's loss, for the horrors my great-grandfather went through. He never even got to meet his daughter. I ring my mother when my sobbing has subsided. I have too many questions that remain unanswered.

"She lived a great life after Jack's death. It didn't define her, Evelyn. She had lost her greatest love, but she knew she had to go on. I wanted you to see that humans can suffer the greatest of sorrows and survive, sometimes even thrive. Jon's life may be over, but yours is not."

"I have so many questions though. What happened to Jack? One moment he was in hospital and the next he was dead."

"Your great-grandfather Jack went back to the front line after being cured of shell shock, only to have a relapse. He was tried for cowardice. They thought he purposefully did not fight. They did not take into account his previous mental health problems. He was found guilty and sentenced to death. Olive also received the letter of his execution, but she never showed any of the family. She kept it quiet until her death, when the letters were recovered. She did, however, continue to write to Jack for years but she never sent these letters."

"It's just so sad, Mum."

"Sometimes life is, my love. Sometimes life is."

53

Amy

I had finally started looking further into Mohammed's case, I could not avoid Zahera's sorrowful eyes and pleas any longer. I knew there was something not quite right about the case.

Apart from a vague childhood connection with a boy who'd converted to ISIS, Mohammed had no links to extremism. He was on his way to a new job; he had a date that night.

Zahera was distraught by the allegations against her brother and their family. Mohammed was the easy answer. He was the only known Muslim on the tube. The police had clearly drawn some inferences. I am not surprised, as we know too well in my workplace institutional racism is still rife in the police force.

There was the witness who said he appeared agitated before getting on the train, and he was seen carrying a large rucksack. This could easily be rebuffed though. Of course he was nervous: it was a new job; his large rucksack contained everything he needed on his new desk.

My opinion was just conspiracy though. I had to provide

evidence. I had to prove them wrong. It was laughable really. If the police looked into my search history this past week they'd likely assume a morbid fascination or link to extremism. I looked at the list of the victims on the tube that day again, and something just didn't add up. Twenty-two dead in total, I'd seen their faces before, of course I had. The newspapers had run emotional pieces on each and every one of them, bar Mohammed. I'd read the reactions of friends and family members. The victims' lives minimised into a three-hundred-word obituary documenting their achievements and their personality with a limited number of adjectives.

I created false scenarios in my head, pictured what the victims' families may look like, what their new family units involved now they'd lost their loved ones – imagined how damaged they all were. It is so hard to picture the lives of these people just from one photo. A photo will never sum up all the components of them.

Celine

It'd started as a support group. I had harboured so much anger surrounding my father's death I needed an outlet: a place I could go and vent my feelings of frustration without fear of being reprimanded. These people, well, they'd eventually become my friends. Sometimes when I was there it was the only time I felt like I belonged. These people had become an extension of my community – they understood.

I remember the first time Jon came to one of our meetings. I was always on guard when new people arrived, but I didn't have time to distrust him because I was so overwhelmed by his charisma. Jon had that easy charm, that warmth that made you feel like he'd saved it all up just until he met you. I was immediately enraptured.

Meeting after meeting I held back until he was seated then manoeuvred myself, so I was close to him. I thought up reasons I needed to contact him; I imagined scenarios of just the two of us, and then, well, then I started to create them.

It has been so difficult since his death. The secrets I held compounded all the sadness I felt. I think back to the final few times I saw him, the distance that had spread between us. I will never know what he was going to tell me that day, if anything. Maybe it was just lunch, maybe there was nothing more to it than that.

I do not feel that I have a right to grieve. It seems unreasonable of me to experience such sadness; which others would believe should only be reserved for his wife. The lover is shunned in these scenarios; their pain forgotten – unwelcome.

Max

After his night with Amy he still couldn't stop thinking of Celine. It had taken a while to find her on Jon's social media accounts. Her account wasn't under her given name. He had to carefully scroll through all of Jon's friends looking for an image of her. He eventually found her. She was as photogenic as she was beautiful in real life. Her dark hair splayed over her shoulders, her deep brown eyes striking in their intensity. She did not have many public photos, but the ones she shared gave Max all the information he needed.

He arrived outside the restaurant early, he recognised it, it was where he and Jon had had their last meal together. There was a bench directly across the road he sat at which meant he could observe her from a distance. He wanted to understand what her role was. He couldn't age her: she might just be a casual waitress here for all he knew. He didn't expect her to open the restaurant, nor did he expect all the staff to greet her as if she owned the place. She had appeared from the flat above the business. She seemed far too young to run her own business.

There seemed to be five of them in total. She busied herself setting tables whilst two of them helped. The other two retreated to the kitchen. She paused every now and again, a look of anguish across her face and rubbed her lower back. Lunch service didn't begin until midday, so he had another hour to burn. He'd come back at twelve, pretend it was a coincidence if she recognised him. It was plausible he had just happened across this rustic little Italian.

Evelyn

I have come to the park in London where Jon proposed. I have the very last of the letters with me. I need to finish reading them; I want to finish reading them. I lay a picnic blanket open where I and my husband once lay.

I stare up at the blue sky for a long time, listening to the birds chattering and children playing. I think about everything that has happened since Jon died, everywhere I've been. How different I now am because of this experience, how it will forever mould me. I roll over and pull the final letters from my bag.

Dear Jack,
How much more could we have served this country? We sacrificed our men, our loves to war and then for your sacrifice they punish you

because of illness. They were the cowards, Jack, they were the cowards, my love.
Yours always,
Olive

❧

November 11, 1918

Dear Jack,
They have declared peace, after all the sacrifice, everything we lost, just like that it is all over. But my world has still come to an end. This is not a world I wish to occupy any longer. I have lost all that I loved, first to war and then now again to flu. It took Kitty, very suddenly. Within the day she had passed. I am alone in this world, my love and my closest friend dead before me, and I do not know what to do, Jack. I'm beyond lost without you. Rosa is the only thing that keeps me going.
Yours always,
Olive

❧

Dear Jack,
My days no longer seem to serve any rightful purpose. Rosa of course keeps me going. She is a spritely little thing, one year old and she seems to be clearer about her direction in the world than me. It is useful she is with me; I must rise, I must dress her and prepare food daily – I fear if it was not for her I would have been swallowed by the slumber of grief that suddenly overcomes me, but for now, whilst I care for Rosa, I cannot allow myself to comprehend your leaving for too long.
Yours always,

Olive

~

Dear Jack,
It has been a year now since the end of the war and I am going to put
my pen down now, sweetheart. It has bought me so much comfort to
write to you, but I fear it is no longer what you would want me to be
doing. You did not fight and suffer so I could sit here in the depths of
misery. You fought so I could enjoy the simple pleasures of life, so our
children could fall in love, walk in the park, swim in the sea. You
fought so we could go on – so we could live. I'm going to live, Jack, I
promise you I'm going to live.
Yours forever,
Olive

54

Celine

I would recognise those features anywhere. My legs momentarily lost their rigidity – the similarities were undeniable, and for a moment I had been looking at Jon again. What was he doing here though? Why would his brother, Max, come to my restaurant of all places? I knew contacting him had been a mistake, but then I was awash with confusion. I went to his table. "What are you doing here?"

I watch him mull over whether to lie and pretend it was a coincidence. "Who are you?"

I did not know what to say to him. I still couldn't tell him the truth. "I'm just a friend, a friend of Jon's, or I was."

"It is just strange I have never heard of you, Celine."

"Sorry, I didn't mean to bother you. I shouldn't have turned up like that. I just wanted to say sorry about your brother." I can feel the tears threatening. My voice wobbles.

Max pushes out a chair and instructs me to sit. There is an authority about him that makes me listen. "Was there something more between you, Celine? I knew my brother, but I didn't know everything. Can you tell me whether you were in a relationship with Jon?"

I hesitate. When I try to speak I cannot find the words.

"I knew it when I first saw you. I knew it. How long?" Max takes my silence as an admission of guilt.

I do not have the energy to deny it. "On and off for a year or so. He never said about me?" I knew it was indulgent to ask and of course he wouldn't have.

"No, no he didn't. He was too busy pretending he was married to Evelyn, I assume." There is a bitterness in his tone.

"Sorry, I know it was wrong. We just couldn't help ourselves."

"Oh, that sounds like Jon. He never could."

It is a mistake, the more I tell him the more questions he has.

Amy

I'd been scrolling through the victims' social media accounts for hours now, I'd drunk half a bottle of red wine and eaten a bag of popcorn – I really needed to look at my diet. It was Friday night. I knew I should be out in the city – busy, socialising or visiting an exhibition, but I'd become consumed by this case: I thought about it every waking hour. Zahera's eyes and her resolute stare stuck out in my memory, her absolute conviction her brother was innocent. Everything I'd uncovered about him substantiated her beliefs.

The usual memorial posts and shared photographs of happier times were the most recent on their social media accounts, but I wasn't interested in that. I wanted to look further back, long before the attack. I wanted to see if there had been another person of interest on the tube that morning that the police had missed.

Lucy Vassay's Instagram was open. I stared at the screen,

moving the photos up and down. A snapshot of her daily life lay before me. Lucy was thirty-eight-years-old, single by the look of things. An accountant, she'd been on her way to work. Her Instagram portrayed city breaks, champagne up the Shard, multiple new pairs of shoes, girlfriends and lunches. There were a few images of a dog from around Christmas time, probably belonging to her parents as it looked like she'd returned there for the festive season. Her last post was a picture of a beach with a countdown of eleven days in the centre. Three days later she'd been killed.

I find it strange how lives are presented online and how I can decipher so much about her in death, yet nothing at all. These were just the snapshots she wanted to depict – I wonder about the sum of her rather than the image. There are no comments to suggest this woman was anything but just on her way to work.

I spend the entire evening looking at the victims. I even ended up looking at their friends. Most of the victims have private accounts or it is only very limited what I can view. Tiring, I decided to look into one more of the victims before turning in.

Jon Mullens' profile was open. He was familiar, I didn't know why. Maybe he just had one of those faces people recognised. He was devilishly handsome, a twinkle in his eye that shone through the camera. I'd succumbed to men like him before. I bet all he'd had to do was smile and mutter his name and women would have been weak.

His life appeared as I imagined it would: idyllic. Images and images of expensive European breaks; the beautiful wife; the designer apartment; the successful job. Their wedding had been a few years previous and looked like it was an image taken from the pages of *OK!* magazine: a chateau loomed in the background. I tried to look at his wife, but her account was private, bar her profile picture: Jon and her with wide open smiles. She looked nice.

There was nothing much to report on Jon. He looked like anyone else in their mid-thirties of wealth living in London. It was difficult not to be jealous, but then I remembered his fate. He had around 400 followers, but he appeared to have only followed a select few, idly I clicked on the list of these accounts.

I took a deep intake of breath. The list of people he followed was littered with far-right support groups; clearly a Britain First supporter. Tommy Robinson's activists were also listed. It amazed me how many people held these views – these groups would have had a field day publicly when "one of theirs" was killed by a young Muslim, but there was nothing on any of these groups about Jon.

Maybe he was just a voyeur? Interested in their views from the side lines. Maybe they were entirely unaware he supported them. Exhausted from my searches I retired to bed, where my dreams were fretful, and I woke every few hours with a metallic taste in my mouth that reminded me of fear, yet I had no idea what I was afraid of.

Max

He is angry. How dare his brother do this to Evelyn. Of course, he would never tell her. He could not bear to inflict that pain on her. The woman across the table from him is clearly upset, but he feels nothing towards her. He has no sympathy. He will not comfort her: she was not Jon's wife. He can understand the temptation. She is strikingly beautiful. But a whole year! She wasn't even a momentary fling. Jon had conducted the affair for way longer than he could have imagined.

Max has lost his appetite, but a waitress places the meatballs he had ordered in front of him. He thought he'd devour them, but now he just wants to leave. He pushes them around his plate. He has so many questions. He knows many of them will go unanswered. "How did you meet again?"

"Friends, through friends."

"Which friends?"

"Just some of the men he works with." She will not meet his gaze. She is lying. Max can tell. He knows all of Jon's friends – or he thought he did.

"So, why now? Why did you really contact me?"

"I don't know really. I think I just wanted to be connected to Jon again, in some form. I still can't believe he has gone."

"With all due respect, his wife can't either and she is my priority."

Celine winces. "There is something else. I don't really know how to say it. It wasn't meant to happen."

"What? What wasn't meant to happen?" He cannot believe it. Of all the things Jon could have done, it is the worst. It would absolutely break Evelyn's heart. He sits speechless for a while. He orders a large beer and then another. He does not know what to say – what to do.

Evelyn

It is strange the loss I feel now I do not have the letters to read. I suppose I was on a journey of grief with my great-grandmother, albeit in a different lifetime. I have decided I need a change. I cannot go back to weddings, I know that now with such clarity. It will be easy enough to hand them over to someone else in the industry. Maybe I will work with children, if I can't have them, maybe that is the next best thing. I was a teaching assistant a long time ago, maybe I will be one again.

I have packaged the letters away in a velvet-lined box. My mother thinks it's fitting I kept them. I am glad that occasionally

I'll be able to delve back into their lives, their love story. It seems important I remember them and their story, almost as important as remembering Jon's. Maybe I'll put my story into a letter one day for my future relatives. Maybe I'll pen something down so in the future all our stories aren't forgotten.

55

Celine

I found out two weeks after the attacks. I had thought it impossible that the numbness I had felt since Jon died could intensify. This latest revelation made it a hundred times worse. I couldn't understand how it had happened. It hadn't been the plan. Our affair was meant to be uncomplicated; there weren't meant to be repercussions: especially repercussions I couldn't erase. I had no idea what to do with this new information.

I closed my father's restaurant for a week. I couldn't cope with the public. As far as my colleagues knew I had no links to anyone on the tube attacks. I did not have the energy to justify my sadness. I flew out to Italy the next day, renting a house in the Tuscan countryside. I needed a retreat.

It was autumn: my favourite time of year. The light across the countryside was serene. I did not do much over the course of the week, I just let it all sink in. I was enveloped by shock. I occasionally sobbed when reality struck, but mainly I slept. I spoke to the chef daily; I lied about my activities, making out I was doing the opposite of my stagnant reality. I had no idea what to do. He was eager to get back to work.

I couldn't tell the staff. How would I even begin to explain everything? Nobody had known I was seeing Jon. I remembered back to the night Jon had been so upset when Evelyn had miscarried again. I had not thought about the fact we hadn't used protection until my period was late. It took me a while to recall if it could even be possible, we were always so careful.

The sickness had appeared shortly afterwards, coupled with the exhaustion. I spent a lot of time imagining what Jon's reaction would have been. I wonder if he would have been angry, or pleasantly surprised – a sign we should really be together. I have never wanted children.

I concealed it for months, but it was growing more difficult. I wore loose tops. The staff had questioned my energy levels and refusal to drink wine with them at the end of the shift, but other than that my life was quiet, so it wasn't difficult in the early days. But, now my stomach had swelled and there was no denying my pregnancy.

Amy

I have no plans this weekend and the niggling doubt I have missed something when I look at Mohammed's case won't go away. So I've resigned myself to my laptop for another evening. A Saturday evening searching the accounts of the victims for clues lay ahead. There was something niggling at me. I just couldn't place it, but ever since discovering Jon Mullens' affiliation with far-right groups, I couldn't help but consider that there may be more to the attack.

The faces of the victims are pinned on my wall. I am concerned I am getting too invested in the case, but then I remember Zahera and her pleading eyes. The insistence that her brother is innocent. I place a cross next to the faces of the victims I have investigated and found nothing other than a tragic ending.

Thus far Jon Mullens is the only man I've found who has anything untoward in his history. I am certain that his views aren't even a rarity anymore, so may not be of any weight. I feel useless.

Am I just chasing dead ends, also in denial with Zahera about the truth? There is just something about this case that has consumed me. I decide to read the news instead, a distraction from my thoughts. The news is littered with Brexit, Boris Johnson, and the story of Liliana Segre, which immediately catches my focus.

Ms Segre an eighty-nine-year-old Holocaust survivor has been placed under police protection after receiving death threats from far-right extremists in Italy. Liliana in her early life, aged thirteen, experienced the worst kind of human horror. How is it even conceivable she'd face such hatred towards the end of her life? The reason for the personal attacks? She was advocating against hate, racism and anti-Semitism.

The argument that criminalising such poisonous rhetoric stops freedom of speech and amounts to censorship is laughable. These people need to be censored and they need no freedom to incite hatred. Their opinions may be their opinions, but that does not entitle them to a platform to voice them. Did we learn nothing from Nazi Germany?

These assertions of rights are a threat to far more fundamental human rights, that must be protected at all costs. We must not repeat history – we are treading the path already beaten at the beginning of the twentieth century and we need an immediate diversion.

Celine

I am spent by Friday evening, I cannot bear the idea of trudging across the city on the tube for the meeting. My ankles are swollen, my lower back aches and I have an insatiable appetite. All I really fancy is a bath, my duvet and a box set, but I have been avoiding the group for months now and I did not want them to think I'd deserted our cause.

It was just difficult since Jon: everything was a reminder of him, of what I'd lost. I had opted for an incredibly oversized jumper and padded jacket, luckily it was February, so no one would notice my bump. I could conceal the pregnancy with layers.

The group has diminished since last summer. The attack separated those who were serious, and the members who merely talked the talk but were not willing to act upon it. As I approach the tube I sense I am being followed, I do not know why, I turn around, but there is no one there. I am being paranoid. The wind is bitter tonight; the darkness only adds to my insecurity.

I arrive at the small pub late. There are only eight of us this evening. They greet me warmly. I apologise for my absence over the past few months: I receive understanding nods. I had thought I concealed my relationship with Jon well, but now I'm not so sure. I order a glass of wine. I know I shouldn't, but one wouldn't harm the baby and I do not want to arouse suspicion.

I wait at the bar as a blonde woman is served a vodka and lemonade. She ducks her head and passes me. She takes a seat near our table. She unsettles me. I do not know why. Her back is to the group. I shake myself. I'm just being paranoid. Maybe I am overtired, my hormones playing tricks on me.

Amy

I return to my computer the next night. I open my Instagram and see it is still on Jon Mullens' profile, those he follows the last page I looked at. I scroll down again, shocked by these far-right groups that exist in the world.

The far-right is the fastest growing form of online extremism. It is no wonder when you start to look into the excessive amount of online material. The counter-extremism strategy the government currently employs needs an urgent overhaul. This propaganda on either side infiltrates the mainstream too quickly and effectively. Gaps in legislation allow the sowing of these divisions.

The number of prisoners convicted for far-right terror offences is growing at an alarming rate in Britain. Far-right activist groups pedalling their own rhetoric encourage community tensions. They swoop into cities and communities sharing false information about minorities, particularly Muslims. The truth is being distorted so quickly. Civil unrest is a very real threat.

I scroll through those Jon follows again. One name jumps out at me. GeorgeCUnionGB. I do not know why it is familiar. I click on his profile – it is open. It is an array of Union Jacks, photos of Trump and obscene racism. I do not know how I recognise his name. I look through more of his profile, I search his images. I only find one of him, he stares back at me, his face filled with rage.

It is hours later, as I soak in the bath, when it comes to me. George Davies-Clarke. It was the name of one of the victims that day. I jump out of the water, soap suds still all over my body and dash to my computer. It takes forever to fire up. I search the news articles for photos of the victims, all the while loading my

Instagram on my phone, so I can compare them to this man's profile.

The photo of George Davies-Clarke included in the obituaries is the opposite of that on his profile. In this photo, he is smiling – his grin wide and open. He is standing on a beach, the sun glistening on his bald head. His tribute includes a mention of his parents and sister – no partner, no children. He was forty-three years old, originally from the north-east but had resided in London for the past seven years.

My stomach flips as I realise how monumental this discovery is: Jon Mullens and George Davies-Clarke were known to each. They followed the far-right. They were both on the tube that day. They may have been the terrorists that day, not Mohammed.

It is not necessarily a shock. I am aware these groups exist. I am aware of their prevalence, but I cannot fathom why the security services haven't discovered this before me, how they have only focused on Mohammed, and may have missed the most likely perpetrators. It is well known that groups which promote hate crime against Muslims and immigrants are on the rise, so how have they not looked further into these men's lives? How have they not searched their internet history? Why have they not been flagged?

I think back to the case of Alex Fields Junior in Charlottesville, Virginia, in 2017 and how a white man was treated very differently to a "terrorist" of another colour. I do not know why I am surprised. This innate vilification of non-whites as terrorists as opposed to white people is inherent in our justice systems, both sides of the Atlantic.

In August 2017, the "Unite the Right" rally took place in the small American town. Dozens of those opposed to this movement had come to protest. They rallied against these abhorrent humans and peacefully chanted, "Our Streets!"

Behind them a grey Dodge Challenger accelerated. The protestors soon realised the car was not stopping and screamed out warnings.

Fields drove his car into the crowd. People flew in the air, others dived for safety. He came to a halt when his car slammed into a vehicle in front. He then went on to put the car in reverse and tried to escape onto the main road.

Fields killed a thirty-two-year-old woman in the attack: Heather Heyer. He also injured nineteen others. He was charged with murder and hate crimes, but interestingly he was not charged as a terrorist, even though the then Attorney General initially referred to the attacks as meeting the "definition of domestic terrorism". In fact, there have been a large number of cases in America since 9/11 where the Justice Department has not brought terrorism charges against far-right extremists, regardless of the fact their crimes meet the legal requirement to be considered "domestic terrorism".

Domestic terrorism are acts motivated by ideology that are harmful to human life and intimidate civilians, change government conduct or influence policy. It is clear that if Fields had been a Muslim aligned with ISIS the Justice Department would have handled his case very differently. By not treating domestic and international terrorism the same, the government sends out a clear message to different groups about the consequences of their actions. There are clear double standards when it comes to classifying what the US deems as terrorism – it should be a crime charged against all who commit such acts, whatever the colour of their skin, agenda or ideological motivation.

I had paid attention to how Fields was treated by the courts. Months later the case of Sayfullo Saipov, an immigrant, came to my attention. He too had driven a vehicle into a crowd, this time a bike lane in Lower Manhattan. He killed eight people. He had alliances with the Islamic State.

Saipov's crime was very similar to Fields, yet because Fields was motivated by domestic extreme ideology, as opposed to foreign extreme ideology, he was treated and tried not as a terrorist, but rather an angry white man.

I start looking into the other victims' accounts, to see who they too followed online. I have been feeling tense since my discovery, and I want to run it past someone. I do not normally tell Max anything of importance – it is not the nature of our relationship – but I need to discuss it with him. We'd eventually told each other our professions, and as a police officer he seems as good a person as any. I hadn't shared the details, of my work, just that it was in the field of human rights. I changed the subject when he asked what area I specialised in. I never give too much away.

We've met in a bar this Thursday and I cannot seem to quench my thirst for vodka and lemonade tonight. "Max, if you found out something that meant someone innocent wouldn't be framed for a crime they didn't commit, would you come forward?"

"Of course, I would, Amy. It is the right thing to do."

"Even if it meant potentially putting yourself in danger."

"Yes, I would. Why? What has happened?"

"It's just this case I'm working on. I've made a discovery, I think I'm right, but I may be wrong. It just doesn't add up in comparison to what has been reported."

"What case?"

"I can't say. It's not that I don't want to, but I'd rather keep it to myself until I've let the police know."

"That's fine. I am the police though."

"Not the type of policeman I need though."

An awkward silence filled the air, I just wanted to change the subject now. I'm not sure why I'd even raised it with him, but I don't really have any friends in the city outside of work.

Max

He'd been to see Evelyn prior to coming to the bar tonight. She has been avoiding him, but she can only do that for so long. The same old feeling ignited in him when she came to the door of her flat. He had hoped it was fleeting, but it clearly ran deep.

They need to sort out Jon's things this weekend. He knows Evelyn has been putting it off – he had been too. He is hoping Amy will take his mind off what lies ahead over the coming days, but when she arrived she seems agitated, like she had problems of her own, she alluded to a case, but Max did not push further.

Evelyn

Max arrived at my door as the evening was drawing in. I have been avoiding him of late. I just needed some time on my own to process everything that has happened since last August. He is a constant reminder of the husband that is missing and sometimes I find it too difficult.

He had come with a purpose, as Max always does. "Evelyn, we cannot put it off any longer. It is unhealthy."

"I don't see why there is such a rush, Max. It's my flat, so surely I can decide what remains here."

"Evelyn, you don't need his things to hold on to the memories. Jon's clothes weren't what made him who he was. He would want you to let them go."

"I'm not ready though."

"I don't think any of us will ever be ready to say goodbye."

I had agreed in the end. I did not have any fight left in me. I knew that there was no point fighting Max on the subject, because he would win. We agreed he'd come tomorrow.

I spend the night watching sad films and crying, my grief too cumbersome to bear.

56

Amy

I seek out everything I can find on George Davies-Clarke. He worked in security, an army veteran, he had served in Afghanistan and Iraq. He had been suspended from the forces in 2015 and deemed unfit to serve after suffering anxiety, depression and PTSD.

It is a sad tale of a man who had fought for his country and was then discarded without any support.

After he was named a victim there had been articles on him, and a select few interviews with his parents and sister. His sister, Denise, had spoken out about his struggles with mental health in the years since he left the army. I'd googled her name and discovered she did not live far. There was no harm in seeing if she'll allow one more interview.

George Davies-Clarke's sister lives in a tower block in a state of dilapidation. It is an area that I don't often frequent. I took the staircase, and I was out of breath by the time I reached her door.

The woman who appeared at the door looks like she had

lived too quickly. Her face was strained and exhausted. I could hear squabbling children in the background.

She was flustered when I told her why I was there. She was not averse to meeting but I had obviously caught her at a bad time. We arranged to meet the following day in a café near Streatham.

I arrive earlier than we agreed. I like to be prepared. She is late, when she finally flies through the door it is as if she is being chased. The woman seems to be permanently in a state of stress.

"What do you want to know about George?" She is exasperated and has no patience.

"I was hoping to find out more about his time in the forces. What happened when he left?"

"I see. Why?"

"I'm doing a profile on the fallen victims for the *Metro*." It is a lie, but I know she won't tell me anything if I really explain why I'm there. "We obviously want to honour his memory, what he did for the country. We'll of course paint him in a favourable light."

"He fought for this country for nothing. They deserted him. He spent months in Iraq, outside of Baghdad fighting al-Qaida. He lost his friends. He saw men die in the most atrocious circumstances. His equipment failed him; he was worn down by the war. It was terrifying: he never knew if he was coming home or what he was fighting for. It changed him. He wasn't the same George that had left to go to the army aged-eighteen."

"What do you mean, not the same?"

"He was angry, so angry. He was filled with this interminable rage. We couldn't get through to him, he didn't talk about any of his experiences. We just knew they'd been bad. In the early days, he would relay what happened over there."

"But, then he stopped?"

"He withdrew. He just became quieter and quieter unless he was on one of his rants."

"Rants?"

"Sorry, I shouldn't be talking about this. It's not appropriate. You can't print this. I just wanted to explain he wasn't bad. He just didn't get the help he needed."

"If it helps, this can be off the record. That is if you want to talk about it. It sounds like he had a tough time."

"We tried to help: that's me and my parents, but his PTSD was impenetrable. He met these people and... I don't know... things were strange."

"What people?"

"This group, a sort of Britain First group. They filled his head with far-right ideology. They became his focus."

"What was the name of the group?"

"I don't know if it was that organised. That's why he was on the tube that morning, meeting with them we assume, although it was normally a Friday night they met up, but there is no other reason he'd be on that tube line. The strange thing is the people he most hated killed him in the end. I always rebutted him, told him these beliefs were misplaced. He saw all Muslims as terrorists, and now, well now it is how he died – at the hands of a terrorist."

"It is a tragedy what happened that day. Could I ask, did you know any of the people in this group?"

"No, not really. I don't see how this is relevant to the article."

"Sorry. No, it's not relevant to the article, I suppose I'm just curious from a journalistic point of view. Not for this article of course, and George would never be mentioned in relation to them."

"He only really spoke of the woman. I think he had a crush on her. Celine something, I don't know her surname, just that she owned an Italian restaurant in Soho."

In the rest of the conversation I gathered more information on his childhood, relationships, work history. I had to appear interested, when in actual fact all I was thinking about was how I could track this Italian restaurant woman down. I thanked Denise for her time, paid for our coffees and left.

I would send her an email a week later telling her my editor had pulled the piece but thanking her for her time. She'd never know my real motivation.

~

It did not take me long to track Celine down. There were only so many Italian restaurants in Soho. I'd eaten in every one after work this week. I was tired of pasta dishes by the time I located her restaurant.

It is Thursday night; a whole week since I'd met Denise. I have not slept well. I cannot stop going over the links between these people.

I hear someone call her name after I've been seated. She does not serve me, but I can observe her. She is strikingly beautiful. I can see why George would have had a crush on her, I would defy most men not to. She is wearing baggy clothes. A loose jumper masks her figure, but I imagine she is one of those women who need not work out.

The food is nice, I eat slowly; trying to gauge her. There is no suggestion this woman would hold such extreme views. I find it ironic, considering she is clearly of Italian heritage herself. I wonder what led her to hold such beliefs, what happened to her to stimulate such a hatred. I catch her leaning against the counter at one point – her head in her hands. She appears weary.

I do not speak to her that night. Of course, I do not plan on confronting her. She is not going to willingly concede information that may frame her or Jon and George. No, I will have to be cleverer than that. Denise had mentioned that George met with "his friends" on Friday nights. I imagined wherever George used to go on a Friday night, Celine might too.

Evelyn

I opened the door to Max, boxes piled up by the side of him.

"It's time, Evelyn."

I didn't want it to be time. It felt so final though, like erasing all of the concrete evidence Jon was ever in this house. How could it ever be time?

There was nothing I could say to derail Max's plan to sort through Jon's things, though.

Max was methodical, working from room to room. He placed items that were so strongly linked with Jon's personality into one box – his favourite jumper, his pyjamas, his wedding suit, his favourite T-shirt – I assumed for me to keep. I hoped.

He placed the standard shirts, T-shirts, trousers and suits I wouldn't miss too much in bags for the charity shop.

I couldn't bring myself to watch. I couldn't be a part of it. I'd locked one of the wardrobes off. I did not want Max to access it. It was not up for discussion. I was keeping everything in there.

He came to find me after some hours of moving boxes and boxes out of our flat. My mind was in a state of oblivion.

"I need the key, Evelyn."

"No," I whispered.

"Evelyn, where is the key?"

I remained silent. The contents of the wardrobe were private. Max had no business with it.

"Evelyn, I will break the wardrobe door. You cannot live like this. Jon is gone. Keeping his things will not bring him back."

"No, Max. Just, no."

He left the room.

I didn't think he had it in him, I didn't think he'd be so harsh, so brutal with my belongings. I heard him enter the lounge and walk across the room, I could make him out in the corner by the wood burner. I heard metal hitting wood before I realised what he was doing. I ran from the kitchen, a scream hurtling out my mouth. I launched at him from the bedroom door, throwing him into the wardrobe, causing him to fall.

The axe was still in his hand and he'd landed awkwardly on the floor. Jon had always used it to chop wood in the winter. Max looked so taken aback.

I retreated. I scrunched myself into a ball against the wall, sobbing hard, scared of myself. I managed a whisper then, so quiet I wasn't sure he'd heard: "No, Max. My babies. It was our babies' things."

Max

He hadn't expected Evelyn to help, and he was relieved when she retreated to the kitchen to avoid the task. He was distracted as he ploughed through Jon's possessions. Celine was on his mind.

He was so angry with his brother, a wasted emotion given the circumstances, but he could not help it. He did not know what to do about the pregnancy: the child was part of Jon. How could he turn his back on it? But to have Jon's son or daughter in his life, he'd have to expose his brother's affair and that would break Evelyn's heart.

Jon was troubled. Max had always known his brother was hedonistic, he'd had a penchant for women, for alcohol, occasionally cocaine – he hoped that had eased over the years, but he was never really sure. Max wasn't naïve though, he'd known what his brother was like. He still loved him, still accepted him, but he did not understand him. How could he have ever risked hurting Evelyn?

The day passed in a flurry of activity. Max sorted through his brother's clothes. He tried his hardest to remain detached, occasionally he was floored by the memories of Jon – a T-shirt would transport him back to a day spent playing football and drinking ciders in the sun in the park.

He came across the leather jacket late in the afternoon. He hadn't realised Jon had kept it for all those years. He remembered the Christmas he had given it to him, Max had saved his pocket money for months. He knew his brother had wanted it for such a long time. He was overcome with a surge of anger at the loss of him.

He was sick of all of this, sick of his grief, sick of Evelyn obstructing them from moving on. He knew she was hiding more of Jon's things in a wardrobe she'd locked. He was suddenly overcome with pure frustration at the entire situation.

"I need the key, Evelyn."

She refused repeatedly. He could not take it anymore. He didn't think it through when he grabbed the axe Jon used to chop wood for their burner, but he had really had enough.

Evelyn launched at him as he hit the wooden doors. He hadn't expected that. She'd retreated immediately into the foetal position and began sobbing in the corner so he barely heard her whisper.

He felt awful, he knew about the miscarriages, but he'd never realised the extent of her grief for their lost babies. He crouched beside her and rocked her in his arms.

57

Celine

After the meeting, I spent most of the weekend in my flat. I was too tired to work in the restaurant. The chef was annoyed, and I had to feign a stomach bug, even though it was my own business. We were a team and I hated letting them down, but my body was craving rest. The baby has begun kicking. It is an unpleasant sensation and a reminder of this problem. Most the time I try to ignore the impending birth.

Max arrived at my door on the Sunday night, an unwelcome visitor. He wanted to discuss the child and what I planned to do. He mainly talked about his concerns for Evelyn should she find out. It quickly became apparent who he was there for and it wasn't me.

Max

He loads the last box of Jon's belongings into his car on the Sunday night. It has been an emotional weekend and he is relieved to see the back of it. He'd tried to convince Evelyn to join him for dinner, but she had retreated into herself as the day progressed. He cannot help but worry about her, he feels so helpless.

As soon as he gets in the driving seat he knows what he must do.

The woman who answers the door looks like a faded version of herself – the mane of black hair has lost its gloss, her olive skin looks tired, her deep, dark eyes still transfix him, but they no longer glisten. Celine is agitated, nervous. He recognises how strange this situation must be given they do not know each other.

"I just wanted to talk to you about your arrangements."

"My arrangements...?"

Max looks around the room full of art, trinkets and life. There are airline tickets framed and photos everywhere. It is cosy; he has a sudden flash of Jon being between the four walls, but it was almost too obscure to place him here. He wonders how much time his brother had spent there.

"Well, yes. I mean, do you expect us to have contact with the child? I'm sure we can arrange something financially. It's just – it is very precarious with Evelyn."

"I see."

"She has been through so much and to discover Jon was cheating would be bad enough, but a baby, that would be too much – too much for her."

Celine doesn't display any emotion. She seems very disconnected, even to the pregnancy. "Max, it won't be a problem. Evelyn won't find out."

"Okay, well that is that then. I just wanted to make it clear – she is my priority."

"That is very clear, Max."

"Okay, well I'll let myself out."

She nods at him and retreats to her kitchen. When he reaches the street below he breathes a sigh of relief. He just hopes he can trust Celine.

Amy

I hadn't been certain Celine would leave her flat on Friday night – I had hoped she would, but maybe these meetings George's sister knew of no longer happened.

I'd been waiting outside the restaurant since 5pm and Celine appears at eight o'clock. As she approaches the tube she turns around immediately; suspicious eyes. I quietly look into a nearby shopfront and feign disinterest in her. I make sure I take the carriage down from her on the tube, this way I can still see her rise to exit at her stop.

Luckily, the pub she is going to isn't far from the tube stop. I hang around after she enters, before I open the doors. I immediately walk to the bar and order a vodka. I try not to stare at her, but I cannot help it, until she clocks me watching her.

She waves at a table of five other people by the window. I take the empty table nearby but keep my back to them. I take my phone out and begin scrolling through social media, so I look distracted.

I know I've got the right group when they apologise to Celine about Jon. They must be connected. I think back to Jon's Instagram, and how I'd imagined his life so perfect when I first saw it online. But not only was he part of a white supremacy network but judging by the way the group address Celine, he was also in an extra-marital affair.

They speak in hushed tones; it is not the normal group dynamic you'd expect from a Friday night catch-up in the pub. I occasionally hear the odd racist word bandied about, but I cannot decipher their exact conversation. At around half past ten I leave. I manage to jot down the first names of the people in the group – it is a start.

Evelyn

It was a last-minute appointment. I preferred them: it limits the time the bride has to get worked up about her impending wedding. It's amazing what they can think of if they have months, even years, to deliberate.

It has been nearly eight months since Jon's death and going back to work was difficult. I'd felt a disconnect that I'd struggled to bridge. I hope it didn't translate over to the weddings, but I just didn't care enough. Everything felt pointless.

I'd arranged to meet her in a café, just off Notting Hill. The woman who approached me was unbelievably beautiful: a Mediterranean beauty with skin that almost looked illuminous in its perfection. I was entranced. I noticed she was pregnant and could not help but feel jealous.

The details of her wedding so far were vague. She seemed desperate for ideas – she quizzed me on my wedding day: the dress, the cake, the flowers and the venue. She even asked if could see photos at one point. It was peculiar for a bride to show more interest in my wedding than her own.

I opened my phone and carefully selected a few images from my and Jon's wedding day and offered them to her to see. Her eyes welled with tears.

"Are you okay, Celine?"

"Yes, yes. Sorry. It just looks so beautiful."

"Yes, it was." I stared at this woman across from me, confused by her intensity of feeling.

"He was so handsome."

"Pardon?"

"Your husband... he is handsome."

"I thought you said *was* handsome."

"Yes. Yes, yeah I mean he was handsome on your wedding day."

"I see. Sorry, Celine, but do I know you somehow?"

"No. No, how would you know me?"

"There is just something familiar, as if you're familiar with me?"

"No, just what I read online."

I let it go. Maybe she had just presumed I was married. There was just something niggling at me, something not quite right about the way she looked at me, about the tears in her eyes when she saw a picture of my wedding day. She may have seen me in the news after the attack; there were many articles on the loved ones left behind. I do not want a stranger's pity though.

Celine

I had heard so many women tell me: *it's different when they're your own; you can't imagine the love you're capable of; wait until you hold them in your arms; you'll never regret it.* I knew I wouldn't feel any of this. I know you're not meant to admit it, but I wanted my hands back, my time back, my life back. I wanted to go back to work: the restaurant. I wanted to drink wine and read a book, without worrying about this pink mound of screaming flesh that would soon be arriving. I did not want this dissatisfied being sucking the energy out of me.

I had spent the last four weeks thinking about it, weighing up the implications.

I knew Evelyn's job. I wanted to meet her. I don't know what I'd wanted to achieve, I'm not sure what my intentions were, but

I just knew I had to meet her again. She wasn't what I expected. She was stronger than I imagined; more together, considering what the last year had thrown at her.

I shouldn't have gone. I'd almost given myself away, and I didn't want to ruin this woman's life, there was no need to. I hadn't expected to get so emotional, maybe it was the hormones. When Evelyn had showed me the photo of her and Jon it had floored me. I realised I didn't really know him at all. There was a whole other world he existed in. I had just been a temporary fixture in his story, and now I was faced with his widow, and I hated myself for all of it.

Of course, I had known she'd wanted a child of her own. Jon had not opened up much about his marriage, but the night the child was conceived he had told me of their grief; the lost babies; the failed attempts at a family; Evelyn's sadness.

I arrange another meeting with her to confirm the details of my imaginary wedding. I had sent her an email after our last meeting, I told her I wanted to use her services.

She had replied promptly. Her response was polite, but you could tell she was not bothered either way about my wedding. I am meeting her in the same café later in the week.

58

Max

It was the right thing to do. The child would not have contact with him or his family. He hoped the child never discovered who Jon was, it was much easier that way. Otherwise everything would get far too complicated: messy.

It was not as if Jon couldn't afford it; Max had taken care of his brother's finances after his death – Evelyn didn't look into things like that so would not question the money Max had withdrawn to pay Celine off.

Celine was hesitant to begin, she did not understand his intentions, but Max had convinced her otherwise. It was a healthy amount and it meant she no longer needed to work all the hours in the restaurant: at least she could take care of the child.

He felt better for it, knowing the child would be provided for. Morally, he felt awful for the unborn baby being abandoned by the family on his father's side, but he had to protect Evelyn.

Amy

Every time I closed my eyes I was greeted with Zahera's pleading stare. I knew it was a case of gathering all my evidence before I took it to the police. It was a risk, but I wanted to ask Celine some questions.

I arrive at the restaurant just before lunch service. She answers the door suspiciously. "Hello."

"Hi, Celine. My name is Amy Lions. Sorry to bother you, but I was wondering if I could ask you a few questions."

"About what? Who are you?" I can tell Celine is immediately cagey. This is not what I wanted.

"It is just a few queries about an article I'm doing."

The last thing I want to do is tell her about my real job. If she thinks I'm investigating her I know she'll clam right up.

"Right... How do you know my name?" She steps back towards the counter. I can see her literally retreating.

"I understand you may have links to two of the tube victims. I'm just trying to build a bit more of a character profile for the tribute."

"The tribute...?" Celine says slowly, a question hanging in the air.

"Jon Mullens and George Davies-Clarke. They're deceased. I understand you knew them both. You all used to meet up together."

I see the dawning realisation on her face. She drains of colour. "I don't know what you're talking about."

"But I think you do, Celine. It is just a few friendly questions, nothing to worry about. I'm just trying to build a portfolio of all the victims on the tube that day – a better understanding of their lives, their views, their passions."

"Sorry, I can't talk to you at the moment. I'm really busy." Celine closes the door abruptly in my face before I get a chance to rearrange another meeting. Confirmation that my suspicions are correct.

Celine

The idea had been to increase fear, to amplify the capital's feelings towards Muslims. Of course, there would be one on the tube; they were everywhere: the perfect scapegoat for our cause. There were some in our organisation that wouldn't have approved, some who would see the act as too extreme. There were those in the group who I was sure would have reported us.

Jon, well he wasn't as angry. He ranted and vented his frustrations, but I didn't believe he'd ever go as far as we needed. We had to get the ball rolling. It was time for action. We'd just omitted to tell some of our members. George was dedicated, he was willing to do whatever it took. Occasionally I thought he was slightly unhinged, but weren't we all.

It was never meant to go this far. If I'd known all of this would happen I would have stopped it. I could not risk it coming out though, could not face a lifetime in prison – if it came to light everyone would know about the baby, the father. I could not have a child growing up into that, no matter how little I wanted it.

And, now, now I had this Amy Lions at my door asking me all kinds of questions and I know she is aware of my involvement and I don't know who to turn to. I wish I could ask Jon what to do.

Evelyn

She seems agitated as she pulls up a chair. I can properly see the extent of her pregnancy today. The bump isn't hidden by oversized jumpers.

"How far are gone are you?"

"Nearly nine months."

"Do you know what you're having?"

"No. I don't want to."

"Yes, I always thought a surprise would be nice." I momentarily lose my train of thought.

"Are you okay?" Celine is staring at me intensely.

"Yes, yes, fine. So, your wedding."

"Yes, I wanted to meet you in person to say."

"Okay."

"Well, to say, we've decided to postpone what with everything that is going on with the baby."

"Oh, you really didn't have to come in person – it's fine. I totally understand." I'm actually relieved: I cannot muster an ounce of enthusiasm for weddings.

Celine is still staring at me. "It was really nice to meet you though, Evelyn."

"Yes, you too."

I stand to leave.

"You could stay, now I've dragged you here, for a coffee?"

I'm really not in the mood for platitudes with strangers, but then she is heavily pregnant, and I don't want to seem rude. I accept her invitation.

"Two double shot espressos," she bellows across the small café. I think to tell her she shouldn't be drinking caffeine in her condition and then decide against it.

The rest of the interlude is strange. Celine asks me questions about my life, but I don't wish to discuss these details with a stranger. It is too raw. She tries to ask me about Jon and our wedding, at which point I realise I no longer want to be there. I feign a meeting and leave. As I stand she embraces me. "Sorry again, Evelyn, for everything."

"For everything?" I am perplexed by her apology.

"Oh, you know – dragging you here, not getting married, wasting your time, making you meet me twice."

"It's fine." I dismiss her apology. I just want to leave. "Take care, Celine. Good luck with everything."

"You too, Evelyn. You too."

I leave the café, but I can't help but turn around for one last glance. I can't be sure, but I swear she was crying.

59

Max

Work had been busy that week. He was glad he had solved the problem with Celine the weekend previous. Gang-related crime was through the roof and county lines drugs suppliers were increasingly preying on young and vulnerable people – it felt relentless and depressing. This week had been difficult, Max had held a sixteen-year-old boy in his arms after he'd been stabbed, the young boy had been in the wrong place at the wrong time in Hackney and an opposing gang member had stabbed him. Max tried to stem the bleeding but by the time the ambulance arrived it was too late. As he held him in his arms he realised these boys were only children, they'd entered this criminal world before their lives had even begun. He is hoping to see Evelyn again this weekend. He wants to take her out for dinner. He needs to see her.

He finishes tonight at eight and cannot wait to get home to scrub this feeling off. One of the officers suggests the pub, but Max is not in the mood. He still hadn't socialised much since his return to work.

It is as he rounds the corner to his flat that he sees Celine on the doorstep. He is reminded of the first time he saw her there and wished she'd never appeared. Never tarnished the memory of Jon and burdened him with their monumental secret. "I told you I'd transfer the money as soon as the baby arrives. You cannot just turn up here."

"It's not that."

"What is it then?" He senses her panic.

"I need to come in. I need to tell you something. I need your help."

What Celine relays to him is so difficult to contemplate, the information she is sharing with him he can't assimilate with his brother. That was not Jon. That cannot be Jon.

Celine

I watch Evelyn go, as soon as I lose sight of her, I sob into my sleeve. How could I have been so naïve, to think Jon was ever going to leave her for me? She clearly had no idea. I was just another of Jon's secrets.

I pull out my phone, I have been meaning to search her name since she arrived at my flat but have avoided the issue. I'm too terrified of what she'll uncover. She appears on the first page of my search:

AMY LIONS LLB, LLM HUMAN RIGHTS ADVOCATE

She is not a journalist at all. My breath quickens. It is lucky I am still seated as my legs shake beneath the table. What does she know?

It is an automatic reaction. Twenty minutes later I find myself turning the corner to Max's road. I do not know what I am going to do, but maybe he can help me. We have to stop this

Amy before it's too late, not just for my sake but for Jon's memory and the baby's future.

Evelyn

I am exhausted by the time I get home. I find meeting potential brides underwhelming now. I don't seem to care. To concern myself with a bride's place cards or colour choice seems beyond trivial. I know I should stop taking the appointments now I've decided I do not want to continue with this career.

I mindlessly turn on the news. Brexit is still on the agenda. There is talk of a virus in China, which I pay little attention to; these viruses never seem to reach the West. There is a segment on discrimination I allow myself to watch. An interview with a lady who was involved in the London Bridge Attacks in June 2016.

A photo of her had been circulated after the attack and made into a meme, suggesting she didn't care for the victims as she looked at her phone. What they'd failed to share was the multiple other photos of her in distress. I did not understand how people could be so cruel, why would they want to cause such a divide or wrongly attack a woman who has just experienced such an atrocious event. I never understood the need for "us" and "them" – even after Jon died. I recognised it was extremists. It was never one whole religion's fault. These men were obviously evil.

Jon and I had different views. As much as I loved him he was sometimes a bit intolerant. He'd understand once I'd explained, but his default position wasn't always as tolerant and empathetic as I hoped. I pull out our photo albums, I've nothing else to do today than submerge myself in the memories of us.

60

Max

It makes absolutely no sense. He cannot understand this person Celine was describing. Jon could be a little bit racist, a bit right-winged at times, but he'd never get himself mixed up with a group like the one Celine was talking about. It was ridiculous! What did he have to gain? His brother had been intelligent, he'd been to university for a start.

"He was angry, Max. Are you not even the slightest bit too?"

"If you're asking if I'm a bigoted racist who marginalises Muslims, Celine, then NO, no I'm not angry. How could he be so stupid?"

"We thought something needed to be done."

"What do you mean 'something needed to be done'?"

"He didn't know the details. Jon was passionate about the cause, but he wasn't a crusader like some of the other members. He was warier of action."

"What are you trying to say here, Celine?"

"He didn't know what was happening, I kept it from him. You need to know that of your brother."

Max was becoming increasingly agitated. Celine had been nothing but trouble since she arrived at his front door and now here she was again with her allegations and her cryptic clues.

"Shall we have a drink, Max? And, then I'll explain."

"In your condition."

"One won't cause harm, Max. Trust me. You're going to need it."

As Celine speaks his shock increases. None of her information aligns with his brother. It was not the man he knew. He wondered how many secrets his brother had he would never know about.

A fascist though? Max and Jon had been brought up by very liberal parents. His Mum and Dad voted Labour, encouraged equal rights and always advocated against racism. How could Jon hold such beliefs? He vaguely remembered a veiled comment he'd made about Muslims once, but he'd dismissed it as a joke.

He cannot contemplate how racist Jon was. It is as if Celine is telling him about another person, someone he never knew. He'd been disappointed Jon had been having an affair, but it wasn't incredibly shocking. He'd half expected something like that. But the far-right beliefs, the idea his brother affiliated with people like that had disarmed him. Celine had spewed the views and ideas out so easily that he had recoiled at her words. As a policeman it was his duty to protect society against hate crimes, against people like this, yet now he was faced with the reality that one of "those people" was his brother.

No one could find out, he knew that immediately. If his parents discovered the truth it would destroy them, let alone Evelyn. He could not bear to think of the devastation the truth would cause. Max would take the fall somehow. Whatever it took, he'd protect Jon's memory, his name, his unborn child too.

He cannot have him exposed as a terrorist. It is paramount Max protects his brother's legacy.

"But why now? Why tell me now, Celine? What good will come of me knowing?"

"Because I'm in trouble."

"What kind of trouble?"

"Someone knows, I'm sure she does and she's a lawyer and she's asking questions and I can't go to jail... and the baby... and I just can't. This isn't how it was meant to be."

He has no reason to protect her, but the thought of this information being made public was too much to bear. "How can I find this woman?"

"Why, what are you going to do?"

"Try my hardest to reason with her. Does she know you're pregnant?"

"No, I was wearing oversized clothes."

"Do you know where she lives?"

"I know where she works. I have her office address."

"Okay, let's go." He has no idea how he is going to reason with this woman.

Celine

I'd convinced Max to leave eventually: he was too much of a reminder of Jon. It was unnerving spending time with him and there was no point both of us waiting to follow Amy Lions home.

She appeared later in the afternoon laden with files. She was very pretty in a glamorous blonde kind of a way.

I walked behind her at a distance. How misguided she was. I imagined her in university studying equal rights. Did she not get that equality was the problem? We aren't all equal and that is why society is the way it is: because of people who encouraged the idea we were.

I watch her enter her house, before I ring Max with the address. He is naïve to think his plan is going to work; reasoning will never be enough.

61

Max

He can't believe it when Amy answered the door, of all people it was her. He's never been to her house: they'd always gone back to his. It was the case she had been talking to him about. The discovery she couldn't disclose just yet, especially because he was a police officer. How could it be Amy who had discovered that Jon was part of a right-wing group? How could she have managed to put all the dots together?

He can't believe he hadn't thought to ask her what she did, to listen more when she discussed work. But, that is not what they were about. They were casual, there was no emotional intimacy between them. He hadn't even mentioned he had a brother. He liked the fact they could keep the complicated, complex parts of their existence separate from each other.

It took him a moment to right himself. Maybe this could work in his favour, the fact Amy had relations with him, may mean he could convince her not to disclose the information, once he explained the situation, the pregnancy, Evelyn's grief, he was sure Amy would understand.

Amy

I know I need to report all my findings, I need to give my file to the National Counter Terrorism Security Office. They will contact the CPS and make the necessary arrests. It is not every day you uncover a terrorist network, so I wasn't entirely sure what the next steps were. I would drop the file down the station and then ring Zahera immediately. I couldn't wait to hear the relief in her voice that her brother's name would be cleared, that his memory would not be tarnished.

The fact that two of the men who were on the tube that day were part of an extreme right-wing network is too much of a coincidence. I am just bundling all my paperwork into a bag when there is a knock at the door. This is unusual in itself, I do not have the type of lifestyle where I would receive guests unannounced.

Max is on the threshold. I have no idea how he has found out where I live, but now is not the time. He wants to talk. We do not have this type of relationship. This is exactly what I wanted to avoid when I met him. I try to palm him off and make my excuses. But, he pushes past me and walks through to the kitchen.

"Sorry, Max. Now is not a good time."

"It can't be any other time, Amy."

"What is so important that it can't wait? I have to hand in this evidence."

"The evidence is what is so important it can't wait."

"What? I don't know what you mean. You don't even know what the evidence is."

"But, I do. I do know what the evidence is and that is why you cannot hand it in."

"You aren't making sense. How would you know what the evidence is about? No one does. And, more to the point what does it have to do with you, Max?"

"Mullens. My surname. My name is Max Mullens."

"Mullens..."

"Jon Mullens, as in Jon Mullens' brother."

My legs buckle. How could I have misjudged Max's character so much? How was the man standing before me related to someone who held such beliefs? I didn't know what to say. How could this have happened? How had Max never mentioned his brother died in a terrorist attack? Had he always known that this was my job? Was it a plan all along?

"As in Jon Mullens, the case I've been working on."

"Yes, but I didn't know this was the case you were working on. I didn't even know what area of human rights law you worked in, Amy, well until just now. I didn't know about Jon's beliefs, I've just found out myself. I had no idea of his involvement for God's sake. I'm a police officer, of course I didn't."

"I don't think being in the police makes you automatically exempt from being racist, Max. Anyway, regardless of your job apparently meaning you had no knowledge, explain how you suddenly know now, Max. Explain how you are suddenly at my door. Explain what you are doing here."

"You can't tell the police what you know."

"I can, and I am, Max. I'm not letting an innocent young man be framed for a crime he didn't commit. Your brother was part of the terrorist network here. How can you even begin to defend him?"

"You can't, because there is more at stake here than Jon's legacy."

Max

Celine is walking along the corridor towards the kitchen. Amy's back is to her. This was not part of the plan. Although at least once Amy saw Celine was pregnant, she may understand, may realise there was more to this than just his brother's memory. Celine had pulled her coat off, exposing her belly. I indicate to Amy, Celine's presence. Maybe now she'd understand.

"See, the baby, it would destroy my brother's wife if this came out. She didn't know about any of it, the group, the affair, the baby, the terrorism."

"It doesn't matter, Max."

He cannot reason with her, she is insistent she would not allow this other boy, Mohammed, to be blamed. He understands, but he is panic-stricken. He cannot bear the thought of what this information would do to Evelyn.

He frantically tries to convince Amy. He begs her. "Please, Amy. My family have been through enough. This information would destroy them."

"It is the right thing to do, Max. I'm not going to sit on this, no matter how painful that is for your sister-in-law and your family's reputation."

He is distracted. He doesn't see Celine lunge across the room, he does not see her until it is too late. Until he sees her plunge the knife into Amy's neck. It happened so quickly. A confusion of images accumulating in a reality he did not want to be part of.

Amy gasps for air. Blood spurts across the walls. Celine has hit an artery.

Max has seen these stabbings before. As a London police officer he dealt with knife crime. The vertebral arteries are deep in the neck, so rarely is a neck stabbing fatal, but when the knife penetrates far enough it will be. He had seen two other cases where the knife penetrated this far. Amy didn't have long. She collapsed forward and he caught her as she slumped.

He pulled her into his arms, and stroked her hair, sshing her gently whilst all the time he wanted to scream. He applied pressure to the open wound to stem the blood flow. "It's going to be okay." He knew it wasn't. He could feel himself shaking with shock.

He reached into his pocket and dialled, he explained he'd just arrived at his lover's home, the door was ajar and he'd found her stabbed on the kitchen floor.

"No, no signs of forced entry. Please hurry." He relayed the address and hung up. Nothing felt real.

"Go... go!" he shouted at Celine, while shoving the file of evidence Amy had collected into her hands.

She stood there paralysed.

"Celine, I said go now! You were never here."

Amy looked up at him helplessly, the colour draining from her face as she bled out.

"It's going to be okay, Amy. You're going to be fine, you're going to make it through this."

She was trying to speak, trying to decipher how he knew the woman that had just stabbed her. Why he had just let her leave the scene of the crime. He never wanted this to happen, to Amy especially. He had grown fond of her over the months.

He thought of Jon then. He thought about the brother he'd always fought to protect. He closed his eyes – there was Jon, aged eight, his Dad throwing him into the air in a swimming pool; Jon, aged nine, blond and laughing, chasing Max with a water pistol; Jon, aged eleven, starting secondary school, a smirk on his face as he left the house and gave Max a dead arm; Jon, aged thirteen, full of braces and teenage angst, screaming at his mum and dad; Jon, aged fifteen, the desire of every girl in school; Jon, aged seventeen, unwrapping the leather jacket Max had chosen for him on Christmas morning, a wink and a smile as a thank-you; Jon, in his twenties, sneaking into the spare rooms at parties, a girl always hanging off his arm; Jon becoming partner in his company, treating Max to a holiday of excess; Jon on his wedding day, Evelyn so happy, her eyes glistening with tears; Jon hugging him, his laughter reverberating in his memory as he pictured him throwing his head back. Jon. Jon. Jon.

He released the pressure slowly, he didn't want Amy to know what he was doing. He hoped it would be quick. He saw the light fade, he saw her last moment. He sat there holding her and sobbed. He was sobbing as the paramedics arrived. They peeled her off him. They knew it was too late.

Poor, poor Amy. He had not wanted her to be involved in any of this, none of it made sense. It was not the brother he knew. He knew he would never tell Evelyn any of this. She would never know about the woman he called his lover; she would never know about Celine and she would never find out about Jon's involvement in the group.

EPILOGUE

Jon

J on was thinking about the impending tax return he had to submit at the moment of the explosion. He glanced up. A young Muslim boy was directly in front of him. He smiled at Jon: a rarity on the tube. Jon turned away. Everyone knew not to make eye contact on the tube. It was as if the boy was mocking him.

A man just out of Jon's reach began to laugh, it was a hysterical cackling laughter. Jon could just make out the top of his bald head: shiny and smooth. The boy moved closer to Jon. He was alarmed. You couldn't be too careful of Muslims on the tube. Jon tried to make out where the laughter was coming from. It was then he saw what gesture the man was making. It was then he saw the man's arm raised in the air: the Nazi salute.

There was quiet disbelief in the carriage. If he'd looked sooner, he may have seen this man's bag, may have noticed it was too large, too cumbersome. He may have realised there was something wrong.

The young boy looked at Jon, with pure fear in his eyes.

That's when Jon recognised George. What was George doing? He glanced at the bag – what was he thinking? He suddenly understood everything: the hushed voices at meetings, the sudden silences, Celine's desperate interest in his morning tube route and time. He understood everything too late. Jon decided he'd get off at the next stop. He didn't want George to spot him, could not afford to be affiliated with him in public.

He couldn't wait to get off. He didn't want any part in what this may be.

George began shouting expletives, he ranted about immigrants and Islam. He spouted his indignation at the state of the UK. Jon really wanted to shut him up. He had always suspected George of being unstable. He continued his torrent of abuse, as if on stage ready to reach his crescendo.

Not long, Jon thought, *not long and I'll be out on the street away from him.* He glanced at his watch 7.56am. If only he'd got his usual earlier tube. George came closer to Jon and the young Muslim boy. Jon ducked his head, so George wouldn't recognise him. People tried to distance themselves, but the train was too cramped.

He lurched towards them and spat hatred from his mouth at the young boy in front of Jon: *terrorist killer, Bin Laden's brother, brown piece of shit, ruined our country, go home, taking our jobs, we pay taxes for you scum, rapist, murderers, evil, subhuman, ruined Britain, paedophiles.* It was similar to the rhetoric Jon had used in the past, but it all seemed so ridiculous now.

A flash of light, a loud noise emitted, a powerful surge and then it all went black.

Mohammed

Mohammed Osman had been on his way to work. He was anxious to be early: it was his first proper job and he wanted to make a good impression. He'd left his parents at home, kissed his mother goodbye after his prayers, and left the house in high spirits. He hated the tube, he saw how people looked at him, and he was fearful. It was only a short journey, though.

That night he was meeting a girl. They hadn't known each other long, but he was taking her for a pizza and then the cinema: a celebration. He'd worked hard in university and had been desperate to land a place with a good firm, and now he finally had – he'd allow himself to revel in the moment. As he stepped onto the tube that morning Mohammed was thinking about a young girl, her pretty face just out of reach until tonight.

He was imagining all the future nights they may have together. Now he was earning proper money he thought about putting plans in place. He would start saving for a house, if he was going to ask for her hand in marriage he wanted to provide for her.

He hadn't noticed the man with the bald head standing behind him, he hadn't noticed his sneer and smile as he stepped onto the carriage.

Jon was thirty-six-years-old when he was killed that morning in London's fifth terror attack that year. He never made it to work, he never brokered that deal, he never did those dishes, completed his tax return or met his brother – his life was ended in a moment.

Mohammed was twenty-three-years-old when he was killed that morning. He never made it to work, he never met his girl, he never started his new job. His life was suddenly tragically ended. He was the main suspect for one of the worst terrorist attacks in London since 7/7, because he was a Muslim.

March 2020

Celine

Maybe it was a maternal urge, maybe there was some part of me that knew that I needed to protect the unborn child on some level. I had not planned what happened to Amy, and when I recollect that afternoon it is as if I am watching someone else commit the crime. Murder. I cannot believe I am a murderer. I knew immediately I would need to leave London. Everything was too claustrophobic, too dangerous now. I could not risk getting caught. I couldn't bear prison.

The baby had arrived rather suddenly that night. I had not gone to hospital. I wanted to remain as anonymous as possible now. I knew they'd be looking for me before long and CCTV would provide vital clues. I barely had any time before I needed to leave the country. I was weak as I packed my bags and wrapped the baby in a blanket. She was a silent little thing, as perplexed as me that she had arrived in this world.

Even before the incident with Amy, I had a plan for the child. She had seemed so perfect when I met her – Evelyn that was. I knew she would make a far better mother than me. Maybe it was a way of making up for my guilt too, a parting gift for Jon's wife, a part of him she'll always be able to cherish – not that she'd know. I had left a note with the little girl shortly after her birth explaining Max was the father.

I knew Max would never relinquish the child's real parentage. It had been easier than I thought to bundle her up and leave her outside the police station. I had put Max's number on the note, but I knew he worked there so it was guaranteed she'd come under his care. I kept watch until they discovered her; I'm not heartless.

My brothers didn't welcome me with open arms when I returned to Italy that night, but they welcomed me. The restaurant in London I will put up for sale. I hope I will not have to go back to the UK to complete the transaction, although there is talk of travel coming to a halt. An illness in China that is spreading across the continent.

I sometimes think of the little girl. I wonder what will happen to her, but a life with Max and Evelyn is far better than a life with me. In the end, even though she doesn't know, I suppose Jon gave Evelyn the baby she'd always wanted.

Evelyn

Max arrives on my doorstep, bewildered.

"I need your help." He is breathless.

"Okay, with what?"

"Don't be alarmed."

"What is this about, Max?"

"I'll be back in a sec."

I watch him run down the steps to the car, he is obviously struggling to get something out of the seat. For a moment, I think he has gone and bought me a puppy. I'm much more of a cat person.

As he takes the steps to the flat I am flabbergasted. Why does Max have a newborn baby? There are so many questions, but I beckon him inside. I do not want the baby getting cold.

She is perfect. I cannot understand how Max got himself into this situation, but I could not deny she was everything I'd ever wanted. I hadn't known what to think when Max arrived with her in the car seat. I hadn't understood his intentions. That was Max all over, he never really gave much away about how he was feeling, he always appeared in control.

He'd explained his one-night stand at the beginning of last summer. He told me he'd not really thought much of it. A girl off Tinder he described her as, a woman you would never picture a future with. I could not understand how any woman could abandon their baby and leave it with the father to bring up.

Max seemed just as shocked as me. As he'd arrived at my front door he'd looked bewildered. The baby was fast asleep but Max looked terrified.

Of course, he doesn't have anything for her. Thankfully I still have the wardrobe full of baby clothes. Max had not been so cruel to make me relinquish the items that day.

"I'm going to need your help."

"Okay, Max. I can help."

"She's going to need a mother, Evelyn. Every child needs a mother."

I do not know what to say, this unexpected child here with us is everything I had wanted for so long.

"What's her name, Max?"

"She doesn't have one yet. Any suggestions?"

"Rosa. I think Rosa would be perfect." I thought back to my great-grandfather and the daughter, my grandmother, he never got to meet – it seemed fitting.

Max

The weeks that followed Amy's death and the arrival of Rosa, Max found surreal. He could not contemplate how his brother's actions could still have such an impact on his life, even after his death.

He is still in mourning for Amy, he thinks he always will be. She did not deserve her fate. He never saw Celine again after that afternoon. Her daughter had arrived outside the police station the following day with a note claiming he was the father. She was clever in that sense: he could not abandon the child. He would never have done that to Jon.

Evelyn will never find out of course, he cares for her too much. He could not bear her heartbreak. Rosa is a sweet little thing. They have adapted well considering they did not know this was their fate. Max has moved into Evelyn's flat for the time being. There is talk of a global lockdown – Max finds the idea ludicrous, the world feels like a sci-fi movie gone wrong. But at least they are together, learning to parent in their strange new set-up.

The news this morning of Italy had images of people lying on hospital floors unable to breathe. It seemed unthinkable. Reports coming from Europe of this virus terrified him. He turned to Evelyn and he could see the fear in her eyes. "It'll be fine, Evelyn. Don't worry."

"I'm scared, Max."

"I think everyone is, but it'll be okay. I'll make sure we're okay: the three of us."

He thought back to last August and all they had gone through since and where they were now. It would take him a long time to process the past nine months and everything that has happened since Jon's death. Evelyn is cradling Rosa in her arms. He looks down at the little girl and he can see so much of his brother in her. He places his arm around Evelyn and kisses the top of her head: "I promise, Evelyn. It's going to be wonderful."

THE END.

ACKNOWLEDGEMENTS

A big thank you to everyone at Bloodhound Books for all your hard work, dedication and support. Thank you to the directors, Fred and Betsy; my editor Clare; and editorial manager Tara; our publicist Maria; and my proofreader Shirley. I am so privileged to be part of the publishing house.

Thank you to my fiancé, Matt, and all my family and friends for their continued support, particularly my army of bridesmaids – you know who you are! Also, to Ralph, for your constant companionship.

A big thank you to everyone who has taken the time to read this book. I really do appreciate all my readers so much. I hope you enjoyed *Divided*.

A NOTE FROM THE PUBLISHER

Thank you for reading this book. If you enjoyed it please do consider leaving a review on Amazon to help others find it too.

We hate typos. All of our books have been rigorously edited and proofread, but sometimes mistakes do slip through. If you have spotted a typo, please do let us know and we can get it amended within hours.

info@bloodhoundbooks.com

Printed in Great Britain
by Amazon

72374141R00199